A COVENANT
WITH DEATH

BY
STEPHEN BECKER

A DELL BOOK

Published by DELL PUBLISHING CO., INC.
750 Third Avenue, New York, N.Y. 10017

Reprinted by arrangement with
Atheneum Publishers
New York, New York 10016

DEDICATION:
*To Judge Jay Andrew Rabinowitz
who does justly and loves mercy*

*We have made a covenant with death,
and with hell are we at agreement.*
—ISAIAH 28:15

First Dell Printing—February, 1966

Printed in U.S.A.

PART ONE

1 LOUISE TALBOT CHOSE
to spend the last afternoon of her life lounging in the
shade of a leafy sycamore at the split-rail fence before
her home. She was surpassingly alive and exuberantly
feminine, and did not know that she was to die. Her
home was on Mescalero Road in a small southwestern
town called Soledad City. The road was quiet and dusty,
its houses on spacious plots—not because it was a rich
road but because ours was a small and sluggish town.
Here and there sycamores broke the open vistas. Now
and then an automobile chugged in. Orioles sliced the
hot blue sky. Languid cats strolled the road, and languid
dogs ignored them. The iceman passed on his rickety
wagon. His name was Henry Dugan and he was an old
man, a former deputy sheriff, and he did not mind that
his horse was ancient and dilatory, because greeting
Mrs. Talbot, staring down at her placid opulence from
his perch seven feet up, compensated him for his hot,
weary round. He tipped his frayed, stained, wide-
brimmed Stetson, revealing untamed white hair and a
vestige of gallantry; he noted the careless flow of her
long brown hair, the dark and lovely brows, the white
flash of her smile. Henry too smiled, and nodded agree-
ably, and let his gaze wander briefly to her bosom, un-
bound and indubitable within a finespun blouse. She
seemed to notice, and her smile warmed. Then Henry
passed along, not looking back. Henry was an old man.

Mrs. Talbot was twenty-seven and surely the most

disturbing woman in Soledad City. She was wearing
sandals, a short tan cotton skirt, and the white lawn
blouse. Eastern fashions meant no more to us than
Prohibition, and Mrs. Talbot declined to flatten, distort,
or confine. She did not flaunt; she had no need to; she
was merely casual, and that was enough. It was more
than enough for Mrs. Orville Moody, the next to break
our lady's solitude. Mrs. Moody was a meddler and a
harpy, in whom the Mrs. Talbots of this world (there
would be none in the next, of course) provoked ex-
cruciating spasms of righteousness. In black, buttoned
to the chin, bearing a reticule, Mrs. Moody ran the
gauntlet. Mrs. Talbot spoke: "Hello, Mrs. Moody.
Warm enough for you?" Mrs. Moody did not answer. It
was incontestably warm enough for her, though by her
dress she might have been judged impervious. Summer
was not yet upon us—it was May 3, 1923—but the
spring rains were over, and in our corner of the southwest heat was not just a blanket or a slow fire or any
of the standard metaphors; it was a condition of nature,
a liquid medium in which we did not so much walk as
swim and shimmer.

Mrs. Talbot stood alone for some time. Her next-
door neighbor, Helen Donnelley, sewing camisoles for
her mission society to inflict upon aborigines, glanced
out at her occasionally. Mrs. Talbot paced slowly,
smoothed her hair, examined her fence, stooped once to
adjust her sandal; Mrs. Donnelley looked away, thinking
again, as she had so often, that Mrs. Talbot, while a
nice person really, sometimes showed too much. Across
the road, at the Lucases', no one seemed to be home.
When Mrs. Donnelley looked up again she saw Colonel
Oates approaching. Mrs. Talbot was smiling.

Colonel Oates was sixty-two, high church, a Carolina
Oates, retired some years before to come and live
among us. His colonelcy, his pension, and the decora-

tion for valor that he wore on July Fourth and November eleventh were his reward for thirty years of army life. His hair was white and thinning, his eyes were alert, his nose was high-bridged with nostrils like a horse's. He was a snoop, and overlooked no public event or private scandal. He carried a silver-knobbed cane because on his patrician level gold was considered ostentatious. He did not walk: he marched. But he slowed as he approached Louise Talbot, and tipped his Stetson, and then halted. "Good afternoon," he said.

"Good afternoon, Colonel. Hot."

"Yes indeed. You look, ah, cool."

"Thank you."

"Bryan home?"

"No. He's out somewhere talking business."

"Ah, yes, business." The Colonel approved. "He is an ambitious man."

"Yes," she said, and nodded reflectively. He noticed, for the first time, a fine down at her temples. They stood silently, sheltered from the unrelenting sunlight; perfume rose from the flower beds, and perhaps from Mrs. Talbot. The Colonel fanned himself with his hat, and felt younger. "Not much doing on a day like this."

"There's never much doing on this road," she said. "I like to come out and say hello to people. I wish Helen would come out."

"Mrs. Donnelley."

"Mmmm. She's always busy."

"The devil has work," the Colonel said archly.

"I suppose," she said, and leaned forward, elbows on the fence, a hand at either side of her throat; her bosom rested comfortably on the upper rail. The Colonel harrumphed and inspected the sky.

"Not a cloud," he said. She looked up; he glanced down.

"The glare is awful," she said.

"Yes. How can you stay out here in the heat?"

She did not answer for a moment; and then said, "It's shady under the tree. I'm lonely, Colonel, and I like company."

"Ah," he said. "You should have children." He never forgot the remark.

"Maybe," she said, her voice neutral, her expression bland. "I think I'll do some gardening."

"Then I won't keep you," the Colonel said. "Watch out for sunstroke, now. It's been a pleasure."

"Drop by again," she said.

"Thank you," he said, and waved his hat, and put it back on his head, and marched off. He was on his way to the corner of town where the rich people lived, the Randalls and the Frisbees, the Cathcarts and the Owenses and the Chillingworths; he was to take tea with the Widow Bogan, who had fought Indians as a bride and had once owned great stretches of land. These were the "nice people" of the town. Each Christmas they laced themselves into black cloaks or string ties and delivered poultry to the less fortunate, mainly Mexicans and Negroes, and then returned to their mission-style parlors to make reassuring small talk about the deserving and undeserving poor. The Colonel liked them.

Louise Talbot did no gardening that day. She watched him retreat, waved when he turned for a last gesture, and stood thoughtfully at the fence, one foot up on the lower rail. Shortly Juano Menéndez came along in his car, slowing to offer a deep nod that was almost a bow. Again Mrs. Talbot smiled, and Juano saw, in a brief sensual flash, the comfortable bosom and the shadows below, unrevealing yet distracting. He swore to himself ruefully, but did not stop. He was, after all, Mexican; successful, in that he was half the Soledad Laundry and owned an automobile, and sat at ease in the town's masculine haunts and councils; but still Mexican. Nor did he have need of Mrs. Talbot. He was called the alcalde, and in the Mexican quarter he enjoyed the dominion and bliss of an eighteenth-century squire: he was in his early fifties, had seven living children and nineteen grandchildren, and was the unofficial mayor of the Mexican population. He chuffed away, and Mrs. Talbot was once more alone.

Soon Helen Donnelley emerged from the house next door and came, stately and prim, to stand beside her. "Oh, what a day!" Mrs. Donnelley said. "I've been sewing until my fingers are cramped."

"I haven't seen the boys," Mrs. Talbot said.

"Oh, they're building something. Some sort of radio. I don't understand it myself but they have drawings. From a magazine. Bruce says it's something they should learn about. Where's Bryan?"

"I don't know. Somewhere talking, probably. Business." Mrs. Talbot smiled wanly.

"Men think they're so important," Mrs. Donnelley said complacently.

"Aren't they?" Mrs. Talbot was amused.

"Well, of course. But they're so proud of themselves. They little know what women go through."

Mrs. Talbot showed her amusement, and the women chatted as women chat, passing the time, Mrs. Donnelley taller, ample, older, ordinary, Mrs. Talbot placid yet restless, her brown eyes in motion, her hands roving to her hair, her throat, her skirt. When Bruce Donnelley appeared, far down the road, Mrs. Donnelley waved, and Mrs. Talbot seized the moment to primp briefly.

Donnelley approached, advancing slowly in his heavy, solemn stride. He was the town's ranking lumber dealer, God-fearing and hard-working; member of three luncheon clubs and president of one. Success, success. And an elder in the First Presbyterian Church, and he worked at that job too. He spoke seldom. He was hulk-

ing and had hard, flat blue eyes, blondish hair, and a
sharp nose. He seemed powerful and mysterious: he
was armored in principle, and it was not easy to laugh
in his presence. The blue eyes were direct and unwaver-
ing, and discomfited most men. He was a prominent citizen and no one really knew him. We knew what he
stood for. He was the sort of man who would not understand why you might want to know more than that.

"Good afternoon," he said.

"Hello," Louise said.

"Did you have a good day, dear?" Helen asked.

"Yes. Hot."

"It was. I finished another camisole."

"Good." To Louise: "Bryan home?"

"Not yet."

Donnelley was wearing a white linen suit with a
white shirt and a dark necktie knotted very small. He
stood outside the fence, monolithic, turning slowly to
watch another car go by. People came up the road in
knots, twos and threes: the day help on its way home,
Negroes and Mexicans, raising dust, murmuring, nodding deferentially as they passed, proceeding up this
quiet, comfortable road toward the bridge, where they
would cross to the east side of the river and scatter,
north if they were Mexican, south if Negro. Slowly they
passed, ten or a dozen, in groups and yet one group.
They passed. Soon they were out of sight.

The three at the fence were silent for a time. We never knew if Donnelley had simply stood there, a neighbor and an elder, or if he had flashed covert glances at
the lush stranger beside him; we never knew if he had
resented or desired, denied or admitted the heat of
temptation; if his hand, like Henry Dugan's, like the
Colonel's, like Juano's, like so many men's, had re-
ceived and rejected in one instant the heart's command
to rise and touch. Shortly the Donnelleys drifted home;

and after a few minutes more Louise Talbot too turned from the fence, the road, the town, and walked away, erect and lovely, proud and careless of her warm flesh, statuesque and voluptuous in the soft wash of late sunlight. She went into the house, and the road was empty and quiet.

Four hours later she was dead. She had talked and laughed, a lonely sentinel at the roadside, yearning perhaps for some unknowable adventure; four hours later the voice was stilled and the yearning finally appeased. We knew how. In time we knew who, but by then three of us were dead. And when the town knew who, it was satisfied, and turned away, and left me alone to ponder the last and best question: why?

And where was I when Louise Talbot died? At home, a mile from her, wondering whether to spend my life in Soledad City, not yet aware that I could never escape myself. Now, more than forty years later, I am still in Soledad City, in the same home, in the study that was my father's before me. Now my calendar warns me, shrieking 1964; now they call me Old Judge Lewis. In 1923 it was Young Judge Lewis, and a confused young judge at that. I had never met Louise Talbot formally, and had—or thought I had—a sufficiency of problems without her. I was a judge, at the embarrassing age of twenty-nine, because the Governor of our state had called my father friend, a word that meant much to both men; by a kind of nepotism once removed, there I was, one of two judges in our district of the state criminal court, and this account is of my first capital trial. It is also of myself and of Bryan Talbot and for that matter of Soledad City, because geography is more than points and lines, and civilization is more than concourse. Soledad City was the scene of the crime; it was

also the scene of much life, funny and tragic, plain and
fancy. And for those of us who troubled to look, the
glow of that primitive and provincial life, a glow now
pale, now brazen, now ruddy, illuminated the death of
Louise Talbot.

Back east she might have been less noticed and not
murdered. In Chicago, for example, where I had frozen
to death and learned the law, floozies abounded. But a
dozen years before, we had been still a territory, not yet
a state, and law and order had got ranged on the side of
long black dresses buttoned up to the chin, like Mrs.
Moody's. The ladies inside those dresses were vigilantes
of the soul, dedicated to a shrill, maniacal lynch law.
They were mainly Protestant, and relied upon the support of elders and such; Bruce Donnelley, for one. The
town, Soledad City, was about a third Mexican, and the
relatively unembarrassed Latins (of whom I had the
honor to be almost one), to whom the flesh and the
senses were life itself and not enemies to be smote h-p
and th-gh, stood for Sodom and Gomorrah to the ladies
in black. Gringo Roman Catholics were suspect even
when they bore names like O'Brien and Sienkiewicz;
Sunday mornings people like Mrs. Moody would spy on
them, reconnoitering for just one red skirt, just one rose
behind the ear, just one deep neckline. We were a queer
sort of town, part frontier, part plantation, part pleasure, part cruelty, part old Mexico, part clanking modernity, and, as noted, part murder. Some of the men
had been Indian fighters, and some were back from
Paris and Belleau Wood (where I too, shavetail, had
cringed from shot and shell and not killed anybody, or
not noticeably) and trying to get the roads improved
for their Marmons and Stutzes, Reos and Mercers. A
social stew, in short, and the heat kept it at a simmer; a
foretaste of fire and brimstone. The righteous moved in
pools of sticky resentment, concealing perspiration; the

damned peeled off their shirts and sweated in the sight
of their elect brethren. Nights, thank God, were merely
warm; but perhaps three times a year the desert air
flowed in on a south wind and clung to the streets like
hot tar, and then there were fights and knifings and the
tomcatting came out in the open and we all grew slower
and surlier.

The town had once been a minor accretion at the
bend of a clear river; possibly the first settler was a fer-
ryman. The town grew, and prospered, because of pasture to the northwest and mineral flats to the northeast.
Being a judge, and the sole heir of a local idol, I knew
the town well, and had friends in high place and low.
Up where the Colonel took his afternoon tea lived
George Chillingworth, for example. George was about
my age, and made rude jokes about his good family; he
had sung, danced, made a speech in Spanish, and got
roaring drunk at the wedding of Juano Menéndez's
youngest daughter two years before. If I had a best
friend it was George, but we were not really close.
Through high school, yes, but he had gone east to Har-
vard and I to our state college, and we had quarreled
about the war, he saying it was all for the money. That
was a minor quarrel and we always had a good time together but we were both loners by nature. His own
class, all those nice people, called him a socialist.

George owned the other half of Juano's laundry,
which did all the commercial lavage for the town, including my own robes and the napery at the Territorial
Hotel. Menéndez was my friend, too, and the most popular figure in Soledad City (accepted by even the nice
people, and little he cared!). He loved children and was
a sort of year-round Father Christmas, burdened eter-
nally with gumdrops and jelly beans; he told funny stories in the lobby of the Territorial; and he stood drinks
on any pretext—seven nights running to celebrate the

ratification of the Eighteenth Amendment, and seven
nights again at the passage of the Volstead Act, and
even a few days after the murder, when President Harding's trip to Alaska was announced. "We have finally
driven the son of a bitch out of the country," he
shouted. "Drinks all around."

The Mexicans lived up in the northeast corner of
town, and slightly to the south of them stood the abat-
toir, where meat was dressed for local consumption and
some shipped fifty or a hundred miles to smaller towns.
Beyond the slaughterhouse, in the true southeast corner
and basking in the hot, moist attar of bos and ovis, lay
the Negro quarter, and I had a friend there too, William
Carter, but of course "friend" is the wrong word. We
had competed in high school, both excellent in mathe-
matics, each graded always within a point or two of the
other and no hard feelings; and we were both good at
basketball, forwards on the same team, intramural, as
Bill was not permitted to play for the varsity. I had last
seen him perhaps a year before. He had been sum-
moned to jury duty; he was a registered Republican and
his name was on the rolls. He was dismissed just before
the noon recess, a peremptory challenge he said, and
we met on the courthouse steps and we chatted and he
went home. I wish I could say that I was a good fellow
in those days and lived with truth and took Bill's sister
to the church dance or something on that order. No. I
didn't even know if he had a sister, and didn't care.
When I read a month after the murder that a man in
Detroit named Charles C. Brown, twenty-nine, my age
and Bill's, had been sentenced to five-to-fifteen for
stealing twelve cents and three hundred marks (the
marks were worth .001-.275 of a cent), I assumed that
Brown was colored and realized suddenly that Bill was
no safer than he, but I did not trot off to look him up
and have a drink.

The scene of the crime. My town. I have omitted the business center, the stores and municipal buildings, livery stables and later auto agencies, the hotels and restaurants and saloons (and ex-saloons), the telephone building and the cable office, the lumberyard and the depot, the barbershops and beauty parlors. I have omitted the electric company and the Chinese restaurant and the brokerage office, the banks and the dry cleaners, the town hall and the calaboose, the dingy Mescalero Museum and the movie houses. (I have not even told you what state we were part of, because it does not matter; think of a small and sunny state between New Mexico and Arizona.) Or the dozen churches and the dozen gas stations, or the former fancy house now occupied by the state's local representatives: National Guard (first floor; parlor; beer and music) and State Police (second floor; bedrooms) and Veterans' Adviser (attic; towels and sheets). I have omitted much more, mainly people, but some of them will be along soon.

That was the scene of the crime. It was a little society, complicated and unique, vibrating to overtones and undertones, and it was certainly no microcosm, no happily symbolic distillation of America the Beautiful. It was an unpleasant little town except to those of us who could deceive ourselves with amenities and conveniences. It suffered the climate of Timbuktu and probably enjoyed fewer books; even its boosters and service clubs tended to a sheepish reticence; it was in the process of superimposing a cheap, clanging, oily modernity upon a harsh and gritty past; and everyone in it, including young Judge Lewis, was vicious or inadequate or uncomprehending or indifferent in his own way. We did not even boast a green park.

2 BRYAN TALBOT TELE-

phoned the police at 10:34 on the night of May third. His voice was wild; he was sobbing. He had just returned, so he said, from Peter Justin's Bar and Billiard Parlor, where the town's politics took shape, and had found his wife dead, in a bathrobe, bruises on her throat; she was lying in the hallway between the living room and the master bedroom. He called Alfred Harmsworth, our chief of police. Alfred called Doctor Schilling, whom no one ever referred to as Doc, and ran to the Talbots' house, towing a rookie named Tolliver who threw up when he saw the corpse. "That woman," Tolliver said to me next day. His eyes went momentarily blank with horror. Alfred was in his forties, and had been a captain of infantry in France; he had seen it all, legs and heads lying loose, barbed wire festooned with American intestines, but this was worse. "Probably I never laid eyes on a finer figure," he said. "I had to examine her; and I knew why Tolliver got sick. My stomach turned, and the world was kind of fuzzy for half an hour. She looked fine, except for the bruises on her throat. Beautiful. Long legs and that little waist and everything else exactly what a man would specify if he could get a woman from Sears, Roebuck; but she was dead. I would have paid twenty dollars for her in a bathrobe the night before, but now she was nothing. Wood, or marble maybe. Was that all it was, Ben? That she was dead? Was that what made her ugly and me sick?"

"I imagine there was more to it than that," I said. I knew about the Viennese revolution, so I pontificated for Alfred. "You wanted that woman, like everybody else in town—no, no," (he had tried to protest) "I don't mean that you'd have done anything about it even when she was alive, anyway not while anybody was watching, but way down deep all men want all women. Nothing much to do about it and nothing to be ashamed of. And whatever kind your own group decides is jazziest, you want that kind most. And there she was, all laid out on her back for you—but she wasn't even a human being any more. She belonged to nature and not to you. And all the taboos we don't even know we worry about hit you at one time, and below the belt. Spooks and the wrath of God. Evil spirits. Devils that would shrivel your equipment if you so much as let the thought of her cross your mind."

Alfred was nodding. "I felt that way, sure enough. I've watched Doctor Schilling handle all sorts of bodies, and this was the first time I wondered how he could stand it. But I'm the chief, so I couldn't get sick like Tolliver. Tolliver's only nineteen. If that was the first naked woman he ever saw he may be ruined for life."

"If that was the first naked woman he ever saw, times have changed," I said.

"Yeah. Anyway I had Talbot to worry about. And when I got over the willies I remembered that somebody must have killed the woman."

Talbot sat on a couch, pale as death himself, tears running quick and silent down his bruised face. Alfred noticed the bruise immediately, along the left cheek and temple, the skin barely broken and only a drop of drying blood. Talbot stank of whiskey. Every little while he ran the back of his hand across his upper lip

and snuffled. Once he moaned. Doctor Schilling said
Mrs. Talbot had been dead for only twenty minutes or
half an hour, and then he covered her up and went to
Talbot. "Lie down here," he said, and Talbot broke out
sobbing—long, strangled, airless sobs. He might have
been thinking that if he'd stayed home it wouldn't have
happened; he might not have been thinking at all.
Alfred was sweating now, and losing touch. The night
was still and hot and the hallway was bright with lamplight; a painting of a waterfall hung six inches from his
nose, and every indentation of the frame, every contour
of the drawing, every change in color was sharp, glaring, painful; he turned away but it was the same in the
living room: chairs, tables, knickknacks staring out at
him like bright monsters in a nightmare. Then Tolliver
stumbled back in and Alfred was all right again. He
blinked a couple of times and ran a hand through his
sandy hair and took a deep breath.

Doctor Schilling had cleaned Talbot's bruise and giv-
en him an injection. Alfred would have preferred Talbot awake and babbling but no one ever argued with
Doctor Schilling. Talbot began to quiet down, and
Alfred caught him before he drifted off: "When did you
find her, Talbot?"

Talbot answered slowly. "Just before I called." A
pause. "I tried to bring her to." A pause. "Thought
she'd fallen." A pause. His eyes were closing. "Then I
couldn't . . . find a heartbeat. Thought she was—oh,
God!"

"What'd you do after you called?"

"Rubbed her wrists. Water . . . put water on her
forehead." His eyes were shut and his breathing was
quiet.

Alfred couldn't do much more then, but he tried a
last jolt, hoping for a flash of truth from the drugged
mind: "Who did it, Talbot?"

Talbot shivered. "She won't leave me. . . . That fellow Rollins." (Or so Alfred heard it.) "Nobody. . . . Nobody. . . . My wife."

Alfred bent closer. "Talbot: did you do it?"

Talbot was asleep.

"Can you get somebody to stay with him?" the doctor asked.

Alfred looked at Tolliver. Tolliver nodded. He was ashamed of himself. Alfred patted him on the shoulder. "Tolliver'll stay. What about the body?"

"I'll call Parsons," the doctor said. "Unless you want to examine her some more."

"No," Alfred said quickly. "I'll look around the house, but you can take her away."

The doctor went to the telephone and called our Protestant undertaker.

Alfred looked around the house. It did him little good. He found what he'd have found in any respectable establishment: private correspondence, unincriminating; unpaid bills; clothes and food and cigarettes and a deck of cards; towels and sheets and pillowcases; a dressing table heaped with rouges and lipsticks and powders and pomades and perfumes; a supply of perfectly ordinary, unimaginative lady's underthings; a few books, including Andrew Carnegie and a Bible—all the usual, none of the remarkable. Through the living-room window he saw the Donnelleys' lights and shades and shrubbery; and then he craned slightly and saw people on the sidewalk. He went out to tell them what had happened.

There were half a dozen of them, naturally including the Donnelleys. Again Alfred quitted this planet briefly; life and motion ceased, leaving only the ruthless lights and colors, the night sounds, the pale faces like blossoms clustered before him. "There weren't even any expressions," he said. "No eyes, no noses; it was like standing up in front of so many skulls. There was a street light about fifty feet off, and I got to feeling like the sun and moon had gone out for good, and soon that street light would go, and that would be the end of us all." But it was hot, and the sweat tipped over his eyebrows and ran down his nose, which recalled him to life. Helen Donnelley was pale; Bruce was impassive, but his eyes roved for details. He was chewing on a toothpick. Alfred told them, briefly, and asked them to go on home. Helen Donnelley let out one stifled yell and fainted. Bruce's expression never changed. He caught her as she fell, cradled her in his arms, and carried her home.

By noon the next day Soledad City had high blood pressure. Manslaughter was common enough: we had our brawls and blood feuds and outraged husbands just like any other frontier town. What we did not have, or had not had until then, was inexplicable murder by an unknown hand. Death was no less natural to us than to another community, perhaps more natural because we were almost a desert town, and our nut-brown tots, straying a mile, could amuse themselves with the traditional bleached bones: the remains of not only wild cattle and an occasional horse, but coyotes and dogs and cats, vertebrates of all kinds, among whom chance dictated that a few, now and then, would wander dying to the edge of the sandy sea. But this was a crime and a riddle; the crime was a shock, and the riddle was a pleasure. It was like one of the movies we all whistled and hooted at, but with a familiar cast, and with sound: voices, rumor, speculation. "I can't believe it was Bryan," Colonel Oates said gravely. "I cannot believe that a man dedicated to the pursuit of money would jeopardize his future by murder. Not to mention that this was the utterly useless murder of a magnificent helpmeet. Bryan wouldn't even steal. Embezzlement, possibly: a careful, methodical felony. But not the single rash act. Not Bryan."

"He's a gambler," I pointed out.

"Gamblers know the odds," the Colonel said, "and will not make them steeper. What about the girl's past? Before Bryan?"

"Nobody knows much. She's from Dallas. Married five or six years to Bryan. Bryan's from Tulsa. She had an ordinary childhood. Through high school. Considered a bit fast, free and easy, but no scandal. No ghosts out of the past. Alfred's spoken to her parents. So has Bryan. Her father's a ticket agent on the railroad."

"Poor people," the Colonel commiserated. "What a blow. Any scandal here in town?"

I scowled. I enjoy scandal, but being a judge I despise rumor. I don't like to pass it along. Still—"Bound to be. There isn't a man in town who hasn't lusted after her in his heart. Even Cathcart was noticeably gallant at the dinner last year." We were still celebrating—annually and alcoholically—the privilege of admission to the mother republic. Cathcart, Milton D., was our mayor. Nobody loved or hated him. A short, round, bald man in steel-rimmed spectacles, efficient rather than friendly, he was a good mayor. Since he had been in office, which meant nine years, nothing of note had happened in Soledad City. We liked it that way. There had been a war, and electricity, and the streetcar line, and the Prohibition we ignored, and women voting, but all that was maintenance rather than news.

"Yes," the Colonel said. "You should wear a hat."

"What? I have a nice Stetson."

"You should wear it. I know the heat doesn't bother

you much, but when a man wears a hat he can tip it to the ladies. I used to tip mine to Mrs. Talbot, and my reward was a smile and a soft word."

"I never thought of that." Used to, he had said. We accept it, assimilate it, so quickly.

"I heard Bruce Donnelley used to look at her now and then." The shaggy white brows arched.

I knew Donnelley, as people know one another when they are required to attend civic functions together. He liked those functions; I despised them; so his attendance was honest and mine was hypocritical. He had never to my knowledge made a joke, but he had come close once, at a luncheon, when he turned ponderously to me and said, "I wonder just when they mashed these potatoes." I allowed a smile to grace the comment, but it was not answered; he merely stared, grave, stern, as though cardboard potatoes were a visitation of the Lord upon us poor sinners.

"Of course he did," I said to the Colonel. "But not seriously. Not the elder. And so what?"

"Well, he lived next door, after all."

"What does that mean?" I was annoyed. "Assignations by the garbage can?"

"It means proximity," the Colonel said loftily. "It means temptation. It means the bedroom light at night, the undrawn shade."

"It means the Donnelleys' chickens in the Talbots' petunias. Somehow I can't see two hundred and twenty pounds of Bruce Donnelley lurking in a flower bed for a glimpse of raspberry nipple." The Colonel winced. I kept my tone dry. "And if he did? From Peeping Tom to Bluebeard is a long jump."

"I suppose it is," he said grudgingly. "But who would want to hurt that dear lady, and why?"

"Ask Alfred."

"Ah, no." He smiled. "I am going to ask Eulalia. I admire Alfred, but I adore Eulalia."

"You old goat," I said. He was delighted.

Eulalia was my mother, Mrs. Eulalia Morales Lewis, Mexican, handsome in her early fifties, boasting a good mind and innumerable cousins, among them Ignacio, who had a daughter Rafaela, who—no. Later. My mother had been a good wife from 1892 to 1921 to Graeme Lewis, known as Bulldog, who was a good father, the best, long ago a ranger and then county sheriff, a man of great heart who had killed when necessary. My mother was intensely proud of my being a judge, but I was not supposed to know that; our conversations consisted largely of raillery. They were also bawdy; she was a well-read woman of shrewd good humor, and enjoyed quoting my father. Now and then I would remember one of her more salacious (and salubrious) observations while I was on the bench—in state, sweating under the obligatory robe, straining to freeze an expression of mature dignity on a twenty-nine-year-old face—and would be appalled by the masks we human beings wear when we transact our most earnest business. Needing most to be ourselves, relaxed, mortal, receptive to good sense and to the nuances of truth and falsehood, available to the urgent supplications of wisdom and mercy—precisely then we deck ourselves in cold anonymity, that heads may better roll. If judges were required to sit stark naked we would have more justice.

We had been informed of the murder by telephone, at breakfast. We had been quarreling amiably in her large, airy, buff-and-white kitchen. The eggs were fresh, the bacon was lean, the coffee hot and strong; the day was beginning well. She had sat back with a deep grunt of pleasure, her brown eyes clear and at peace, and had lit a thin, black, four-inch stogy. "A good day," she said. "Cooler. Have you asked Rosemary down for the weekend?"

"No. I may. Do you want me to?"

A shrug. "She's all right. A little shy for my taste."

"Your taste is not paramount. Anyway you're a lusty Latin. A dirty Spic lady."

"Like Rafaela. And Rosemary's a nice clean Swede."

"And a schoolteacher," I said. "She has a pretty face and a fine bottom. She'll make some man a wonderful wife."

"You?"

"Maybe."

She blew a smoke ring. "How could I face Ignacio?"

"More coffee, please. You're trying to tell me something." I was jumpy, not knowing what she had guessed.

"No, no, no," she poured coffee.

"Rafaela," I said. "So you can dominate her. You're afraid if I marry Rosemary you'll have to sleep in the garage—"

"We don't have a garage. And it's my house."

"—but if it was Rafaela you could be a nosy old bawd. You think you'd scare her half to death."

"She's already scared," my mother said with great good nature. "She told me. She's scared you like boys."

I was shaking my head in gloomy disgust when the phone rang. She went off to answer it, and talked awhile, and came back looking sad.

"Louise Talbot was murdered last night," she said.

I chased down to my office, which consisted of one-half the second story of a two-story building. Across the hall from me was a ladies' hairdresser. The arrangement was undignified but interesting; I never knew whom I would meet on my way to the men's room, or what vision of factitious delight would grace my exit from same. The ground floor was a drugstore, with soda fountain, notions, newspapers, magazines, bottled liquor with hair-tonic labels, toys and games, and occasionally an all-night poker game in the back room, including me. It was run by a folksy, rubicund gentleman named Geronimo Goldman who described himself as the last Jewish Apache. He was around sixty, and specialized in forgetting to send out bills, weeping openly at hard-luck stories, and giving away free medicine. Also removing cinders and bandaging cuts. "I make it up on the newspapers," he said. He had told me once that his real name was Bernard, that he was from Newark, New Jersey, and that he had moved west just before the war for his health and because he was fascinated by Indians. "Is that why you have that lilt to your voice? Almost an accent. Is that New Jersey?"

"What, New Jersey," he said. "That's what's left of a Yiddish childhood. Plus, plus," the admonitory finger, the toothy smile, "plus my Apache heritage. But the Apaches have no word for herring. Salt fish, they say. You go in and ask for a salt fish, you're liable to get anything."

"Funny," I said, "I don't know that I ever talked to a Jewish fellow. I mean not *as* a Jewish fellow."

"You don't have to say 'Jewish fellow,' " he explained gently. "Just 'Jew.' An all-right word. Being a Jew is honorable work."

"Jew," I said obediently. "Jew." It sounded odd.

"Very good," he said. The rumor was that he supported himself playing poker, and I am in a position to confirm that, but I have indicated my aversion to rumor. The building itself had been put up in the 1880s, and its various occupants worked with a constant sense of impending catastrophe, heightened by the groaning and crepitation of exhausted lumber.

I had two rooms. One was an anteroom where my part-time clerk could read the Police Gazette, and where people could sit when I wanted to impress them by making them wait. The clerk, a bright young ex-Zuñi of twenty-two, had little to do, but he had been graduated from a state law school and a clerkship was traditionally the next step. His name was John Digby, which was his idea of the emancipated form of Jumping Deer, the name given him at birth. He was all right: smart, cheerful, ambitious, you might even say one hundred per cent American. I considered him with an odd mixture of respect, melancholy, and expectation. The respect because he did his work well; the melancholy because he had chopped away his own roots—he had *chosen* a kind of anonymity; and the expectation because I never fully believed that he wanted to be like the go-getters around him, and I kept hoping that he would show up in war paint, naked and greased, with a bleeding goat's-scrotum, full, hanging around his neck. He wore blue suits, black shoes, white shirts, and red neckties. In the year following these events the government of the United States condescended to grant him and his brothers American citizenship.

I have mentioned my work. There was not much of it. Soledad City, all four thousand of us, was a county seat. The county consisted of eleven hundred square miles with a total population of about nine thousand. There was a fair amount of theft, and there were a good many fights, and as the automobiles sputtered in we had accidents and insurance problems; there were wills to probate and an occasional divorce to maneuver; there were town ordinances to uphold and neighborhood bickerings to resolve and imprecise surveys to adjudicate; and there was local politics. Otherwise it was a quiet life. The county had two judges, and we sat alternately, three months on and three off, always in Soledad City; whoever was off performed the lesser functions of justice of the peace and assisted Ira Grandison, the municipal judge, when necessary. My colleague was an older man, over sixty, a former United States marshal named Alvin Hochstadter. I did not care for him at first—he was showy and frontierish, with a string tie, a wide-brimmed hat, white hair, a ruddy face, a promiscuous smile—but he was a fair man and we got along. He knew the law, but I don't believe he ever in his life gave a thought to the philosophy behind the law. Maybe he was better off. He had a vinegary wife who was one of the nice people. Nobody liked her. They had two boys and a girl out in the world.

I waved to Geronimo—that was how he signed himself, by the way, even checks—and ran upstairs. I opened the windows and took off my white linen jacket and sat down at my desk and called Alfred.

"That's right," he said. "Around ten last night. Strangled, looks like. No idea why, and it could have been anybody. No evidence one way or another. I'm afraid Bryan's in for a hard time."

"No criminal assault, I take it. Why Bryan?"

"That's right. No real reason," Alfred said, "except that, well, he was there, he was around. And he was drunk, and he said some suspicious things. He's a strange fellow," and I could almost see Alfred frown and fret, sadly yearning for a neatly classified criminal like a walking delegate (they were coming to be called "union organizers" and their presence in Soledad City contravened a municipal ordinance) or a drunk and disorderly.

"Go slow," I said. "You know that's not enough."

"Of course I know," Alfred barked. "Sorry. I mean

that it's only a possibility. He was closest to her. He'd been drinking again and he had a bad bruise on his face. And you never know what goes on in a marriage. There was talk about her and various people, just talk as far as we know. Of course even if it was true, I don't suppose a man goes around killing his wife just because she's, uh—"

"Flighty."

"That's it." He sounded at once relieved and embarrassed.

"All right," I said. "It's in your hands. And the District Attorney's. Get the coroner's jury together, and the grand jury if Dietrich wants it. If you make an arrest get your man to me or Hochstadter right away. And Alfred—"

"What is it, Ben?"

"I don't know how to say this, and I don't mean to rile you, but remember about confessions. Don't be clubbing anybody."

"Ben," he said, "you ought to be ashamed of yourself. I've never done that. Not even with—not with anybody."

"You've never had a first-degree murder either. I didn't mean any harm, Alfred. Just a caution."

"All right. Forget it. I'll keep you posted."

"Thanks, friend. I'll see you later."

Alfred had called me Piggy until I was twenty or so; I was a stocky little black-haired black-eyed boy. Then he decided I deserved better, college boy and all, and switched to Ben—my full name is Benjamin Morales Lewis. Everybody called me Ben. My mother called me Judge when she felt I had done something egregiously stupid, which was, come to think of it, often.

Now I had nothing to do. I leaned back and thought about the Talbots. I had never spoken to the deceased, and only casually to her husband, so there was not much to think about. After a while I derricked out my father's silver watch. It was 8:20. I called Rosemary at her home. She had left for school. I waited twenty minutes and called her at school. She was in class; for long distance they would fetch her. I waited. I tapped my fingers on the oaken desk. I looked out at the bright, dry, dusty day. I thought of Louise Talbot, and then of Rosemary dead, and did not like it. Then I heard her voice and my legs tingled and I was not a judge any more. "Hello," I said. "Hello, hello, hello."

"You miss me," she said.

"Come for the weekend."

"All right. But I'm shameless. I wish you wouldn't wait until Friday."

"I didn't realize," I said. "I didn't even know it *was* Friday. I hope you didn't have any other plans. Anyway I asked you last week."

"You are a fool," she said. "But there are certain things about you I like."

"Tell me. I have all day."

"This is the principal's office." Her voice was suddenly crisp and neutral, but I was slipping into a kind of moony drunkenness.

"And he just walked in. Watch his free hand. All right. Tell me tonight. I'll be at the station."

"Fine," she said, and then quickly, "lovely."

"Yes," I said. "I love you."

"Well," she said brightly, "I'm sure all of us here feel the same way."

"That's fine. Bring everybody along."

"Then we'll consider it arranged." I could see the principal frowning.

"Yes indeed," I said. "And I hope you will allow me to express the general feeling here by indicating to you our extreme pleasure that these preliminary discussions have borne such—"

"Goodbye," she said pleasantly, and hung up. My palms were wet.

It was at lunch, at the Territorial, that I spoke to the Colonel, and after lunch, in the bar (the sign on the wall now stated "Reading Room"), that Alfred achieved his conversational catharsis. When Alfred had gone back to his office at the jail I loitered, greeting friends and absorbing gossip. There was only one topic and no one said anything original or illuminating. I had no wish to go home and listen to my mother pontificate. She would be wise, irreverent, full of insight, and— worst of all—probably right. She could keep. At about four I went to my office and called to see if all the trains were running on time. They were. I pulled out a book, at random, and found myself reading about Cooley v. Board of Wardens (12 Howard 299), a decision handed down by the United States Supreme Court in 1851 governing the employment of harbor pilots in the port of Philadelphia. We were five hundred miles from salt water, but a good judge is ready for anything.

I am embarrassed, remembering all this; but I will not apologize.

3 THE WEEKEND PASSED
pleasantly, which is the old-fashioned way to describe
two nights of Dionysiac revels and two days of adoles-
cent mooning. The clear suspicion had now assailed me
that marriage was not a matter of grave and careful de-
liberation, but a deed one went ahead and did: a simple
yes or no, please. The corollary suspicion was nastier:
that I did not want to marry. Despite much evidence to
the contrary I still thought of myself as a young man of
middle-class rectitude, and I was uneasy; the age of
carefree liberation was not yet upon us, and morning-
after remorse was not yet archiac and unmanly. Guilt,
in short, but something more, too, on the order of an
esthetic betrayal. There she stood, or sat, or lay, a
brown-eyed Viking, a boreal beauty whose absence left
me in pain, and yet in whose presence I could not take
the natural and desirable final step; a step to which I
could find no let, stop or hindrance either in the nature
of man or in the immediate ambience. What braked and
bound me? No visions of a lost freedom; the world of
the mind was open to me and I had even, as the saying
went, been to New York, not to mention Paris. No crass
ambitions; Soledad City was tawdry and provincial but
not ignoble, and being a judge seemed all right, sus-
taining rather than creating, with time to wonder and
to read and to enjoy life. Still, Rosemary's voice was a

bit high for my taste. Nonsense. It was an awful voice, tiny and piping and breathless. ("A small but unpleasant voice," they said of one soprano; yes.)

Well. Foolishness. I knew I would need, soon, to think deeply about this. Responsibility, it was, and this time I did not have a jury or a precedent to assume it for me. I was tired of tiptoeing, of leaving my love by the dawn's early light. I liked to lie with my lips in her hair and my eyes shut against the dazzle of sunlight on her ivory haunch, the one French novelists invariably called the "hanche galbée," the loveliest of curves in a curved universe. But, but. Well, nobody was rushing me.

And while I rose on a Sabbath morning, stretched, groaned, touched my toes, blinked, felt the blood course and the bladder press and the lungs fill and the brain prickle, a mile away dust descended to dust and ashes to ashes as Louise Talbot was buried. The Colonel attended the funeral; he attended everything; and he described it later. Martin DeKalb's horse-drawn hearse, and the two hired Pierce-Arrows behind it, three or four private cars behind them. The clip-clop along a shadeless road and the cars stalling one by one in a senseless and random rotation so that the line of them died and lurched and died again and stretched and shrank like a drunken snake. Then the cemetery, the cortege passing through the gates at about nine-thirty and crawling up the one dusty road and halting. Bryan Talbot got out of the first Pierce-Arrow and stood by the casket. Mr. and Mrs. Hoyers, parents of the deceased (and here the Colonel shocked himself and us by a monumental slip of the tongue: "the bride's parents," he said), emerged from the other hired car and stood across from Bryan, not looking at him or speaking to him. And after the brief service in the pitiless morning sun, the pastor's meaningless comforts, Hoyers sweating under the arms, his wife sobbing softly, Bryan blank and glassy—after the few mourners had comforted parents and husband and the gravediggers had returned to fill the hole—then the small group dispersed slowly, and the Colonel smelled sweet grass and heard birdsong until the cars started up and the smell became the smell of exhaust and the birds were frightened into silence. But the old soldier noticed again that the Hoyerses and Talbot did not speak, or look; just disappeared into their cars. So he snooped about, and discovered that the Hoyerses were staying at the Territorial and planned to be in our city until at least Tuesday; not at the house, not with Bryan, and Emil Dietrich had paid them a call. Which the Colonel duly reported, with flashings of the eye and archings of the brow and whinnies of delectation.

On Monday, May seventh, the newspaper informed us that an Army monoplane had flown across the country, without stopping, from Hempstead on Long Island to San Diego, in twenty-seven hours; and that there had been earthquakes in Turkey and Chile. On Tuesday it informed us that the grand jury was considering the murder of Louise Talbot. "I think they were wrong about her," my mother said that night. We were sipping coffee on the veranda. It was a warm night and the new street lamps were sparking and sputtering; lizards crawled and locusts chirred and far off a voice whooped; relentlessly, suicidally, a moth assaulted the screen. When I was a young boy we had heard distant coyotes barking into the still night air; but no longer. "She may have been a cold woman, and trying too hard. Marriage is supposed to be fun. If it isn't—and it may not have been her fault—a woman is liable to do any crazy thing. That husband of hers never looked like much."

"That doesn't make him a murderer." Bryan Talbot, who is, in a twisted sense, the hero of this narrative, looked like very little. Pleasant enough; I liked him all right; early thirties, five feet nine, light brown hair, humor in the eyes now and then; a graceful carriage; all in all, a superior municipal employee, maybe a junior water commissioner, or a superintendent of schools. He was neither. He had a shrewd mind but he drank too much and was not steady. He was, for lack of a more precise word, a free-lancer. A dabbler. Real estate. A small automobile agency for two years, after which he was bored and sold out. The whiskey traffic, which he handled openly for a while, as a business; no one bothered him. He had helped, on the business end, to plan the first and only streetcar line in town; he conferred with lawyers, criticized contracts intelligently, rode in the third seat on the inaugural trip from Town Hall to the Mexico Road, and then declined a position as director of the line. Colonel Oates had asked him why. "For a gold dollar four times a year?" he answered. "I'll tell you, Colonel: it's a dead end. The fun's over. I intend to move on sometime soon. Denver, maybe, or California. I'm shooting for bigger things. Fifteen thousand a year."

"Fifteen thousand!" The Colonel was shocked; anything over three thousand was superfluous in Soledad City.

"Yes," Talbot said firmly. "I've got a damn good mind for business. I have no trouble making a living. And if I can swing just one big deal, I'm on my way. I know what people think of me." He grinned. "Not much of a sticker: go into something, wrap it up, hop right out again. Well, they're right. As soon as the deal is made, as soon as it turns into just a job, I lose interest. I'm an entrepreneur. I was born to fees and not to wages. I went to college, and got out with honors, and I want a lot of the good things in life."

"Go get 'em," the Colonel had said. "You're a cocky young fellow, aren't you."

Nor did that make him a murderer.

"He's a good Presbyterian," I said to my mother. "What should she have married? A weight lifter?"

"You'll never learn. If I've told you once . . . strength is nothing, gentleness is all. Still, you're right. He was a good Presbyterian. That whole road's full of churchgoers. Not much fun. And the Talbots were right next door to an elder."

"Bruce Donnelley."

"Yes. There's a man I really don't like. Your father once said that when the Donnelleys pulled up the shades in the morning it wasn't to let the sunlight in; it was to show the neighbors that they weren't copulating in the daytime."

Bruce Donnelley again, with his carefully knotted necktie and his detachable collars, like a Wall Street fellow. A man no one knew because he was all surface. Silent, powerful, and heavy-laden, a cornerstone of the social edifice. I remember wondering what he thought of the murder: was he outraged, or only annoyed? Uncomprehending, or grieving mute with the wisdom of those-who-know? A strange sort of municipal colossus: the marmoreal Moses, chairman of the moral board. And murder next door.

"Colonel Oates thinks Louise Talbot was a volcano," I said.

"Poor Sebastian," she said. "Poor epicene Sebastian," a strange adjective but strangely accurate. "He told you that to make me jealous."

"Maybe so. He said he wished *he'd* been her next-door neighbor twenty years ago. Then he said, 'Better yet, forty-five.' "

"Forty-five years ago," she mused. "That's sad. Still" —she cheered up—"he was perfectly right. Boys of seventeen, if they are intelligent enough to take tutoring —"

"Oh, my God," I groaned. "Why don't you go bake an apple pie like everybody's else's mother?"

Thursday the grand jury indicted Bryan Talbot for the murder of his wife, and Alfred Harmsworth went out and arrested him.

The indictment was made public at about ten in the morning. John and I were in the office, fanning ourselves and sifting esoterica. "Suppose there's a gas explosion because of a leak in the line, the line the company installed, but in the contract of sale the customer waived redress. Suppose he's badly hurt in the explosion, hospital, lots of bills, property damage. What can he do?"

John looked grim. "Did he receive a consideration for the waiver?" I nodded. "He could still fight it," John said. "If the gas company was a public utility the waiver might be against public policy." He brightened. "Ha!" he whooped. "Trespass! The gas company has no right to invade the house, outside the line, with its product."

"How do you get money out of them for trespass?"

"You don't," he said. "You—" and he shut up when the telephone rang.

"Ben." It was Hochstadter. "They've just indicted Talbot and Alfred's gone to get him. I thought you might like to be here for the hearing."

"I sure would. Half an hour?"

"Yes. See you."

I told John.

"No kidding," he said. "How'd they do that? Something we don't know about?"

"Circumstantial, I suppose. That's allowed, you know."

"I bet it's more than that," he said. "Sex somewhere."

"You savages are always thinking of the one thing," I rebuked him. "However," and I felt a sudden excitement, "we may have first-degree murder on our hands. You'd better come over with me. You won't run into many of those around here."

"You bet," He sprang to his feet. "First-degree. Wow."

We clattered down the ancient stairway and into the sunlight, which slowed us immediately. John was a good fellow to be with on a morning like that: broad and tan, extravagantly healthy, bright-eyed, flat-nosed, fine teeth, and with the look of a man who believes that the only surprises life will offer are very funny jokes. Eager and optimistic. We walked easy and fanned hard, and soon we were at the courthouse.

The courthouse had once been an indoor market, more than a shelter and less than an edifice. After the war a market building became almost superfluous and thoroughly inconvenient. Superfluous because truck farming diminished, retail stores proliferated, and canned goods became popular and cheap; inconvenient because the center of town proved—in our Lilliputian economy—the only tract sufficiently uncluttered by residences to qualify as a "business district." Some of the livery stables became garages and the gasworks became a power plant. Our newspaper, the *Trader,* went from eight pages to sixteen, contracted to reprint "Mutt and Jeff" daily, ran a weekly book review by someone named Adeline Hawkins Pearsall ("The rule is," Geronimo told me, "that women with three names are awful writers and women with two names are all right," and in my lifetime his hieratic wisdom has required little correction), and a lesson in auction bridge. The *Trader's* editorials were generous and humanistic, incoherent, often fiery, occasionally bilingual; though the national news was late its datelines were never falsified because the newspaper's proprietor, Mr. Edgar Musgrave, was a man of pepper and probity. Also of small elegance and less syntax. He bumbled, and sweated beneath a Damoclean imminence of libel suits, averaging two or three retractions a week. He had no prudence, utter integrity, and an appalling innocence. He had composed and published one imperishable headline, cherished by only a few of us but with fierce and undying gratitude: a dentists' convention had come to town and he had headed the story ORAL CONGRESS THIS WEEKEND AT TERRITORIAL HOTEL.

But I was describing the courthouse. It had begun, sometime before 1900, as a great shed, rectangular and flat-roofed with simple wooden pillars in front. (I recall it as having then resembled the very oldest Greek temples, all post-and-lintel; but when I was a boy that comparison would not have leapt to mind.) A massive rectangular solid: wide doors and no windows in front, an unbroken row of huge windows down each side, a bare wall at the back. The windows, separated only by thick studs, began three feet off the floor and went up eight more. That was a lot of window; but they had admitted light and served as loading ports.

The remodeled building, dating from 1913, was not radically different, and it had a certain demented charm: the floor was four feet higher at the front. The contractor had decided it would be simpler just to tilt the building up. So it was necessary to negotiate half a dozen steps to reach the front door. A second wall had been added some eight feet in from that door, with a men's room at one end and a ladies' room at the other of the corridor thus formed, and room for a desk or an armed guard or a voters' registration team. All the fixtures here had irregular bases like boot heels to compensate for the tilt. The toilets, which faced the rear of the building—at least in the men's room—were set on slanted wooden pedestals so the seats would be level. A short man could let his feet dangle. A carnival atmosphere, like drunken women in spike heels. Double doors opened into the rear of the courtroom, and the floor continued to slope all the way to the bar of justice, which supplied the effect of an amphitheater: rows of wooden benches with tilted bases and level seats, stepping down to the pit. The bench, or altar, was itself level, fittingly. Behind it was the original rear wall of the building, and behind that an addition had been erected, an extension, three rooms: Hochstadter's chambers and mine, and between them an attorneys' room. Each with toilet and washbasin. The windows remained huge, admitting a dazzle of light, but now they seemed to rise as they approached the bench, adding to the majesty of justice. They were usually closed; unless we were granted a good breeze, the air without was warmer than the shadowed arena within.

John and I went up the steps and into the empty courtroom and down the aisle and around the bench, past the exhausted American flag. I knocked at Hochstadter's door; he rumbled something, and we entered. The Judge was seated at his desk making no pretense at work; he was playing with a cigar lighter shaped like a flintlock rifle, snapping it on and off, and when we had said good morning he put it down. "Well, this is a fine kettle of fish," he said. That was his style. "Sit down."

"What happened?"

"I'm damned if I know just yet. But the indictment's returned."

"Who did Dietrich call?"

"Now that's interesting. He called the neighbors, the Donnelleys and the Lucases, and he called her parents, and Bryan, and a fellow named Rawlins, all the way from Dallas."

"That's her home town."

"Yes. But who is the fellow? There's something here we don't know about. And a doctor from somewhere. Here it is"—he shuffled a handful of notes—"a doctor named Hanford Selma. Also from Dallas."

"Dietrich must know a lot that we don't."

Hochstadter nodded gravely, frowning at Life and Death.

"Our own little Eden," I said. "Thank God it's your three months."

He leaned back and stared coolly. "Why do you say that?"

I raised a placating hand. "All right. I'm sorry I said it. I just don't feel up to a capital case yet."

"Yet? You've been a lawyer for three years and a judge for one, almost, and you've had it very easy. I hope you won't squirm when the larger responsibilities come to you."

I almost flushed, and felt deep anger, surely obvious for a split second; then I laughed and gestured at John and said, "Please. Not in front of the hired help."

"Sorry," he said. But his eyes were still grave and cool.

"Somebody coming," John said.

We waited, and after a few seconds even we non-redskins could hear the footsteps. A knock; the Judge rumbled again; the door opened and Alfred walked in with Tolliver and Bryan Talbot and Oliver Parmelee. We all said good morning. Oliver Parmelee was the town's most distinguished lawyer, who had been admitted to practice before the United States Supreme Court even before we were a state, and who was courteous enough never to say aloud that he, and not Hochstadter or—how much less!—I, should be on the bench. He was about fifty, a prissy man with minimal hair and four grown sons and a mysterious liver ailment; he was quite pale.

We were all looking at Talbot. The room was too small, nine by twelve beneath the high ceiling, and seven of us were crowded together. Talbot seemed sullen, but it was he who broke the silence: "I did not kill my wife," he said in a low, tight, emphatic voice, the words spaced and clear: "I did not kill my wife." His bruise was almost healed, barely a flush on the skin.

"The grand jury has not convicted you of murder," Hochstadter said, "and you are not on trial here. The grand jury found that there was sufficient evidence to warrant your standing trial. Alfred has arrested you— at least I assume he has."

"Yes," Alfred said. "I booked him just now."

"Very well. This is a preliminary hearing and the only legal action taken here will be setting bail. I'm sure Alfred's told you, though, that anything you say from now on may be used against you."

"I did not kill my wife," Talbot said, and his face was inflexible; his eyes glittered. He was hating.

"If you'll all be seated," Hochstadter said. "Three on the couch, there. Oliver, this armchair. We're a bit crowded, I'm afraid." He threw back his head and ran a hand over his silvery hair and pursed his lips solemnly. "Alfred, if you'll summarize."

"Yessir," Alfred said. He reached forward to slide a thin sheaf of papers onto the desk. "I have here the substance of an indictment handed down this morning by the grand jury—all the numbers and descriptions are there, and the dates—charging Bryan Talbot with the willful and premeditated murder of his wife Louise Talbot. They indicted for first-degree but I guess you and the jury have some leeway there. Acting on the bill, I've arrested him and have now brought him before a magistrate as required by law."

"Very good," the Judge said. "And I assume, Oliver, that you have been retained by Mr. Talbot?"

"That's correct," Parmelee said, and his voice was huge, always a surprise: a great operatic basso, though he looked like a breathless, paunchy tenor. "We'll answer to the indictment and plead at the proper time, and we now request that Your Honor set bail and a date for the arraignment."

"Yes. Now you understand, Mr. Talbot, about bail? Ordinarily, for a lesser offense, you may not leave the state, and you are required to be available, that is, findable, so to speak, whenever the authorities require your presence, failing which you have committed a further felony." Talbot only glowered. "I am empowered by law to set an extremely high bail for a crime of this magnitude, or to deny bail altogether, because obviously any further felony would not weigh heavily on the mind of a man guilty of first-degree murder."

"I am not guilty of first-degree murder or any murder," Talbot grated with the same baleful intensity.

"Please, Bryan," Parmelee said.

"You may not be," Hochstadter conceded. "And you are a citizen of some repute. I will set bail at five thousand dollars. Unless there was eyewitness testimony before the grand jury."

"No," Alfred said.

"I'll go that bail myself," Parmelee said immediately.

Hochstadter's eyebrows arched. "That's highly irregular."

"But perfectly legal," Parmelee said. "It's my feeling that this indictment is outrageous, as I think you'll agree when you've seen what it's based on. I am absolutely persuaded that Talbot is innocent."

"However that may be," Hochstadter answered, "I'll take your signature here for the bail." He drew a pincenez from his breast pocket, adjusted it, peered down at the papers, and scratched away with a pen. He reminded me of celluloid cuffs and sleeve garters.

When he was through Parmelee signed the paper, and Alfred stood up. Hochstadter nodded, and Alfred and Tolliver clomped out. "I'll talk to Dietrich today," the Judge said, "and arrange for a formal arraignment as quickly as possible. How's tomorrow morning at ten? You and he"—he was addressing Parmelee, and continued to nod at Parmelee even when his words were for Talbot—"can get together and decide how much time you want before the trial. Mr. Talbot, under the circumstances I'd like you to stay in Soledad County, and preferably in the city. When I've read the minutes I may decide to set a new bail."

"I'm not going anywhere," Talbot said. "I did not kill my wife."

"That's all for now," Hochstadter said.

"Come along, Bryan." Parmelee took Talbot by the arm, bowed slightly to the Judge, and led his client out of the room.

For several moments Hochstadter stared down at the papers on his desk as though the whorls and chicken tracks expressed a truth of great importance. He shook his head. "It's no fun," he said bitterly. "You go along now. I want to call Dietrich and see what the hell this is all about."

John and I left him there. We were much sobered.

The next morning Talbot pleaded not guilty. Hochstadter and Parmelee and Dietrich conferred and the Judge announced that the trial would begin on Tuesday, May 22nd. Emil Dietrich announced that he would prosecute personally, which was no surprise. He was the county District Attorney. The fire of his political ambitions had been banked during the war when his name alone disqualified him for public adulation; the high school had discontinued its course in German and the good ladies of the town labored long on wristers and mufflers for our side. But Dietrich was once more a first-class citizen and a candidate for practically anything. His announcement was not good news for Talbot. I noticed again how quickly we all assumed that an indictment was a conviction; by Friday afternoon a dozen townsfolk had asked me why Bryan would do a thing like that. "He didn't," I said; and they were startled and asked how I knew and I had to add, "until the jury says he did, he didn't. You remember that."

"That's right," they said, recalling. "But just suppose he *did* do it: why would he do a thing like that?"

I gave up. The world was too much with me, from Hochstadter on down, and I was not a peripatetic sophist approachable in the public streets and available for hourly preachments. My telephone rang every few minutes. John told people I was studying documents, which I was not—what documents? The bail bond? I knew little more than any courthouse loiterer: a handful of citizens had spoken under oath to a properly constituted body of solemn soothsayers, who had offered a hypothesis "in which, after the fashion of prophecy, the past is clear and historical, the future is dark, enigmatical, and erroneous." Politely, bland and impassive, John said, "That was Colonel Oates. He said he'd heard something absolutely amazing about Louise Talbot."

"I'll bet he did. I agree with you today, John. That man is an old biddy."

"I have nothing against him," John said. "He is a perfect example of the superior paleface but he keeps it to himself. He does not accuse me openly of eating dogs, cats and human flesh; but I can't help what my instinct says about him. Anyway, he'll see you tonight."

"Oh, fine," I said. "Rosemary's coming down. All we need is an evening with the old folks."

"Singing some of the great old songs. Judge——"

"What is it, John?"

"What do you think about Bryan Talbot?"

I remember closing a book, Fitzgerald or Sinclair Lewis, and standing up. "I don't want to think about Bryan Talbot," I said. "I don't think he did it because I never think anybody did it and I shouldn't be a judge, I should be a game warden."

The noble aborigine picked his nose awhile and then spoke. "The savages of the north, less civilized than my own people, tortured those who broke the law. If the victim died without whimpering, he was innocent. If he confessed, he was executed. Is that what you want?"

"We did that everywhere," I said gloomily. "No. It isn't what I want. I'm going out now. Close up when you want to and I'll see you Monday."

"Yessir," he said, and I took my Stetson and left him. Downstairs Geronimo poured me an ounce of bourbon from a Style-Nouveau reagent bottle and informed me that the sister of John D. Rockefeller, Jr., had been released unraped by bandits in Shantung, though her ten companions remained in durance. "Only the men have been molested," he said gravely, and we drank to Oriental delicacy.

After dinner I treated myself to a boisterous Mexican brandy. La Belle Eulalia had charred a steak beyond recognition, in the Spanish manner, and had then performed her customary magic: the meat tasted of juices, of garlic, of forest and field and bubbling spring. I whined in beggar's Spanish that we were always eating beef and why did we never have beans, and so forth, and the ladies were polite enough to laugh, sipping red wine and gazing fondly at their idiot companion. (My mother was proud of her ancient wisdom and high critical sense, but when I lapsed into Spanish, my mother tongue in the deepest sense, learned at the dug, she yielded to the most naïve maternal affection.) Rosemary was tall, blonde, with a hint of future plumpness, rich and quiet, luxe, calme, et volupté. She transported me (among other transports) to the eighteenth century, and to rural England. She was the squire's daughter, elegant, accomplished in French, spinet, needlepoint, and minuet, but not yet so far from the barnyard that she was above a rousing gavotte or a surreptitious tousling. Except that she was a good Lutheran, and sometimes bleak. Sometimes glum. (I, of course, was the wild, ruddy, black-haired horseman, flaying hounds, dropping grouse, downing claret and siring healthy bastards all over the manor.) But oh that voice! How could she teach, with that voice? I lisped in numbers, and the numbers came; I squeaked arithmetic. She taught third grade, and I suppose they were all tiny sopranos, so no one noticed.

That night I tried to focus on marrying Rosemary. (I assumed that she would have me.) I came to no conclusion because my mind wandered. It wandered to France and to Mexico. To a girl from Rambucourt who looked something like Rosemary and whose endorsement had won me the respect, cheap and stupid, of my fellow officers and gentlemen; and to Rafaela with whom I had milked goats on a hot day, wondering why the somber glance of a skinny fourteen-year-old could make me feel gangling and uncouth. I glanced at Rosemary's divine amplitude for reassurance and inspiration. She was pink and tan and sleepy, and her long hair was braided in a golden coronet.

The brandy was almost gone, and I was beginning to think of bed—so was Rosemary, I hoped—when the doorbell bonged. (It was a real bell, relic of a mission in Mexico razed by frenzied farmers half a century earlier.) I admitted Colonel Sebastian Oates, who went immediately to kiss my mother's hand and to present her with a bunch of rosebuds. "Sebastian," she said, "you are a gentleman. My son's idea of gallantry is tickling a housemaid. This home is the richer for your presence."

Colonel Oates beamed goatishly, cast a glance of ferocious superiority in my direction, and proceeded to his next goddess. "Miss Bergquist," he said. "Sweet Rosemary," and kissed her hand.

"That's for remembrance," I said, bored.

The Colonel vented a series of sniggering noises, intended, I supposed, to be devilish. "You're a bookish lout," he sneered, and let go of my girl to march to a wicker chair beside my mother's. He sat down in one swift geometric motion, like a carpenter's folding rule; he was still at attention. The room was not constructed, or decorated, for such rigidity: it was dim, with tan walls and dark brown beams, and its furnishings— couches, chairs, tables, lamps, books—were well used, comfortably aged. Even the reds and yellows in the Indian carpets had faded gracefully. "A cigar," he offered. I declined. He did not offer one to my mother. He did not know she smoked (any more than she knew —I hoped not—of the nocturnal migrations in her own home) and would not have believed it if he had seen it. "Well!" he said. "Anything new?"

"Not since this morning," I said.

"Rosemary." He barked the name. "Has your beau told you all about it?"

"Why, Colonel," Rosemary fluted primly. "You mustn't compromise me. If you mean Ben, he told me that Bryan Talbot was charged with murder."

"He was indeed." The Colonel beamed. "A horrible business. Horrible. And the story behind it, the facts, the facts—even worse. Depravity. Sordid, sordid."

I sighed aloud, and poured him a brandy in silence. Handing it to him I tried to seem concerned and just: "Colonel, you could only have heard what you are about to inflict on us from a member of the grand jury. They are supposedly bound to silence. If you listened, you helped a man break his oath. If you repeat what you heard, you are betraying the spirit if not the letter of the law."

"That's right," he said. "Well spoken, lad. You've done your duty. I shall say no more."

"Good."

"I hear President Harding is going to Alaska," my mother offered, "and will return by way of the Panama Canal."

"Joseph Conrad is in New York," Rosemary chirped, "on his first visit to the United States."

"A dangerous man," the Colonel said grimly. "There is venery in his books. I read one called Lord Jim, and a story about a man with a boat. Mr. Conrad has little respect for law and order. And one thing leads to another, you know. Give me Owen Wister any time."

To my mother I said, "Your friend," in obvious disgust.

"You are young," the Colonel snapped. "You underestimate the baseness of man. Bryan Talbot, for instance. I'd like to know exactly what he was in the habit of reading. Any man who could do what he did—"

"Are you trying to say that Joseph Conrad is an incitement to murder? For God's sake. And Talbot's only indicted, not convicted."

Rosemary glanced from me to him and back, dreading brouhaha; but the old gentleman, in his white linen, with his bloody military mustache and his ramrod back and his piercing blue eyes and his god damned old woman's mind and old woman's tongue, his glossy tan, the deep wrinkles bracketing his nose, the sleek fine white hair carefully parted and the imitation regimental tie, sat there nodding his iron head. I did not like him.

"Not to murder," he said loftily. "But to contempt for the decencies, which may lead anywhere."

Oh, Jesus. The decencies. He was off now and not to be stopped.

"I regret having to mention this before ladies," he began, and he regretted it as an undertaker regrets, "but Bryan Talbot, four years ago, brought an unmentionable disease into his home."

After a moment I said what was always said, "It's no worse than a bad cold."

"It was much worse," he said quietly. "He communicated it to his wife, who had no choice but to undergo an operation that deprived her forever of the opportunity to bear children."

After another moment I said, "I'm sorry," trying to keep surly resentment from my voice.

"It was after that that she became promiscuous," the Colonel said. "It was after that that she took a lover, with whom she transgressed on her periodic visits to Dallas, ostensibly to see her parents."

Rosemary avoided his eye, and mine; she was pale. My mother sat frowning.

"And it was as a result of *that*," the Colonel finished, only the slightest of flourishes in his voice, "that Bryan Talbot strangled her."

Which killed the weekend. When the train chuffed away Sunday night I realized with relief, with shame, that marriage had not been mentioned. And walking home sadly, past Bosko Boskovitch's grocery, dark this Sunday night, past Magratan's hardware and Wapelo's stationery store and Lew's Hand Laundry, crossing Houston Road and striking for the bridge, I saw him. Peter Justin's Billiard Parlor was open but no one was playing billiards. The huge overhead lamps with shades like coolie hats showered yellow light on half a dozen men in the midst of whom Bryan Talbot stood gesticulating as he spoke. All I could see was a white shirt and a broad red necktie, red galluses, and the florid, intense face with brilliant flame-blue eyes. Peter Justin stood nodding, a beefy man, size nineteen neck they said, needing a shave, hair thin and plastered flat. I heard the rapid, businesslike voice but could distinguish no words, and I passed along quickly like a hitchhiker putting behind him the gate to an insane asylum. Thank God! I thought. Thank God this is none of my worry!

And so I reached home, lusts appeased and love not yet reduced to memory and longing, and slept the sleep of the just.

4

JUDGE ALVIN HOCH-
stadter always made solemn efforts to radiate distinc-
tion, and always failed. Silvering hair on a massive head,
set off by his invariable black string tie, afforded him an
initial advantage on which, sadly, he was unable to im-
prove. His voice was soft, his body flabby, his roguish-
ness infrequent and elephantine: the total effect was one
of amiable and weak dignity.

George Costa, bailiff-sergeant-at-arms-tipstaff, closed
the doors at the rear of the full courtroom. Harvey
Bump, court clerk and recorder, oyezoyezed nasally,
and Hochstadter emerged from the wings. We rose; he
sat; we sat; and on a dusty yellow morning, with bands
of sunlight streaking through the rippled panes and stip-
pling the motley audience, Judge Hochstadter faced the
state, the defense, and his public.

It was Tuesday, the twenty-second of May, at ten in
the morning, and Louise Talbot had been dead for almost three weeks. No delays had been moved; Dietrich's case was, he said, as tight as it would ever be,
and Parmelee was sure of an acquittal. Hochstadter had
misjudged him altogether, telling me a week earlier,
"Parmelee'll move for a change of venue. Then he'll
fight the jury. He'll bring out that they've heard the rumors and he'll move for a change of venue again. He'll
object and object to make a record. Oh, he'll be trouble, all right."

But Parmelee was no trouble at all. He was almost

silent at the arraignment, and when the trial opened he
sat composed, still pale and presumably liverish but
quite calm. Talbot was sullen but not withdrawn, and
looked about him often. He met my eyes now and then,
and I nodded, and he nodded back. (I was in the first
row of spectators, a corner seat.) My fellow onlookers
craned and whispered and shuffled their feet and flapped
at the heat with straw fans and newspapers. My own
fan, a handsome and sturdily hemmed concoction like a
straw ping-pong paddle, bore the name of the funeral
parlor from which Louise Talbot had been buried; it
had been presented to me, with suitable expressions of
sympathy, at my father's funeral. He had been county
sheriff for nine years and had died of a heart attack
playing poker at Peter Justin's, with good whiskey in
his belly and a good cigar in his mouth and five worth-
less cards in his right hand. He had been a foursquare
Welsh Methodist though a heavy drinker and my mother, a bad Catholic, was certainly not the woman to let
him backslide posthumously. The Reverend Doctor
Wesley Arthur Jones had missed the point of my father's life but had given him a rousing send-off. If my
mother's genius hovered about me in the presence of
women—natural enough, I insist—my father's ghost
murmured when I was in court; he had been one aspect
of the law and I was another. I will not bore you with
platitudinous episodes from my childhood in which
Bulldog—he resembled one, a big one, and ruddy—
taught me justice; mostly he taught me not to inflict
pain, and very often that was what justice meant. Or
rightness, and if justice was not rightness, how
could it be justice? That was why you shot a crippled
horse. That was also why you drank during Prohibition.
Because sometimes justice and rightness did not seem
to be the same. Justice was public and rightness was
private and if they were not the same you chose right-

ness and did not inflict pain. He killed fish quickly though he had been told that they did not feel pain. A gut shot was unjust and he worried over one gut-shot antelope for many years, referring to it when he was depressed or drunk, but did not worry at all and only snorted when I was taken in flagrante with the younger Owens girl, both of us thirteen and in flagrante meaning that her blouse was wide open. Her chest was much like mine.

He would have snorted again but without approval watching our fellow citizens scramble for places in the courtroom. The air was golden with the bright unquenchable gleam of prurience. Fishing trips were cancelled, shops unattended; the public squares—two benches in a patch of dust, most of them—were deserted, save the courthouse square, which had become a picnic ground: couples, old men, women with babies. Sandwiches and water bottles. White-throated swifts and white-bellied sparrows hopping and flashing from sycamore to sycamore. The people were quiet enough, and I do not mean to offer the impression that they were bloodthirsty, but nothing since the war had so stirred the town, and even the war consisted largely of band music at the depot. Tolliver, Alfred's young constable, had helped Talbot to the defendant's chair and had then gone outside to keep the courthouse steps clear. In the courtroom the lucky ones peered at Talbot, rustled newspapers, buzzed and whispered and fanned. I chatted briefly with Edgar Musgrave, whose topics ranged from Bonar Law's resignation a couple of days before to a judge in Houston who had granted two hundred and twelve divorces in two hundred and forty-five minutes. Edgar said it was easy because most of them were uncontested. One was interesting, granted to a woman who had been dragged out of her house in Goose Creek the previous January and flogged by five men in disguise.

"Damned cowards," Edgar said. "The Klan, I bet. Like those Chinese bandits. Know what they did last week?"

"No."

"They held up a train and took three prisoners, and then threw them off a cliff as a warning, because they think the government's stalling on the ransom for those captives. Damned cowards. There was an earthquake in Quito. Lot of people killed. I didn't know Talbot wore a wrist watch."

"Yes," I said. "And a straw hat."

"He could appeal if he had to," Edgar said. "Can't get a fair trial in Soledad City if you wear a wrist watch and a straw hat. Smokes cigarettes too. Prejudiced jury. Damned cowards."

"You're behind the times," I said. "Wrist watches are all right now. Since the war. Hardly the place for those old turnips. And a lot of people smoke cigarettes. Anyway an appeal is mandatory if he's convicted."

"Coffin nails," he said. "You know the best story this week?"

"What?" The courtroom was almost full.

"Harding appointed a colored man to be collector of customs in New Orleans, and the Louisiana authorities wouldn't stand for it and made him quit. So Harding reappointed him. That's pretty good for the old boy, hey? And the best part of it is the man's name." I waited. Edgar grinned. "Walter Cohen. Isn't that something?"

"I don't believe it."

"God's truth," he said. "Walter Cohen. Those Louisiana people have no poetry, that's all. If they throw him out again, let's give him a job here."

"Or send them Geronimo," I said, and Edgar whooped gleefully as Harvey Bump stood up.

Now this trial, and my account of it, need some

gloss. A good trial is, as you know, consummate drama.
It helps a drama if there is a triangle (Agamemnon,
Achilles, Briseis) or if the crime is Everyman's secret
dream (Oedipus) or if there is a radical involved, a free
mind in Brownian motion against the walls of the tin
box called society (Socrates). But only one trial in a
thousand is even interesting, unless you care for arcana,
the priesthood of lawyers performing before the hallowed symbols (flag, Bible, robes, water pitcher) and
chanting ferociously in a dead language. Otherwise the
usual trial is a contest in chicanery, but at least it is a
contest, and chicanery is often less inconvenient than
unchecked crime. And even the dullest trial pits man
against man, mind (however shallow) against mind,
and is therefore a diversion, not as exciting as a good
cockfight but superior to whist. The presumption of innocence, politely maintained even in the face of absolutely Euclidian demonstration, makes the contest.

But in its undercurrents Bryan Talbot's trial was not
so much a diversion as a community bloodletting. Parmelee could not have foreseen how sharply the town
would react. For the space of three or four days all the
normal hostilities of an American town were translated
into the language of Bryan Talbot's alleged crime. And
those hostilities were not merely the platitudinous fric-
tions of a mongrel population; they were, suddenly and
astonishingly, open passion. Or so it seemed to me. An
outsider might have seen the gloating and gossiping and
horrified repugnance as the normal reactions of placid
burghers to a crime that repelled and attracted them
equally. But watching the watchers I sensed more. A
deep pleasure, for example, among the Mexicans because this monster was a gringo and a Protestant, and
the Mexicans had lived through generations here knowing that to Talbot's kind a Mexican was not simply a

Mexican but the embodiment of Latin lust, consort to the Whore of Babylon; Catholicism itself was somehow like a fat woman flirting with the Devil. And among the Negroes because clearly there was no way to blame this enormity on a black man, and we all knew—but no one dared say—that we kept Negroes where they were and how they were not because they were evil but because we were and it was easier to ignore that by inventing a reservoir of exotic and enigmatic ruffians. And among the "best people" because they could conveniently and righteously disown Talbot, hate him and fear him openly without feeling at all immoral or unChristian; to them he was like a naked baby in a front yard, a red shirt at a funeral, burlesque, a colored Congressman from Chicago, or a boy and a girl in the back seat of a Locomobile. Solidarity had come to the town, and Bryan Talbot was the common enemy, and everyone had a reason to be happy. Bryan Talbot had sinned against God and broken ancient laws, and for a few days everyone else in Soledad City felt virtuous.

Normally jurors are reluctant to serve. The variety of their excuses, the imagination and industry lavished on them, would do credit to a surrealist. The veniremen are all indispensable at their offices, plants, stores, or farms. Their wives are sick and they have many children. They have weak bladders and are unable to sit still for more than an hour. They have strong opinions on the crime at issue and would be unable to render an unemotional verdict. A business deal six months in the making is to be consummated this week. Their religion does not permit them to assist the state in punishing evildoers. They are friends of one or another lawyer, plaintiff, or defendant. They are subject to headaches that warp their judgment. They are recovering from typhoid. Their mare is about to foal or their prize black-and-tan to throw a litter. They are on a special diet for rheumatism. They become hysterical when locked in a room. They have boils and cannot abide wooden benches.

Normally. Not this time. Never since have I seen so many able-bodied Americans oppressed by a surplus of leisure and asking only to devote their hours to the state. The venire facias had been answered by thirty of the most eager public servants this side of William Jennings Bryan, who had just been elected a commissioner by the Presbytery of Southeastern Florida.

The first two veniremen were accepted without a murmur, upright citizens named Sawyer (an engineer at the waterworks) and Meldrum (a butcher).

Dietrich had no questions.

Nor had Parmelee. Not even about capital punishment.

Hochstadter almost let his eyebrows rise. There was a gentle buzz in the audience; Hochstadter rapped once, and the next candidate was introduced. His name was Diego Gutiérrez.

Dietrich had no questions.

Nor had Parmelee. Not even about capital punishment.

Hochstadter looked thoughtful.

In twenty minutes six veniremen had been accepted. The seventh was a Mrs. Arthur Dodd.

Dietrich had no objections, but Parmelee challenged for cause.

Hochstadter nodded; he seemed relieved. "Please state the cause."

"The victim of the crime was a woman; accused is a man."

"And you feel that a woman might be swayed by her emotions."

"That is correct."

"The lady may be excused," Hochstadter said. Mrs. Dodd looked as if she would weep. "I'm sorry, madam. I believe counsel's point is well taken. May I ask"—he turned to Parmelee—"that you state your grounds more fully in the future."

Parmelee bowed. "Of course, Your Honor."

And that, incredibly, was that. Parmelee challenged another woman, who was dismissed; and the jury was complete, with two alternates, in less than an hour. Parmelee had challenged no man. He was sure. He was staking everything on one roll. He worried me.

Emil Dietrich's opening statement was a model. So far the town had nourished itself on rumor alone, and the spectators awaited confirmation of Talbot's depravity; Dietrich did not disappoint them. There were men leaning forward, avid, bright-eyed; there were women who refused to look at Talbot or even at Dietrich except sidelong but who emanated prim attention. "The means, in this case," Dietrich said, "was a pair of human hands. That Bryan Talbot had the opportunity is obvious; indeed that *only* Bryan Talbot had the opportunity seems equally obvious. It is the moral obligation of the state, however, to demonstrate a motive; and because—we admit this—there were no eyewitnesses, it is the state's obligation to prove to you beyond question that the motive was of such emotional force that it could, and did, impel the defendant to the most extreme and irrevocable of human actions: murder." And so on, for a minute or two, after which he digressed: "You must understand what first-degree murder is. Judge Hochstadter will instruct you further on that, later; for now I will say that first-degree murder is deliberate homicide by a human being who is sane within the legal definition and who has premeditated the act. That is, who has thought about it beforehand. There's one tricky point here. He doesn't have to have thought about it for months, or weeks, or days, or even hours. If the idea comes to him and he thinks about it for as much as five seconds, the murder is premeditated; the law assumes that *any* time for thought is sufficient time for a man to think twice, not only about killing but about the *wrongness* of killing. About the consequences.

"Now I will tell you more exactly what the state will prove. The state will prove that in 1919 Bryan Talbot contracted a social disease." He paused; utter silence. "That he communicated that disease to his wife Louise." Another pause. "That as a result she was obliged to undergo surgery, more precisely an operation called a hysterectomy, as a natural result of which she was barred forever from bearing children." I thought his pause here was not for effect; it was as though even he, after the days of preparation, was not ready to absorb such facts. But he may have been wishing that he had some women on the jury. "That as a further and later consequence, in her resentment of her husband she took at least one lover, with a strong probability that it was more than one; and that her husband's motive for killing her was a violent resentment of her promiscuity coupled with a deadly sense of his own guilt in the tragic course of her life."

He was on dangerous ground, and knew it, and shifted immediately. "I suppose you are now thinking of certain 'unwritten laws,' by which traditionally a man discovering his wife in adultery is considered to be justified in taking violent action. Although the state believes that written laws are more important than unwritten, the state nevertheless acknowledges the strong emotions that may possess a man at such a time. But"—and here he gazed at each juror briefly—"the state will prove that it was not a sudden, instinctive reaction to one incident that motivated the accused. We will prove that Louise Talbot's infidelities had occurred over a period of two years and more; that her husband knew about them and therefore condoned them; and that it was no single instance that drove him to murder—that, indeed, his wife had not been away from him for many weeks before the murder. The state will prove that this husband, who acquiesced in his wife's infidelities for a long time, coldly and deliberately murdered her with absolutely no immediate provocation, out of his accumulated resentment of a situation which he himself, more than any other human being, had brought about. It was willful and premeditated murder."

He was silent for a few moments, and then drew a long breath. When he resumed his voice was more official. "The state's case, as you will see, does not rest on any firsthand, eyewitness evidence of the murder. It consists largely of what is called circumstantial evidence. Now: there is a superstition, a wrong belief, a misapprehension, very commonly held about circumstantial evidence. People who do not know the law will tell you that you cannot convict on circumstantial evidence. That is very simply not true. This kind of evidence—that is, evidence that sets the time, place, method; evidence that *excludes* other possibilities; evidence that is a net, in which it is obvious that the accused is caught, rather than a searchlight pointing directly at him—has been, in more than half the serious criminal cases in which I have been involved, the evidence on which the prosecution based its case. It is not too much to say that without circumstantial evidence courts of law would be paralyzed, and justice would be utterly impossible. The judge will, I am sure, have more to say to you about this later on."

Dietrich flattered the jury adroitly. His voice was just barely emotional; he was not leading them on a crusade, but was admitting them as thinking men to the processes, the intimacies, of the law. He was making citizens of them, and the solemnity of their faces proved his success. He went on, discussing the murder itself. He did not point out that the death sentence was mandatory upon conviction; Parmelee would play upon that in his closing statement, in the classic effort to remind men that they were not God and that even a legal execution would leave blood on their hands. Dietrich finished in a low key, reminding the jury that we had not been a state for long but were no longer a territory, and that the existence of law, and of respect for it, was one great difference between barbarism and civilization. The law, and not the visceral preferences of the population: I thought of Gibbon and the wry smile with which he must have written "But patience is not the attribute of zeal; nor can the arts of a court be adapted to the freedom and violence of popular enthusiasm." He meant another kind of court, but he spoke true.

Well, Dietrich had a good jury: not crusty old cattle barons or domineering male heroes, but the butcher the baker the candlestick maker, spongy men of the middle class who, taking their wives in adultery, would be more likely to sulk than to shoot. Parmelee would get nowhere with the unwritten law; but I suspected that Parmelee did not intend to bring it up.

Hochstadter recessed until two o'clock and I went home to lunch, avoiding the Colonel. I had chicken salad and beer, and resumed the morning's events for my mother. She was somber, for her, but requested details; her Wednesday night mahjongg group, she said, would want to know everything. And she was writing to Ignacio, who missed me.

By which she meant Rafaela.

Cousin Ignacio was Ignacio Montemayor, and he was a distant cousin who owned property in the state of Sonora about a hundred and fifty miles southwest of us on an unambitious river. He had a married son, Ramón, and two married daughters, Julia and Marta, and an unmarried daughter, Rafaela. His first wife had died fifteen years before and his second wife, an Indian, about five years before. He had not married a third time. His correspondence with my mother was European: respectful, formal, newsy letters in an elegance of phrase and hand that died with the nineteenth century. We visited perhaps twice a year before the war and then more often; after my father died, my mother took comfort from the bosom of the family, though it was a skinny family and a bony bosom, only Ignacio and Rafaela left to tend the estate. We always hired a car and left early, allowing six hours for travel and minor repairs. We entered Arizona and roared from Douglas to Bisbee to Nogales. At Nogales we rested because we could get a drink just by crossing the street. Nogales must have been the most cheerful of Prohibition towns: half in the land of the free, dry, and half in sodden Mexico. From Nogales we aimed straight at the Rio Concepción and then followed the river to Ignacio's, bouncing along a track that put me in mind of Central Asian trade routes. A caravan, camels and yurts and pointed turbans, would not have surprised me there. By the time we reached Ignacio's we were encased in dust, half blind, and stiff in the joints. Two hours later we were clean and refreshed, pumping a powerful red wine into ourselves and chatting in barbarous Spanish, all but Ignacio, who was phatic: he communicated in elemental bursts of sound reinforced by the jiggling, bobbing, or oscillation of hands, shoulders, feet, hips, and head. He was just too lazy to bother with consonants.

The Montemayors were far more important to me than I knew; and when I think back I can remember almost nothing of what was said. I remember the land, the vine-covered slopes and the field of maize, the groves along the river, the higher slopes where Ignacio and my father had hunted desert rams, the gardens near the house and the formal fishpond, and the homes of Ignacio's tenants, or fellow farmers, or dependents—the relationship was never clear. I remember a town some fifteen miles down the river, with an alcalde and a guard post, and neither the mayor nor the soldiers really sure to whom they owed allegiance; and a priest who was quite sure, which outraged Ignacio, who hated priests. It was an adobe town with a beautiful stone church that lacked a bell. The bell had been carried off for smelting years before in a local Jacquerie. I remember the cantina there, beaded curtains, dark inside, many flies, but cool, and tequila slowly invading the eyes and brain so that the walls and bottles and bartender shifted from dark green to purple and preposterously to dark yellow and the day outside the door was bright red through the hanging beads and even the voices took on tints, murmured browns and grays and a clanging orange and the dirty pink of a shrill laugh.

I remember Rafaela only dimly in those early days. She was eight years younger than I and slightly wall-eyed; wide-set eyes, almost black and diverging slightly. Rafaela loved all living things and sulked when the men hunted. We paid little attention to her, a girl; but now and then her grave composure was disquieting even to adults. I condescended to her for many years because she made me feel like a child. Her voice was dignified, its tone level; she spoke slowly and firmly, and she never lied.

All that too was my life; how much of it, Bryan Talbot may have taught me.

Juano Menéndez owned—flaunted—a Stanley Steamer, and at twenty minutes of two he barged into the courthouse square on his burnished throne. The automobile itself was almost silent, emitting a gentle ffft-ffft-ffft, but was usually followed by a pack of yelping hounds; apparently the Steamer gave off a hiss, or a whistle, beyond the range of the human ear but irresistible to dogs. This day Juano came to a stop almost surrounded by small children, and with cheerful resignation he dismounted, plucked a large sack from the seat, and poured an inch of chestnuts onto the boiler. The children, all shapes and colors, watched in silence and greedy awe. The automobile hissed delicately, an outsize samovar. I stood beside Juano and contemplated the pagan, hungry eyes of tomorrow's leaders, the white teeth, the torn shirts and the varied pigments, the bare feet, the scabby knees, the grimy wrists and elbows, the loving effulgence of sunlight on young hair. The day was bright, hot; the square lay in a peaceful bath of tropical balm, Juano was stocky, black hair turning white, his skin dark and leathery; he was health itself, and well-muscled health, and even in lazy repose he emanated strength. "This looks bad," he said. "What a bad thing."

"If it's all true," I said.

"Mmm. I hope it's not. But what else? What a bad thing. Will they hang him?"

"If he's found guilty he has to hang. It's the law."

"A bad law," he said. "Maybe not. She has no brother to do it, and her father is an old and weak man. I saw him."

"You think private revenge is better than the law?"

He considered. "I don't know. When the law does it, everybody shares. The law does it for you and me. But you and me, we don't really care about that woman. We weren't really hurt that she died."

"Yes we were. Because it could have been us. Anybody. For different reasons. She died for all of us."

"Well now," he said, "for all of us? You make her sound like the Christ." He plunged into the thicket of children and extinguished the fire. "All right," he called. "First, one for everybody. Then you can fight for the rest." The dogs had drifted off. "You know who is most nervous?" he asked me.

"Who?"

"Willie Waite."

"My God. I never even thought of him."

"He was drunk again last night. Which is not unusual, but he looked bad."

I sighed. "He gets paid for it, but I don't suppose that makes much difference."

"A pension. Until now it was a pension. More than a dollar a day for doing nothing. But you're right. The money doesn't help."

Willie Waite was about forty-five, with a slattern for a wife and two unhealthy little children. He had been a ranch hand, salt digger, prospector, guide, dishwasher, handy man, hostler, and even, in days long gone, towel boy at Consuelo's, an establishment of blessed memory of which I will have more to say. He was a man of no accomplishment, no character, no eccentricity; he was just Willie Waite; and he was also the official, state-appointed, one-and-only hangman of Soledad County. The hangman has never been in demand socially, and the old custom of hiding him behind a black mask was a good one. With the mask he was anonymous and therefore surrogate for us all; without it he had his own identity and absolved the rest of us. With it he could do his day's work and go home and tell his friends he'd been fishing; without it he had no friends. It was, come to think of it, not much different with soldiers, or anyway enlisted men; we paid them to do our killing and then locked up our daughters when they came to town. They were crude and not civilized like the rest of us and did not have a home with a garden. I had not seen Willie Waite for months. He was a member of the Ku Klux Klan and, some said, the junior kleagle or whatever in our county.

"Let's go in," Juano said.

"It's full," I said. "Have you got a seat?"

"A cousin," he said. "He was there this morning. This afternoon I take the seat and he goes back to work. Luis Nava. You know him. The bean merchant. He runs the cockfights."

"I know him," I said. "I think he is my cousin too in a complicated way."

Juano clapped me on the back. "Let's go, cousin."

Dietrich spent an hour or so establishing Louise Talbot's presence—and the probable absence of anyone else—at the house on the evening of the murder. (It was here that Mrs. Orville Moody contributed her observations, and the Colonel, and Henry Dugan.) He was working chronologically with his witnesses, establishing the time and place and mood before he even established the crime. Helen Donnelley took the stand late that afternoon and I saw for the first time that she was attractive, almost beautiful; overlooked and ignored by us rakish masculine chaffers because she was, after all, in her forties, because she had, after all, two children, because her husband was, after all, an elder; and beauty, to us local studs, was under thirty and virginal, like Charlie Chaplin's blessed damozels. Mrs. Donnelley suffered another disadvantage: if a man thought of her at all it was as Louise Talbot's next-door neighbor. She was a tall woman with a sturdy, uncompromising figure; her hair was dark brown and her eyes were gray, and her nose was straight and fine. The thought touched me that Rosemary would be not very different in twenty years: an inch or two more here and there, and with those inches a softer warmth and a deeper heart. I liked Helen Donnelley. She spoke directly and without obvious emotion. Yes, she had chatted with Louise Talbot, from about five-thirty to about six. She had then greeted Bruce, who also spoke briefly to Mrs. Talbot. No one else had joined them. She had seen Colonel Oates stop by earlier. Louise Talbot had been placid and friendly.

Dietrich paused then, and nodded, and asked suddenly, "Have you ever seen Bryan Talbot drunk?"

Mrs. Donnelley hesitated, and spoke slowly: "I have seen him when he had been drinking. I don't know about these things, and I can't say whether he was drunk."

"Very good," Dietrich said. "How did he behave?

Was he pugnacious, friendly, sullen?"

"Objection," Parmelee said. "Calls for a conclusion."

"Sustained," Hochstadter said.

"Did he ever pick a quarrel when he had been drinking?"

"No."

"Laugh excessively, become boisterous?"

"No."

"Fall down?"

"No."

"Talk gibberish?"

"No."

"I want to phrase this next question carefully." Dietrich smiled. "To your way of thinking, did Bryan Talbot behave in a noticeably different manner when he had been drinking?"

Parmelee did not object.

Again Mrs. Donnelley was careful. "I would say, yes. His—well, his emotions were *more so*."

"That is, heightened."

"Yes. He hardly ever showed affection, in public I mean, when he was sober, but one day when he'd been drinking he went over to Louise and gave her a big kiss right on the mouth, and hugged her. She had to break loose from him because he was squeezing her. And that same day he started to make a speech against the Democrats, and he got terribly angry."

"But he knew what he was saying, and he was coherent."

"Oh, yes."

"Thank you, Mrs. Donnelley," and Dietrich turned to Parmelee and said, "Your witness."

And Parmelee never even mentioned liquor. I frowned; but I thought I understood. Parmelee would not plead drunken impulse, but he would not deny intoxication either; he believed that Talbot was innocent, drink or no drink, and he believed that he could prove it. So he spent his time establishing two points: that the Talbots had never quarreled noticeably, and that they had been good neighbors. Which points, to Mrs. Donnelley's knowledge, were true; so Parmelee thanked her and sat down.

Dietrich hurried forward. "Mrs. Donnelley: do you say that in the time you were the Talbots' neighbors you never heard a whisper of complaint, never a hint of quarrel, from your friend Louise Talbot?"

"That's right."

"But you know married life: isn't it fair to assume that there were at least minor disputes, coolnesses, differences of opinion?"

"Yes, I think so."

"And you never heard the slightest breath of any of that from the Talbots?"

"No. Not at all."

"Thank you, Mrs. Donnelley."

"Thank you, Mrs. Donnelley," Hochstadter said. "You may step down now."

"Bruce Donnelley," Dietrich called, and the elder took his wife's place on the stand. He walked like a bear: strong, solid, with heavy, even steps. The reliable, phlegmatic American: he seemed unblinking. He also seemed slow-witted, not volatile.

He confirmed what his wife had said.

"And you did not see her go into the house?"

"No."

"Then you saw no one else with her?"

"No. Of course not. I only saw her for half a minute."

"And never again?"

Bruce shook his head heavily. "Never."

"Thank you. That's all."

Then Parmelee stepped forward and repeated with Bruce the line he had taken with Mrs. Donnelley. Bruce maintained firmly that no whisper of trouble had escaped the Talbot household. Dietrich also repeated himself, and sat down smiling. It was a rare enough moment: each attorney had scored a point, and each felt his own victory to be the more important. Parmelee had shown that the Talbots were outwardly happy; Dietrich had tried to show that their façade was utterly impenetrable and therefore that anything at all might have been roiling the household.

This was quite unappetizing to the spectators. Dietrich was, in his fussy, overcareful way, trying to anticipate the defense's contention that some unknown party had spoken with Louise Talbot, that somewhere in Soledad City there had been a man with reason to return, with lacerated emotions, with a continuing and passionate interest; and he had tried to define Talbot as an erratic, but not unbalanced, drunk. Within limits, he had succeeded; but only within limits. Louise Talbot's private life remained private, and Bryan remained a figure of woozy doubt. Still, the jury was left with an impression that Louise Talbot was home alone most of the time, and that her life in Soledad City was quiet and full of Bryan. And she had done no entertaining on the day of her death.

Dietrich spent the last hour of the day on the crime itself: let them think about it overnight. Alfred testified, and Tolliver, who was officious and exact and contributed nothing, and Doctor Schilling. Dietrich played on Talbot's bruise; the doctor said that it had been "fairly fresh," incurred certainly "within the half hour," and Dietrich favored the jury with a faceful of hypocritical sorrow. The doctor went on to say that Talbot had been drunk, and in shock. The deceased had been strangled but was otherwise unharmed. Otherwise unharmed!

Parmelee could do little with these witnesses. Alfred and the doctor agreed that Talbot's babbling might have been meaningless, but Alfred managed to hint that it was important, would bear further thought, and seemed incriminating. Doctor Schilling admitted that the bruise was more than a scratch, but would not say that the victim could not have inflicted it. The rest of us believed what we wanted to, and what I saw at the time was Talbot drunk, seizing a woman, ignoring her frantic blow, and tearfully taking revenge on God knew what unnamed oppressors for God knew what unnamed oppressions. That is, I could see the act, but I could not see why; not even after Peter Justin testified.

Justin might have plunged us into chaos by declining to mention liquor. We all drank but were not required to incriminate ourselves, and the Fifth Amendment was still as valid as the Eighteenth. But he spoke freely, and I learned later that Dietrich, no enemy to schnapps, had promised him an informal, and highly illegal, immunity. Justin said phlegmatically that Talbot had drunk about half a bottle of bourbon in two hours. Straight, with chasers. Justin had turned him out at ten minutes of ten: Talbot was wobbling, and had picked a fight. Senseless, and with a total stranger, who had seen a dark and lovely woman in the streets earlier and was congratulating Justin on the local talent.

Talbot lurched toward the man and said, "Just keep your mouth *shut*, buddy."

"Easy, Bryan," Justin said. "He wasn't talking about Louise."

"The hell he wasn't," Talbot said. "They all do. Where you from, buddy? Dallas, maybe?"

The stranger, imperturbable, gave Talbot obscene instructions, and Talbot lunged but Justin had him by the back of the shirt and threw him out amiably.

Parmelee followed this testimony with barely suppressed excitement, which died abruptly when Justin went on to say that the stranger had sat drinking until midnight.

"Did Talbot mention his wife again?"

"Just as he was leaving."

"What did he say?"

Justin looked at Talbot here, and the first gentle grimace tightened his features. "He said, 'Damn that woman. *Damn* that woman,' and then he went on out."

"And that was the last you saw of him that night?"

"It was."

"Your witness." And Dietrich sat down.

Parmelee cross-examined with skill. Delicately, establishing but not defaming his client's character, he allowed Justin to make it known that Talbot was an habitual drinker but not a drunkard, and that in his year of drinking he had committed no act of violence in Justin's presence. The spectators were disappointed, cheated; they had hoped for more.

But when Hochstadter adjourned at a quarter to five the courtroom emptied slowly, amid bombination: tomorrow the strangers would testify. Tomorrow there would be talk of death and fornication, of bitter laughter and bitter tears; of tragedy. Soledad City, our wholesome middle-class American town, would be lined up three deep for good seats.

5

AND THE NEXT MORN-
ing I had troubles of my own. It was another fine day, a
bit too hot but not oppressive, and on my way to the
office at eight-fifteen I admired the high-school girls
who crossed my path: blooming, tan, those white teeth
and clear eyes, and they seemed to smell of prickly pear
and blue grama grass. They reminded me of Rafaela
because I had watched her grow up, from an ignored
infant to a lovely chiaroscuro little girl, and she too
smelled of the grasses and pines, even later when she
was a tomboy repairing baby birds or riding home with
a hurt lamb across the saddle. We had examined the
lamb together and Rafaela smiled shyly, as another girl
might who had just finished sewing her very own ging-
ham dress. Later Rafaela could do that too and once
we sat for two hours while she hemmed and I read, and
every few minutes she looked up, dark eyes in a lovely
Old World face—wasted on me then—to smile that
same shy smile. But these girls, in the streets of my
town, were a different breed; they traveled in flocks.
Most of them wore white middy blouses. The boys were
in jeans and had their sleeves rolled up. In my day
twenty years earlier—over sixty years ago now!—the
authorities had experimented briefly, requiring linen
jackets. Parents had repaired to the then Judge, a man
named Crown, threatening to sue because their children
did not own linen jackets and the public school system
of the territory had no right to demand expenditures

over the usual taxes. The territory had been edging its way into Supreme Court decisions and the legislature was tired of rebuffs, so Crown simply notified the Board of Education that a linen jacket, or anyway requiring one, was unconstitutional. The Board then laid out almost four hundred dollars for eighty linen jackets of various sizes that were given to the boys. So the parents threatened to sue for misuse of school funds. They quieted down when the Board promised not to buy any more, and as soon as the first batch wore out we went back to khaki and denim. Nowadays children have to buy their own neckties and pens and accident insurance and God knows what. One of my grandchildren was required to pony up a dollar for something called a class terrarium. A thousand square miles of desert, salt flats, cottonwood groves, farmland, pasture, and good solid diorite mountains within a day's ride, not to mention bats, rats, shrews, carrion beetles, and ant lions, but the class needed a terrarium. City Hall is *still* full of lizards, but the class needed a terrarium.

Anyway I reached my office at about eight-thirty and saw a stranger waiting outside the door. About my age, short and stocky, dark and hard, and as soon as he spoke I knew he was from back east, Illinois or Indiana maybe. "Good morning," he said. "Are you Judge Lewis?"

"Good morning," I said. "I am. Let me get this open and come on in."

"My name is Gorman," he said.

"How do you do. Had breakfast?"

"Oh, yes," he breezed. "I start early."

I grunted, never having considered early starts particularly virtuous and preceded him into the office. I waved him to a chair and sat down while my face took on magisterial lines. "Can I help you?"

"My identification," he said, and slid his wallet toward me. Gorman, Francis X., Treasury Department. Special Investigator. Et cetera.

"A Federal man," I said. "What is it? Trouble at the bank?"

"No sir. I'm what most people call a Prohibition agent."

"Then I won't offer you a drink," I said lightly. "Do you mean to tell me you're looking for violations in a little oasis like this?"

"The law's the law," he said. "Everywhere."

"Everywhere in this blessed republic," I emended. "Not in civilized countries."

"Well, of course." He smiled as if I had made a joke. "And you're not far from the border."

"Do you know what they say?"

He smiled again. "What do they say?"

I spoke wearily. "They say that people are drinking far more now than they did before Congress called their attention to liquor."

"I'm sorry to hear that," he said, and he astonished me by mimicking, quite gently, my professorial tone. "Unfortunately, my obligation is to uphold the law, and not to lobby against it."

So I smiled too. "All right. Have you come to me for information, or do you want me to sign a warrant?"

"Well, maybe both. I need at least one witness who's not an agent. I never used to; but they've got us tied up in so much litigation now that I couldn't make an arrest alone if I was drowning in the stuff." He was wearing a blue gabardine suit, much frayed, and his shirt collar was dirty. He pulled out a package of Spuds and lit one without permission. Then he remembered me and offered the package; I declined silently. "I'm pretty sure the Territorial Hotel is serving liquor," he said. "They told me no last night, but they have what they call a private reading room, and there was a lot of noise coming from it and it smelled like a saloon to me. I'd like you to come over there with me."

"Right now?"

"If you don't mind."

"They don't have to let us in, you know. And I think if they saw me, a judge, walk in with a stranger they might be very polite and very uncooperative. That is, if they really have the stuff."

"How about a search warrant?"

"That's possible," I said. "Ah. Just in time." John was loping through the doorway. "Mr. Digby, Mr. Gorman." They nodded. "Mr. Gorman is from the Treasury Department. A Prohibition agent. He and I are going to draw up a search warrant and go over to take a look at the Territorial. In about fifteen minutes. I may be some time, so I want you to get to court and occupy my seat for me. We've got a murder trial in progress," I told Gorman. "First-degree. Haven't had one of those in this county since statehood." I turned again to John. "And on the way drop off and tell Ettore the examination will be nondiscriminatory because admission to the bar is a right and not a privilege. In this or any state. Go along, now."

"Right away," John said. "Pleased to have met you, Mr. Gorman." Gorman nodded pleasantly, and John skipped off.

"What is he, an Indian?"

"Zuñi," I said. "A good clerk. Smart. Works hard."

"I'll be damned. Got a lot of Mexicans around here, too."

"That's right." I was scribbling at the warrant.

"They much trouble?"

"They're all anarchists," I explained. "Knife throwers." I did not look up. "Wife beaters. They keep pigs. Sleep all day."

"Must be rough," he said.

"Yes." I blotted the warrant. "My mother's the worst of the lot. She smokes cigars. Not only that, but they're all Catholics." I stood up. "Shall we go now?"

He was a lot redder than John. And I remember thinking of Cousin Ignacio then, possibly because it was preposterous that he and Gorman should inhabit the same planet.

Cousin Ignacio was a polished primitive, with a beard and dirty nails, and a black cigar, dead or alive, in his mouth; and in the library of his house was a billiard table probably a hundred years old. Ignacio weighed some two hundred pounds, most of it sideways, and he bowled through the lanes, gardens, and fields of his busy estate like an officious cannonball. He possessed a fine private library, maybe four hundred serious volumes and nothing after 1850, the second Calderón, and Ignacio had not read a book since running away from the Brothers in 1880 or so. Reading was a woman's occupation chez Montemayor and Rafaela had read all those books by the time she was eighteen, including a few not written for young ladies. My mother brought her books in English. Julia and Marta had also been great readers before they married. Ramón had never read more than the financial pages in his life; he lived in Mexico City and made money, appearing at Christmastime with bolts of cloth and boots and mysterious novelties like toothbrushes and hair tonic. He had a wife and children and they were always welcome but otherwise no one paid them much attention, or to Ramón either, who could support just so much pastoral simplicity and always made plausible excuses after three or four days.

Ignacio and Rafaela lived alone except for thirty or
forty friends, companions, employees, stockholders
—who knew what they were?—who ran the farm. Ignacio cared for his manor, his wine and cigars, his
anticlericalism, his horses, and his family, in approximately that order. He liked women too but they were
a condition, an environment, and not a category. He
was dark brown with a thick head of black hair and
the eyes of an eighteen-year-old, black and snapping, and I imagine he had tumbled every woman
on his estate and his tenants, who called him Don
Ignacio but also called him a blockhead and a mule
when he was wrong, did not object, or did not object
strongly, or did not seem to object. Who could object
to rain or thunder, and what good would it do? Objections glanced off him anyway; he was a good man
but mindless and his eruptions of lust or anger were
blind, unthinking, and not too frequent. He hardly
ever spoke except to manage his farm or to be polite.
The obligatory courtesies at my arrival and departure emerged in the form of laryngeal grunts and
gurgles accompanied by nods, smiles, flutterings of
the hands, offers of red wine and black cigars. I always drank his wine and smoked his cigars; his life
on the farm was truly a life and not a collection of
disjointed aspects and activities, and the wine and
cigars were integral. The wine, from his own grapes
and probably his own bare feet, was dark red and
quite harsh even after years in the bottle, so he kept
most of it in casks and he and his friends drank it up
every year. He had been told that it tasted much like
Corsican wine but neither he nor I had ever drunk
Corsican wine. We drank plenty of Ignacio's, though.
When dinner was over and we were alone at table he
usually opened another bottle, and when it was half
gone and we were either drowning in the juices of

the maduro or choking to death in its smoke Ignacio would croak something like "Nnn. Ggg. Quieres?" and jerk his head toward the library, which meant, "Would you care for a game of billiards?" After the game he would nod in pleasure, shake my hand, and trundle off to bed; he was up with the sun. Then Rafaela would join me in the library and blow out the candles. I don't believe Ignacio ever knew, or would have cared.

Rafaela was a boy by day, on horseback many hours, visiting friends, watching stock, tending hurt lambs and such. Not a classic tomboy; she had never hunted or fished or bothered with adventures. But she wore trousers and shaps. She was of average height and build but extremely graceful, and would return to the house in late afternoon to change; for dinner, and for the evening, she was a lady. A very beautiful lady, and the cool efficiency with which she rode or set a splint or quieted a baby was never inflicted upon me. Only that occasional sense of my own inferiority. When I left for the war she was a child and when I got back she was still a child, but only because she was just seventeen and an old friend and I was fresh from the ripeness of Paris, and when I was twenty-five ripeness was all. I was polite and cheerful for a couple of years, visiting three or four times with my parents and then with my mother. Ignacio was heartbroken when my father died. My father's Spanish was only fair but to Ignacio words were a superfluity; he and my father rode together, worked together, and spent hours hunting. When there was nothing to hunt they shot at targets and drank wine and careened home in roaring good spirits. I was a disappointment to Ignacio because I did not replace my father. I slept a lot in a hammock and read the old books and one day I noticed a stun-

ning black-haired black-eyed dinner companion in
her early twenties staring carnivorously at me. It was
Rafaela. That made me more than ever a homebody.
She was wearing a long dress that evening, dark
green brocade, with a pale green shawl; and she
warmed me with eyes that were no longer wall-eyes
but had become what the Italians called gli occhi di
venere, the eyes of—well, what? Venery, lust, lechery, passion; but in Italian it was a compliment.
We went riding next day and fetched up in an elfin
grot, and I shut her wild, wild eyes with kisses more
than four, and ravished her; or would have, in
Fielding's glorious words, had she not by a timely
compliance prevented me. After which she snubbed
me for several hours so that I arrived in the dining
room morose and confused, trying to be natural but
nervously fearful that I had violated every possible
rule of human behavior, from incest to simple social
regulations like not pinching the chief's daughter in
his own tent. But between soup and chicken she
laughed in delicious mischief and I knew she had
been playing some woman's game. When I was sure
it was all right I grew jealous and wondered who had
preceded me, but I never asked her. I told myself
that I had no claim on her. What I meant, and eventually discovered, was that I did not want her to assume a claim on me.

So she was my south-of-the-border lollipop, and
the only woman I ever knew with whom love was
friendly.

I reached the courtroom at nine-fifteen. Mr. Gorman had said, "I'm very sorry," as we left the office.
I said I was too busy to indulge "the nice sensibility
of honor, which weighs the insult rather than the in-
jury," and he said "What?" and I patted him on the

back, and we found nothing at the Territorial, and Ettore winked at me as we passed through the kitchen, and Mr. Gorman vanished from my life, none too soon. Something on that order befell us every three months or so, and we had been caught more than once but nothing ever came of it, and we found it easier to anticipate such investigations than to quash later actions. We had no objections to the Volstead Act in principle but many in practice. Washington was a long way off and we all felt that we could manage nicely without the Great White Father. Since our full initiation into the Union we had benefitted to the extent of one war and the Eighteenth Amendment. And as far as I could see that was all. My mother thought we should have applied to Mexico or set up an independent state under Pancho Villa.

John slid out of my seat, but I motioned him back and squeezed in beside him. He thanked me with a glance and we turned to the proceedings, which were barely under way. An elderly gentleman was being sworn. "Clement Hoyers," John whispered. Her father.

Clement Hoyers, duly sworn and identified, proved to be a ticket agent for the railroad. He was gray and apparently dyspeptic, belching frequently but with delicacy. He was also grief-stricken and vengeful. Having established, to no one's satisfaction, Louise's virtue before marriage; having revealed that he had opposed the marriage because Bryan was not steadily employed; having sniffled a bit and pulled himself together, he entered forbidden territory at Dietrich's bidding.

"Please describe the tragic events of nineteen-nineteen," Dietrich told him. "I know it will not be easy for you. And I want to ask you to repeat only those conversations in which you participated."

Oliver Parmelee rose slowly. "Your Honor," he drawled, "I object to this as irrelevant. I realize that counsel wants to establish a background of conflict and unhappiness, but I'd like to point out that half the marriages in this world survive in spite of conflict and unhappiness, and that the District Attorney is asking us to believe that a general condition—like marriage itself—goes to prove motive in this case. I don't ask for an offer of proof because I assume I'm right about what he's after. I say it's immaterial."

A general condition. Like marriage itself. Sad and discouraging words from a father of four. I resented them on Rosemary's behalf, and glared at the back of his neck. Did he believe it? Did I? I had sensed it, the heap of dust left by friable passion, the murderous daily routine, the cold bed; had sensed it in law students married young and soon sorry, in the fussy and resentful child bride deceived and insulted by hairy reality; or years later in the heavy, sullen husband bringing home his sour stomach, turning with distaste from his expanding wife and her inevitable flowered print, eating his supper and communicating in grunts. Sensed it, but not believed it. Never, for example, with my Rosemary! Behind the drabbest façade, I thought, still stood the fancy house. Or half believed it, realizing after a time that I was lucky because my father pawed my mother cheerfully and often and the sound of hand slapping fanny was in our house a triumphal and celebratory clash of golden cymbals; but also that I lived in a world where that might be rare. I could never be sure whether I had been made privy to a loving way of life or asked to stake my future on an illusion. Parmelee thought it was an illusion, half the time, or so he had just said; and he was objecting to Dietrich's hint, soon to be magnified, that out of so general a disillusionment could come so specific a murder.

Hochstadter denied the objection. Parmelee had expected that, and subsided; he was making a record for his appeal.

"Well, in September of nineteen-nineteen," Hoyers began, "they'd been married about a year and a half, when Louise came home to Dallas one day. She was kind of moody and sad—"

"Objection," Parmelee called out.

"Denied," Hochstadter said. "Go on, Mr. Hoyers."

"Well, she wasn't happy, I could tell that, and the first night home we heard her crying in bed. I wanted Sarah to go see what was the matter but Sarah said tomorrow, it's just marriage, those things happen. We had our fights too," he said with visible embarrassment, "so I figured she was right, it was just one of those things. Next morning I went to work, and when I got home that night they was *both* crying. So I said what's the matter, and I went over to Louise and tried to give her a kiss, but she said don't kiss me, and got up and ran up to her room. So I asked Sarah. And after a while Sarah calmed down and said she'd tell me after supper. I said no, now. But Sarah said if I tell you now you won't eat your supper. So I said in that case I won't eat my supper anyway, it's already too late, so you better tell me. I always had a bad stomach. So she did. She said—"

"Objection, Your Honor." Parmelee was on his feet again. "Witness is about to repeat a conversation that took place between two other people. His wife is on the state's list and can testify herself. I think the District Attorney is working toward a cumulative effect by repetition."

"He's allowed to do that," Hochstadter said.

"Yes, but not by hearsay."

"He can tell us what his wife told him," Dietrich said.

"Not conversations," Parmelee said. "Not when the substance is in what his wife said."

Hoyers belched audibly.

"Just a minute, gentlemen." Hochstadter thought it over for a few seconds. The audience sat still, alert. "Come up to the bench, will you?"

Parmelee and Dietrich joined him. He told me about it later. "I said to Dietrich, 'You know, Oliver's half right. There's a point where you're not really asking for testimony so much as prejudicing the jury. If you want to establish facts, I suggest you do it as economically as possible.' Economically. I thought that was a good word for it." The Judge smiled, pleased as a poet. We were in his chambers that evening, just after adjournment, and he was waving a cigar. "Dietrich thought I was being rough on him, but Parmelee was happy enough. He looked at Dietrich then and said something strange: 'Emil,' he said, 'I'm going to tell you something you won't believe: Talbot didn't kill his wife.' Emil said, 'I know you think that, and I'm glad you do, but you're wrong as hell.' So I said, 'You can talk about that later. I'm going to sustain this objection.' "

They returned to their tables and Hochstadter announced, "The objection is sustained."

Dietrich said, "Your Honor, I'd like permission to excuse this witness for a time and call Mrs. Hoyers. After which I'd like to recall this witness."

"That agreeable, Mr. Parmelee?"

Parmelee hesitated and then nodded. "Yes, Your Honor."

Hoyers was excused, and his wife was sworn. She was a strapping woman—Louise Talbot's rude proportions were not her father's contribution—with a squarish jaw, small eyes, gray hair, and a little black hat with a black veil dotted by white flowers. Her voice grated, not high and squeaky like Rosemary's but shrill and brassy.

She repeated much of what Hoyers had said. Then Dietrich asked her to tell us in her own words what Louise had told her. She took a deep breath as though she wanted to compress it all into one sentence. "It was late that afternoon. Louise had been moping around all day. Finally she busted out crying again—she was never very, uh, emotional, and I knew something was really wrong." Parmelee stirred, but gave up and leaned back. "Finally she dried her eyes and told me. She told me that her husband—" Mrs. Hoyers came to a full stop and looked around her. She addressed Dietrich. "I can't say this right out in front of everybody."

"Yes you can," he told her. "This is a court of law, Mrs. Hoyers. We're concerned with truth here, and we discuss matters that don't get discussed outside. Just use your own words, and don't worry about technical phrases. You can use your daughter's exact words if you can remember them."

"All right. I'll try," she said. "She told me that her husband had been with another woman—"

"Well, now, that's hearsay too," Parmelee objected. "What Bryan Talbot told his wife is for Bryan to bring out."

Hochstadter opened his mouth but Bryan spoke. "Oh, let it go," Talbot said impatiently. "It's true."

Even Hochstadter was shocked. In the audience eyes widened; I believe they all held their breath. Parmlee sat down and Hochstadter never even ruled. Mrs. Hoyers glared wildly at Talbot.

"Please go on," Dietrich said gently. Parmalee was staring at his client in some anger.

"She said he'd been with another woman and caught a disease and brought it home and given it to her." Mrs. Hoyers bowed her head.

"And what was the disease?"

"It has a long name. I forget. Clement called it the clap." I find it difficult now, several wars and modern novels later, to convey the horrific echoes of that word in the sudden, ugly silence. The word reverberated; swelled; glided and swooped and eddied in the hot, dusty air. Hochstadter adjusted his string tie. The jury stared into the middle distance.

"Gonorrhea," Dietrich said softly, and a hundred solid citizens experienced immediate relief. Thus, the proprieties; the comforts of a dead language. A rose by any other name often smells sweeter.

"That's right," she said. "That was it."

"I see. And what else was said that evening?"

"Well, we didn't say so much after that. It was like we couldn't believe it. I spoke against her husband some."

"And what did she say to that?"

"She said things like 'How could he?' "

"And that was all that was discussed that evening?"

"No. Oh, no. Before we went to bed I told her we'd see the doctor the next day, and I gave her a separate tooth glass."

"Your family doctor?"

"Not exactly. A surgeon. The one who did my appendicitis.'"

"And his name?"

"Selma. Doctor Hanford Selma."

I remember Parmelee fidgeting through all that, and reading the record I can see why. He knew the story; was willing to stipulate the entire setting and background, once Hochstadter had denied his objection to it; and resented not only Dietrich's tedious melodrama but also his own helplessness, the impossibility of counterattack; none of this was at issue.

Eventually, and with the help of an affidavit submitted to evidence, Dietrich brought before the jury approximately what the Colonel had so avidly learned and industriously reported. My classic little joke is now obsolete; a clap may be cured in two or three days, but a bad cold lingers for a week. In 1919 pharmacology was primitive; as Dr. Selma's affidavit explained, the possibility of extensive infection made imperative major surgery, a hysterectomy, removal of the uterus, in order to avoid serious and possibly fatal complications, one of which was called gonococcic salpingitis. There was no question of Selma's probity or of the need for surgery. Louise Talbot recuperated at her parents' home, and the infection disappeared; within a month her blood was normal, and toward the end of October she left for Soledad City, exercising, as Mrs. Hoyers specified, her father's privileges and paying only half fare.

She returned to Dallas in March for a two-week visit, and notified her parents that she had decided not to ask for a divorce. Talbot had promised to reform; he had been drunk and out of town, and it would never happen again. She did not trust his promise but was, apparently, still bound to him by the residual strength of their early love; and he had also promised that he was "going places" and would "make it all up to her."

And Dietrich dropped it right there. "Thank you, Mrs. Hoyers," he said; and to Parmelee, "your witness."

It was a cute touch. He left Parmelee with almost nothing to question. When Parmelee, doubtless feeling that some show of resistance was necessary, began by asking, "Mrs. Hoyers: was it your impression that there had been serious discussion and a true reconciliation between husband and wife?" Dietrich was on his feet immediately.

"Objection," he said. "That obviously calls for a conclusion, and witness is hardly qualified to comment on conversations that took place several hundred miles from her."

Hochstadter sustained him.

Parmelee tried again: "Would you say that by March Louise Talbot had forgiven her husband?"

Dietrich's head snapped up; his hand twitched; but he thought better of it, and waited.

He was wise to wait; Mrs. Hoyers said, "No. He was kind of on probation." She nodded sternly, pleased with the word. "On probation. She was giving him another chance, but I wouldn't say she'd forgiven him."

"Did she say she planned to leave him, or had been considering it?"

Mrs. Hoyers hesitated. "Well, no. She never said that. She was mad at him at first and he made her very sad, but she never said she'd leave him. Of course she thought about a divorce right away, at the beginning, and I told her I thought she should get one, even though we've never had any divorce in our family at all, on either side, but I can't say she ever made up her mind to do it."

"Would you say she still loved him in March?"

Dietrich made the same old objection, and Hochstadter sustained him again.

"I'll ask it another way: did she tell you she still loved him?"

"No. But she said it was hard to leave a man and she had no place to go. I told her she could come home to Dallas."

"And what did she say?"

"She said, 'And then what? Go to work and be an

old maid? Who'd have me now?' "

"Then she had decided to try to make a go of it
with Bryan Talbot."

"Yes," Mrs. Hoyers said, and Dietrich, who was
up again, never had a chance to object because Parmelee said, "Thank you; that's all," and sat down.

Dietrich took a moment for thought. "How often
did you see your daughter after that?"

"Objection," Parmelee roared. "That isn't redi-
rect at all. The District Attorney has started an entirely new line of questioning. We can't chop this testimony into little pieces and bat it back and forth
indefinitely."

"Cross-examination went to the question of Louise
Talbot's later emotional attitude," Dietrich said. "I
have a right to go into the matter."

"An offer of proof," Parmelee said.

"I intend to show that Louise Talbot returned to
Dallas often for the purpose of seeing a man she was
fond of; which would tend to show her alienation from
her husband."

"Well, that was for direct," Parmelee said grumpily.

"The District Attorney is within his rights," Hochstadter ruled. "Objection denied."

Dietrich turned inquiringly to Mrs. Hoyers. "I don't
remember the exact question," she said. He repeated it.
"Oh, yes," she said. "Well, she came home about every
three months after that, for a week or two at a time."

It was on her visit in March that she had run into an
old schoolmate, Jack Rawlins. Mrs. Hoyers tried eager-
ly to fill in the details of their meeting, and Parmelee's
objections were sustained. Dietrich persevered, and the
pattern emerged. The two had met by chance, and afterward Rawlins had squired Louise to movies, to
dances, to dinners; Mrs. Hoyers reported his arrival at
the house bearing posies, repeated Louise's comments

on their evenings together. Parmelee sank deeper into gloom; further cross-examination could only hurt Talbot. But John sensed something I had missed. "He's losing them," he whispered, and I saw that he was right. The audience were fanning themselves, scratching themselves, shifting in their seats; the jurymen were leaning back, some slumped, relaxed and not rigid. They were in part relieved, now that the unmentionable had been mentioned and left behind; in part—I thought —willing to sympathize a bit with Bryan, whose wife had taken a woman's revenge.

Dietrich too looked about him, and knew, but went on calmly. The dilemma was only temporary. He had to establish the rift, the continuing quarrel. There were two sides to any quarrel, and that was the risk he had to take, but a momentary sympathy for Bryan would not serve to exonerate him of first-degree murder. He finished quickly. Perhaps he did cut it short; perhaps, with Rawlins on his list, he had no need for lengthy comment from Mrs. Hoyers. He thanked her again and turned her over to Parmelee, who had sense enough to let her go.

Hochstadter recessed for lunch.

Alvin Hochstadter and I walked together to the Territorial, nodding at friends, the Judge tipping his hat. "Hot," he said. "Damned hot under that robe." Joseph Hawkins led us to a table and held our chairs, and without a word brought us bourbon and ice water. I peered about for Mr. Francis X. Gorman and did not bemoan his absence. "They are making a hash of this trial," Hochstadter said. "Parmelee was right, and Dietrich should have planned better. Can't have them popping on and off the stand like that."

"Trouble is," I said, "Dietrich's got two different stories to tell. And Parmelee wasn't ready for this first one. He isn't sure what to do about it."

The Judge lingered over a long draught of cold water. "Aaaah," he exulted. "You know, that pitcher on the bench warms up in half an hour. In an hour it's like swamp water. We ought to have blocks of ice and some electric fans blowing out over them. What you going to eat?"

"Cold ham," I said.

"Good idea," he said. "You were late this morning." I told him about Gorman.

"Hoo," he said. "And Bettmann the Federal judge. God save us if he's ever replaced." Bettmann was a stern, wrinkled old bibber who had, since Prohibition, developed and exercised a fanatical devotion to the rights of the accused. "God save me if *I'm* ever replaced. I come up again next year." We were appointed on what came to be called the Missouri Plan: every four years the voters got a chance to throw us out. They never did. The proposition on the ballot was phrased in our favor, and it was much easier to vote Yes—provided there had been no financial scandals—than to vote No and have to worry about a new and unknown evil. The natural conservatism of people who disliked all government. Financial scandals were unlikely. We were paid six thousand dollars a year and in 1923, in Soledad County, that was extravagant. I could have been comfortable on half of that; but then my mother, cushioned by what my father had left her, maintained the house, on which her taxes were five dollars a month.

We chatted, and Joseph brought the ham, which was good: pink and firm and lean. With it we ate the house salad, tomatoes and sliced onions in a kind of brine. Tangy. Over coffee Hochstadter said, "And what the hell is he going to ask the old man now? The woman's covered it all but he's got to bring the old man back and it isn't fair to Parmelee. If Dietrich has no more direct, then Parmelee's got to cross-examine with a witness in between. God damn it! I should never have let him do that. Dietrich may have maneuvered himself right into something reversible, and lose it all because he couldn't keep his timetable straight."

"Parmelee agreed to it," I said. "I don't think they'd come near reversing on that. It's hardly substantive."

"They've reversed on procedure before, and often." He shattered his own gloom with a wide grin. "Well, they've reversed me before, too, and I'm still here. I've been through worse. I bet you don't know what I was before I was a marshal."

"No, I don't." He sounded like a boy and I was interested.

"Hoo. You wouldn't believe it, looking at me now, a fat old man in a white shirt, but I rode shotgun between Dallas and Santa Fe. It was the emptiest, longest ride in the world and the only company was real live scalping Indians and the toughest outlaws outside of Wall Street. I only did it for eight months and then I quit. Got so I couldn't sleep. Hayes was President then."

"The Wild West," I said, and smiled appreciatively.

"It was wild enough for me. There was no honor among thieves, believe me. The easiest way to get rich was to shoot a man in the back and take his money. The only thing that kept the killing down was that as soon as you had the money somebody was likely to shoot *you* in the back. I hated it. I was scared all the time. I once saw a man acquitted on self-defense because half a dozen witnesses swore that if he hadn't bushwhacked the victim, the victim was going to bushwhack him. That, was around eighteen-eighty. They talk a lot now about self-reliance in the old days, and believe me you needed it. Although," he added thoughtfully, "there were limits. With the Comanches riding, self-reliance was not quite as useful as the United States cavalry."

"Like most virtues," I said. "It was a virtue only as long as you could afford it."

"Hoo," he said again, brows rising. "You're too young to be saying things like that. You're supposed to still believe in truth and honor and such."

"I do," I said. "But I don't call them virtues. I call them necessities."

He laughed from the belly. "That's better. Don't ever change your mind."

Dietrich did come back to the old man, and among the spectators several women wept. Parmelee sat dour and motionless. "Mr. Hoyers, did your daughter ever discuss with you her inability to bear children?"

Hoyers gulped. "Yes."

"What did she say?"

"She was worried about Sarah and I. She was our only child, you know. She was worried because now there wouldn't be any grandchildren. We used to joke about her having lots of kids to keep us company in our old age. She told me how sorry she was that she wouldn't now, and we both cried some." In demonstration, a tear slid down his cheek.

"I'm sorry," Dietrich said. "Your witness."

Poor Parmelee! Nothing he wouldn't have stipulated, and therefore nothing he could destroy, and the only object of attack a weeping old man. "I can see that you feel very strongly about this, Mr. Hoyers. I'm sorry to have to keep you here, but I'll try to be brief." Hoyers nodded and swabbed at his eyes. "Of course I don't expect you to have much sympathy for Bryan Talbot. But I want you to try to remember if anything was said back in nineteen-nineteen, or subsequently, by Louise Talbot, that indicated understanding of Bryan Talbot, perhaps even forgiveness."

"Only that it wasn't easy to leave a man. That's all I remember."

"No suggestion that there might have been two sides to the tragedy? No sympathy at all for Talbot?"

"No sir." Hoyers straightened up. "It was his fault, all right, and there wasn't anything to be said for him. Not then or ever."

"Not by you or Mrs. Hoyers either?"

"No sir. That's a bad man. I wish she'd never married him. She should have left him right away and she might still be alive."

Parmelee turned to the Judge. "I move that the last answer be stricken from the record."

"Granted," Hochstadter said immediately. "The jury will disregard witness's outburst. His answer to the question was 'No sir.' Mr. Hoyers, please confine yourself to simple and direct answers."

"Then it would be fair to say," Parmelee went on, "that the opinion you formed when Louise came home to Dallas in nineteen-nineteen is the opinion you still hold? Of Bryan Talbot."

"That's right. I haven't changed my mind about him."

"And yet your daughter went on living with him, and the only reason you remember her stating was that it was hard to leave a man."

"That's right."

"You are a Protestant family, Mr. Hoyers?"

"That's right. Lutheran."

"And while you don't approve of divorce, you are not forbidden by religious belief from seeking divorce."

"That's right."

"Then you ask us to believe that Louise Talbot went on living with Bryan Talbot for three and a half years after the tragedy, being his wife, keeping his home, eating with him three times a day and sleeping in the same bed with him, going on vacations with him and doing his laundry, celebrating holidays with him and going to the movies with him and just sitting quietly with him, when she might have divorced him without violence to her beliefs? Failing that, separated from him? And you ask us to believe that she had never forgiven him, that she never loved him for a minute?"

"Objection," Dietrich said wearily. "Counsel is making a speech. It sounds like a summation. And what question is witness supposed to answer, exactly?"

"I'm trying to establish a sharply prejudiced attitude on the part of the witness," Parmelee said. "The question is, whether witness asks us to believe all that, or if not, what part of it."

"Denied," Hochstadter said. "Go ahead, Mr. Parmelee."

"Answer the question, please," Parmelee said patiently. "You really think all that was true?"

"Yes I do," Hoyers said, frowning, his jaw jutting.

"Would you admit that your own shock and resentment might have prevented you from forming an accurate idea of your daughter's emotional state?"

"No sir. I knew how she felt. Her husband was a bad one, and she knew it."

"Then why did she stay with him?"

"I told you why." The old man was angry, which pleased Parmelee; counsel was no longer brutalizing a tearful father.

"Because it was hard to leave a man," Parmelee repeated. "Would you agree that you, robbed of grandchildren and suffering for your daughter, might have been blind to, unaware of, the emotions actually alive in her marriage? The accommodation, the reconciliation that would have been natural and inevitable between two people who continued to share each other's lives?"

"I don't understand," Hoyers burst out. "If she still liked him why would she come back to Dallas and go out with Rawlins?"

Parmelee was silent for a good fifteen seconds, gazing impassively at Hoyers while the jury repeated his questions to themselves and slowly, confusedly, constructed a dubious image of Louise Talbot: at home with Bryan, resigned if not cheerful, then playing the floozy in Dallas.

"You hate Bryan Talbot, don't you?" Parmelee asked.

"Yes I do," Hoyers said.

"That's all, Mr. Hoyers."

"Nothing further," Dietrich said.

"You may step down," the Judge said.

"I hope he hangs," Hoyers said, and descended to the beat of the gavel.

The spectators had perked up. A current of doubt animated them, reinforced by Parmelee's show of strength. Sunlight streamed in from the west now blinking off a hundred straw fans. Hands on his cane, chin on his hands, the Colonel hunched forward, nodding, the superannuated ephebe, his eyes bright and avaricious. Far to the rear Bruce Donnelley fanned himself, a cleft of distrust between his brows; heavy, stolid, righteous, he seemed a jury unto himself. As Hoyers left and Rawlins was called, a gossipaceous murmur rose and fell; Hochstadter ignored it, sensibly. When Rawlins was ready and George Costa had proferred the Bible Hochstadter rapped twice, and the murmur died. Rawlins swore to tell the truth.

He was handsome, well set up, with wavy dark hair, dark brows, small eyes, a blunt nose, a square chin. Twenty-seven years old; he might have been a mechanic who had just been promoted to salesman and would someday own the agency and carry his then two hundred pounds to Rotary meetings and smokers. He spoke with a marked drawl and tried to use the language properly. He told us that he had seen Louise Talbot for a week or two at a spell perhaps three times a year, in Dallas; that they had danced or dined out or seen a movie almost every night; that he had urged her to leave Bryan, and she had long refused; that she had told him, finally, in the summer of 1921, of her operation and barrenness, and though he had said it made no difference to him they had agreed not to mention divorce and marriage thenceforth.

Rawlins made a fine impression. He was average. The jury liked that. He was respectful and spoke to the point. When Dietrich asked how intimate the relationship had been Rawlins paused becomingly and dropped his gaze; then looked directly at Dietrich and said, "It became very intimate." And the jury nodded without prurience, because Rawlins was average and therefore Rawlins's sins were average, and every man in the jury box understood. No visions here of Byzantine orgies, of pernicious acrobatics with ancient names, specifically outlawed by embarrassed statute; this was wholesome and domestic and star-crossed.

"Did you ever have reason to believe that Bryan Talbot knew of your relationship with his wife?"

"Yes," Rawlins said. "When Louise told me about the rest of it she also told me that she'd told him about us, and that she was going to be a free woman. She told him that—"

"Objection." The audience sank back, frustrated. "What Louise Talbot told her husband is not for this witness to say."

"But what she told this witness *is* for him to say," Dietrich cut in swiftly. "It goes to the nature of their relationship. If he's misquoting her, defense can bring that out later."

"Denied," Hochstadter said, and mopped his face with a red bandanna.

"You may continue," Dietrich said.

"She told him that she'd try to be a good wife in other ways but she needed a kind of love he could never give her now. Those were her words, her very words. A kind of love he could never give her now. She was a very . . . *sweet* girl. She said she had fun with me, and not much fun otherwise. If you don't mind my saying so, she said this city, Soledad City, was dull, not much to do and she didn't have many friends, and it was all right as long as she was happy with her husband, but not after the . . . trouble."

"Did she ever tell you how her husband had reacted to her decision?"

"Yes. She said he was mad—very angry." He corrected himself with some delicacy. "But there wasn't much he could do about it because he still loved her. Also he had some sort of commercial dealings here and if the story came out he'd be ruined."

A few of the jurymen glanced at Talbot: the complaisant cuckold, the moneygrubber.

"He was very angry. Did she refer again to his anger?"

"Oh, yes. Every time she came home to Dallas he blew up. Sometimes I thought she enjoyed making him angry, just a little. She giggled once telling me about it."

"But she never again mentioned leaving Talbot, or marrying you?"

"Oh, yes," Rawlins said brightly. Fans were stilled; Harvey Bump looked up from his notebook. "The last time I saw her. In February. She said she'd had enough, and she was going to leave him soon, and would I wait a few months more."

When Hochstadter had restored order, Parmelee asked for a recess. He seemed ten years older, and I thought with alarm of his liver.

6 BRYAN TALBOT TOOK
the opportunity to go to the bathroom, and he dragged
Parmelee after him up the slope like a man leading a
mule. Bryan was talking all the way, flinging words
back over his shoulder; his businessman's face was crim-
son, his eyes snapped darkly, fury radiated. Parmelee
was grim. Tolliver went along with them and he told me
later that in the men's room the two had ignored his
presence and jawed hotly. "Your wife was a teaser and
we've got to bring that out," Parmelee said, or words to
that effect; and Bryan's answer was "She was a damn
good wife and that two-bit dance-hall Romeo is a liar,"
or words to *that* effect. Bryan denied absolutely that his
wife had ever mentioned leaving. "We were back together," he told Parmelee. "She ran off like that to hurt
me and I knew it and I took it because she had *something* coming to her, but it would have ended. I know it
would have. We were better all the time." Then he buttoned up his fly and said, "That Rawlins is going to kill
me if you don't break him down. You get after him.
You show him up. He's a damned liar." Bryan washed,
and slapped cold water on his face.

Parmelee tried hard. He cross-examined until five,
rooting in every cranny of Rawlins's life, but he was up
against invincible candor. Rawlins remained courteous,
soft-voiced, and forthright. Even when Parmelee re-

quired him to supply details of his courtship, Rawlins complied straightforwardly. "No sir. I have a one and a half room apartment of my own, in a new building. Six stories. It's not like a boardinghouse with one entrance for everybody. I can come and go as I please, and with . . ." (long pause) ". . . *whom* I please."

And later, "Yes, sir. We spent many hours together like that. She was my girl. We were happy together."

"I suppose you'd be shocked," Parmelee said, "if you heard that she'd had still another boy friend."

Rawlins was barely contemptuous. "I wouldn't be shocked, sir. I just wouldn't believe it."

"But you knew that her relations with her husband were normal. That is, physically."

"Yes, sir. I know that. I never liked it, and she knew I didn't."

"Did you ever show anger?"

"Well, a little. More like . . . annoyance."

"And how did she react?"

"Oh, she laughed and told me not to mind, just to think how much fun it was when we were together."

The Colonel looked ferocious at that, an avenging angel, as though he had discovered a corporal in the officers' latrine. Juano was in slack repose with an expression of canny sympathy. Tolliver made heroic efforts to appear jaded. Bruce Donnelley was bleak and withdrawn, like a wary mud turtle. The rest of the audience was hot but tireless.

"Did it occur to you that she might also have laughed when she angered her husband?"

Here Rawlins hesitated, and then said, "Yes."

"But it did not occur to you that she might be the kind of woman who enjoyed playing one man against another."

"No sir."

"Or that she might lie to you as you assumed she lied to her husband."

"She didn't lie to him. She told me she told him all about it."

"Ah. But did she lie to him when they made love; when she sighed; when she embraced him?"

"She never talked about that," Rawlins said sullenly.

"Of course not. But did you never think about it? Did you suppose that at home with her husband she was stiff and unyielding and hostile?"

Rawlins sulked.

"Answer the question," Parmelee snapped. "Did you suppose that?"

"No, I didn't," Rawlins said. "I tried not to think about it."

"And were you yourself cold and distant when you were in bed with another woman?"

"That's none of—" Rawlins cut it short with a glare.

"You were about to say, that's none of my business," Parmelee went on in reasonable tones. "But I really think it is. She, after all, was married to another man. Your own friends were just that—merely friends. Did she object to your other affairs?"

"I certainly object to that question," Dietrich said. "Witness's relations with anyone but the victim are hardly relevant."

Parmelee was healthy again; he glowed. "Oh, come now," he bellowed. "I believe this witness has lied about a good many things and I'm trying to find out just what kind of complicated man he is. Do you want me to take him at face value? Then why let me cross-examine?"

"That's enough, Mr. Parmelee," Hochstadter said. "Objection denied."

"Thank you, Your Honor. Now then, young man:

answer the question."

"She didn't know about them," Rawlins said quietly.

"I thought not," Parmelee said. "Then it is your contention that you, in spite of other lady friends, preferred a woman who was not only already married but barred from motherhood—and to such a degree that you asked her to leave her husband for you. And that she, who understood much of life, was totally ignorant of your other, ah, liaisons, and had promised to leave a man with whom she had been through a shattering time, and who was making a good life for her, and in whose home she was at least outwardly happy. Is that what you claim?"

"Yes, sir," Rawlins said. "That is what I claim."

"You were willing to forgo children?"

"Yes, sir."

"And you never thought that in a few years you might change your mind; that when the blush was off the rose she would be in her thirties and without prospects if you tired of her; and that she might have foreseen that?"

"No, sir. I believe we would have been happy together."

"I find it difficult to believe that Louise Talbot shared that opinion," Parmelee said. "I find it difficult to believe that she was unaware of your complicated love life. And I find it very easy to believe that she was playing with you, teasing you, lying to you, and never intended at all to leave her husband for you. No further questions."

Parmelee sat down and heaved a sigh of exhausted satisfaction. For an hour he had wended a thorny way, needing to prove that Louise Talbot was a cheat and a teaser, and even to imply that there might be yet other men involved; but needing also to leave room for the belief that she had reconciled herself to life with Bryan, such as it was. He had done well, but the ultimate obstacle was insurmountable: twist and turn he might, but he had no reasonable alternative to the state's contention that Bryan Talbot had murdered Louise Talbot. Bryan might have had a motive that no other man could know, and the couple's troubles warranted any speculation. Battle for battle, Parmelee resisted well; but he was losing the war and we all knew it.

I called Rosemary that night. "Hello," I said. "It's Ben."

There was silence, and then she said, "Hello," and then there was silence again. I closed my eyes. I knew that "hello." I had known it for many years. It was the hello that preceded empty excuses. The silence before and after was a paraphrase of "You must be that young lawyer who annoyed me at the party" or "Oh yes that clodhopper from someplace out west" or once "You're another of those American officers who call French-women roundheels." With that sort of hello the telephone became an instrument of the devil, and I went on in a dry, defensive tone. "How are you?"

"All right." Another silence.

"Oh, for Christ's sake," I said. "Something's wrong. Can you tell me what?"

"Nothing's wrong."

"Oh, come on."

"I'm just very busy," she said. "I've got examinations to prepare. It's the end of the term."

"Rosemary, Rosemary," I said. "Have I offended? What is it? We're way past this kind of conversation. Please. Tell me."

After a moment she said, "Oh, I don't know, Ben. I

just don't know. I want to be by myself. Is that so unreasonable?"

"Yes. It's damned unreasonable. Three days ago you loved me until you could hardly talk."

"I know." I thought she might have smiled. "Give me a chance, Ben. Call it the natural contrariness of women. I just don't feel like coming down there again."

"And you can't tell me why? Better than that?"

"No. I feel awfully tired." She sounded like a child. I calmed myself.

"All right. Suppose I come up there?"

"Friday?"

"Yes."

"Where would you stay?"

"For God's sake, Rosemary! The town is full of hotels. I can get a guest card at the Bench Club. I'm not going to barge in and take over your bed. What's the matter with you?"

"Nothing," she said. "It's always that, isn't it? Well, all right. You can come."

"Such enthusiasm," I said.

"Oh please stop it. Sometimes you're like a little boy."

That was unanswerable. I said, "All right. We'll talk about it Friday."

"Goodbye," she said.

"Goodbye," I said, and hung up.

I stomped back to the living room and poured myself a pony of brandy and sat down rudely, spilling some of it. My mother was out clacking tiles around a mah-jongg table, and thank God for that; whatever I needed it was surely not the superior wisdom of a mercilessly possessive widdy-woman. I was sore as hell. What clairvoyance did women require anyway? I had not forgotten her birthday; she could not possibly be pregnant; a rival was out of the question, because she would have been pleasant and gay and forestalled my visit somehow; then what was it?

I drank the brandy too quickly and burned my stomach. After a time I said aloud, "Ah, the hell with it." After a longer time I called Geronimo to ask if there was a game, and there was, and I threw on my jacket and trotted down to the drugstore where I said hello to Geronimo and Juano and George Chillingworth and George Costa and Bill Needham, who was the head of our high school music department and whom I had not liked for some time. He was a skinny blond with glasses and an intellectual snob who scoffed often and prefaced his words of wisdom with phrases like "As Chaucer says." His instrument was the trumpet, and I warmed up to him when I caught him in a dirty shirt blowing his heart out with the Mexicans on Christmas Eve; and finally I knew he was my friend when he told us that he had worked his way through a Baptist college playing in a burlesque band.

Anyway I lost fourteen dollars in the next four hours. I still think seven seats make a more interesting game than six.

Thursday morning, much purged of evil and nursing no resentment, still bewildered of heart but clear of head, I divided my attention between the destiny of Bryan Talbot and the ebb and flow of Rosemary. Talbot was, I am sorry to say, momentarily more interesting. Dietrich rested the state's case and Hochstadter denied Parmelee's motion for dismissal, a traditional formality. Then Parmelee opened for the defense.

I did not think much of his opening, but it got to the jury, all right. He was almost folksy. "Fifteen years ago," he said, "there lived not far from here a man named Buck Andrews. Anthony Andrews. They called him Buck." I remembered. Parmelee looked at me suddenly, and went on looking at me, thoughtful and calm as though he had been put in mind of something else altogether. The jury followed his glance but could make nothing of it. "Mr. Andrews raised sheep," he went on finally, "in a small way, up on the Ribera Flats and the hills up north. One year he had a lot of trouble; lost about twenty sheep in a couple of weeks. Their throats were ripped out. There hadn't been any mountain lions up there for years, or wolves, and anyway lions dragged off their kill, but none of Andrews's were missing. And wolves killed to eat, but none of the dead sheep had been eaten. So he looked for coyote sign but there wasn't any; only dog sign, and when Andrews found his dog all bloody one night he took him out and killed him. It happens. A dog goes wild, turns into a sheep killer. Andrews got a new dog. And one day a week or two later Graeme Lewis rode through on his way to Mesa Tinta for antelope and in a swale behind a ridge of rock he found the biggest dog he'd ever seen, some sort of mastiff, dead for several days but killed by some animal that gashed him here and there and finally got to his throat.

"It wasn't hard to figure out, and Andrews was pretty upset. If this big dog had killed his sheep, why hadn't he stopped to feed? If his own dog had killed the big one, why hadn't his own dog been cut up some? Maybe the sheep dog had been the killer, and the big one tried to muscle in and got killed for it. Maybe. Maybe not. Andrews fretted about that for years. When he died in nineteen-twenty he was still fretting about it. Of course he was sorry he hadn't looked around more. He was sorry he hadn't asked for help. He was sorry he hadn't even thought to pen his dog up awhile and see if the killings would stop.

lived with their troubles—including Mr. Talbot's drink-ing—for almost four years. Mrs. Talbot's alleged at-tachment to another man began maybe two years ago. Now how come, if he's supposed to have killed his wife, which he didn't, Bryan Talbot waited so long? To plan it? To find some clever, foolproof way of doing the deed? To cover himself with a good airtight alibi? To arrange a complicated intrigue? Nonsense. This murder was a direct, unconsidered assault; and if Bryan Talbot were involved in any way do you think he would have failed to contrive some careful method of keeping him-self out of it? Bryan Talbot, as I hope to show, is a man of some worldly knowledge, who has traveled a bit, who is accustomed to complex business dealings, and who is far less emotional and impulsive than the aver-age man. I do not think it unreasonable to say that if he put up with the alleged situation at home for two years or more it was not because he was 'biding his time' but because he hoped that it would eventually work out. I want to talk later on about the complexities of married life—some of which I am sure you are familiar with; about the habits of marriage, the concessions made by both husband and wife, the mingled trust and distrust, love and hate, excitement and boredom that can exist under the same roof; and the way in which love, an elusive, indefinable, variable emotion, can support and sustain even the most troubled relationship. No." He shook his head gravely. "I suggest that in the Talbots' marriage there was a strong love, a love that had suffered much but had kept them together through very serious difficulties. I repeat: Bryan Talbot did not kill his wife. Everything brought out by the District Attor-ney in support of his charge can also be interpreted as proof that Bryan Talbot could not possibly have com-mitted this crime."

It was glib; but I must report that right here I began to feel uneasy.

Parmelee went on, and on, and stopped only when he had begun to repeat himself and to bore people. By then it was lunchtime, and we recessed. The lines were drawn, and clearly. When we returned Parmelee and Talbot were conferring in urgent whispers. Parmelee pursed his lips, shuffled papers, frowned. He had the courtroom's attention; mine not fully because I digressed to note Hochstadter (intent, eyes bright), Dietrich (calm but I believe he had not yet decided what he would do if Talbot took the stand), Juano (impassive but somehow sorrowful), the Colonel (tense, like an old maid playing lotto), and Bruce Donnelley (expressionless and remote).

Parmelee glanced again at Talbot and said, almost casually, "Bryan Talbot."

Murmurs and whispers, and the fans beating like surf. Bryan Talbot took the stand, Hochstadter rapped thrice. Talbot was sworn.

Parmelee stood squarely before his witness, his client, his ward, his prisoner, like the Commendatore brooding down upon Giovanni, and spoke in almost the same sepulchral bass: "Bryan Talbot, did you kill Louise Talbot?"

Bryan looked him in the eye and said, "No." He then turned his head, flicked his glance over the jury, and said again, "No."

Barring a hint of rehearsals, it was effective, and Parmelee allowed several seconds of silence. Dietrich did not play the game, and broke the silence in shrewdly good-humored tones: "Your Honor, I do think counsel might establish the witness's identity a bit more formally."

"Nonsense," Parmelee said, but after a few seconds, he asked Talbot to give his name. It was a childish bit of needling on Dietrich's part; customarily witnesses identify themselves before testifying, but it hardly seemed—although—now that *is* strange. After forty years as a judge I cannot tell you at this moment whether or not the law requires that a prisoner, testifying in his own defense, identify himself.

"Mr. Talbot, I want you to tell me if the account given by Mr. and Mrs. Hoyers of the tragedy that struck your marriage was, essentially if not in detail, true."

Bryan's face tightened but he said, "It was."

"And for a time it threatened your marriage."

"For a time, yes."

"Did you love your wife?"

"I did, very much."

"Did she love you?"

"Yes. For a while, when that happened, she didn't. But she did before and she did after."

"Did she ever threaten directly to divorce you?"

"Yes."

"When?"

"Just before she left for Dallas for the operation."

"And subsequently?"

"Never."

"Never?"

"Never."

"But a witness has testified that she told him of her decision to leave you, only four or five months ago, or three, and that she had so informed you."

"That was not true. He was lying. Anyway he looked to me like a—"

"No, no, no!" Parmelee interrupted. "Mr. Talbot: just answer the questions. Do you understand me?"

Bryan subsided. "Yes."

"Good. Now: you have heard Mr. Justin testify that

on the night your wife died you left his billiard parlor at approximately ten minutes of ten. You telephoned the police at ten thirty-four, forty-four minutes later. Chief Harmsworth has testified that it should take a man no more than twelve or fifteen minutes to cover the distance. I ask you now why you took so much longer."

"Well," Talbot said, "I'm afraid I don't know for sure."

"You had been drinking?'"

"Yes."

"Were you drunk, in the usual meaning of that word?"

"Yes. I suppose so. I wasn't steady, and I don't remember much of the walk home. I remember stopping to sit on a bench because I was dizzy."

"Did you fall down?"

"Yes. When I went to sit I lost my balance. I hit my head on the back of the bench and then fell on the ground. For a while I didn't feel like getting up. Then I pulled myself up and sat on the bench."

"Until you felt better."

"Yes. I remember that much because the dizziness got worse when I sat down but after a minute I felt better. Then I felt worse again and I thought maybe I should make myself throw up, but I got up and walked instead."

"And how long had you been on the bench?"

Talbot shook his head. "I just don't know."

"You then proceeded home?"

"Yes."

"And how soon after you arrived did you call the police?"

"A minute or two. I'm not sure. I tried to revive her first."

Parmelee zigzagged. "You were married how long?"

"Five years."

"Did you ever strike your wife?"

"Never."

"What were your plans for the future?"

"I planned to make a good connection in a larger city, perhaps Denver or Oklahoma City, or even on the West Coast. I am a businessman and I wanted to make money. I think I would have started sooner except for the trouble at home, and then there was always something doing in Soledad City so it didn't seem urgent, going away I mean."

"Did your wife approve of those plans?"

"Yes. She was not happy here and was eager to leave."

"Then you would say she looked forward to the future."

"Yes."

"Did she ever threaten to leave you for good?"

"Only at the beginning of our trouble. Not after that."

"Did you ever have words about another man?"

"About that Rawlins fellow. I told her he was no good for her, that he was a small-town dope and she was a big-city lady, or would be when we got there. That she ought to stop punishing me."

"Did you ever have words about anyone in Soledad City?"

Talbot paused here; not because he was in any doubt, but because he knew how badly Parmelee wanted to establish a contact between the deceased and someone—anyone at all—who might have had reason to strangle her. "No." He was almost defiant.

Parmelee nodded. "Mr. Talbot. Those of us who knew Louise Talbot were aware of her great beauty. We also knew that she was much talked about. She was attractive in a rather uncommon way. The impression has been established that you were envied by many men. Were you ever made aware of that envy?"

Talbot nodded immediately. "Oh, yes. My wife was the most beautiful woman I've ever known, and now and then someone would compliment me on her looks. I don't know why people compliment the man in those cases, but they did. I suppose because the husband always seems to own his wife."

"Would you say that occasionally that envy, that admiration, was accompanied by desire for her?"

Dietrich rumbled to his feet, objecting even before he was up, and explained: "Counsel wants to establish the possibility of an unknown party who might have been involved. That's his right. But I don't think he can ask witness for that kind of conclusion. If he wants, we'll stipulate that there's usually desire between the sexes."

That was funny only because it was part of an exchange between two middle-aged lawyers neither of whom—earnest, well-fleshed, sweating a bit—could be imagined sparking a belle; they were nice homey fellows who managed one waltz and fell asleep over the strawberry shortcake. But the courtroom rocked with laughter in a sudden, gusty release of lust: blood lust, sex lust, laugh lust. The gust died quickly. A woman had been killed.

Hochstadter sustained the objection, and Parmelee made his questions more specific, but Talbot was no help. Any number of men might have desired his wife, but he knew of nothing. Only Rawlins. Parmelee droned on, industriously threading a woof of insinuation on the warp of Talbot's denials. He digressed again, and often. He retraced the route of Talbot's evening, of Talbot's marriage, of Talbot's frequent but peaceable drunkenness—"more amatory, it would seem, than homicidal"—and of Louise Talbot's life. He chugged into random corners, switching himself onto new tracks without warning. On and on and on, as though he knew that every hour spent in court prolonged Talbot's life by so much; that every redundant question answered repetitiously comported the infinitesimal possibility of a turning, a slight detour that might lead to confusion if not exculpation. Or that every crawling hour was a buffer between the jury and the crime; in his droning voice, in the enervating heat, in the passage of time lay forgetfulness. That day was wearying; Harvey Bump might have been writing in his sleep. By four o'clock there were empty seats in the courtroom.

I lapsed into an unprofessional catalepsy, slumped uncomfortably against the hard wood like a politician in church, and trying to maintain the same expression of interest and dignity. Lacking discipline, my mind drifted off to Rosemary, snubbed her coolly, returned to Talbot, drifted off again, meandering through the past, greeting ladies, reviewing lost opportunities, tabulating hanches galbées. It was nothing so dramatic as death provoking lust, though I have noticed at funerals that the fitting answer to death is living flesh, and even in my old age female mourners sometimes take on a beauty and an availability in my mind, as though we were all starting fresh now; the graveyard smells of cut grass and ripe blossoms, and every shrub swells, exfoliates. No. A hardwood bench is the death of affection, and my slumbrous fantasies were without heat or purpose. I was simply bored. Because Parmelee was accomplishing nothing, and perhaps even sealing a doom. Everyone in that courtroom believed Bryan Talbot guilty; they might sympathize, they might admire his brave deception, but he had committed one great sin, and they knew he was guilty of another. Parmelee had at best introduced possibilities, but no sane man lives by the possible. Nor does he live by the certain. He lives by the probable. If he lives by the possible he is sick with fear, and if he lives by the certain he is sick with power. Most of us are not sick. We live by a reasonable, lazy sort of common sense, which is another name for the probable and is often inadequate but preserves us from God and the Devil alike. Talbot was guilty, all right. We were sorry about that, as decent people always are. The Colonel said later that even if Talbot had not murdered his wife, he had made the murder inevitable by his earlier sin.

Parmelee finished at four-thirty, and Hochstadter offered to adjourn and leave cross-examination for the morning.

"If the Court please," Dietrich said, "I'd prefer to cross-examine now. I'll be brief."

"Well," Hochstadter said, showing surprise. "All right. Go ahead."

Dietrich just looked at Talbot for a long time, maybe a minute. Then he said, "Mr. Talbot: you would like us to believe that a stranger, at any rate a third party, attacked and killed your wife."

"It's the only explanation," Talbot said.

"Then can you tell me why, except for a bruise on your own face, there were no signs of struggle? Or why, as Doctor Schilling testified, there had been no criminal assault?"

Talbot shook his head. "No. I can't."

Again Dietrich just stared for a time. Then he, too, shook his head, but with weary disgust.

"When you got home that night," he asked, "why did you call the police and not the hospital?"

"I—well—I thought the police would bring a doctor. And I couldn't find a heartbeat."

"You knew she was dead."

"I thought she was. I was afraid she was. I don't think I knew what I was doing, exactly."

Dietrich nodded, and then looked at the floor and

said quietly, "I think you knew what you were doing. Exactly."

Hochstadter struck the remark from the record, and Dietrich said, "No further questions," and we all went home. I had a headache.

And that was all. Poor Parmelee had no allies. Friday morning he delivered his endless summation as I sat peeking at my father's watch—gift of the Civic Club, Soledad City, in Honor of His Fiftieth Birthday, August 10, 1910. The Law Is Light. The watch seemed to run badly that day, evenly enough at nine but slowing steadily. At about eleven I was seized by sighs and tremors, and one desperate, languishing exhalation, half yawn, half groan, caused my neighbor, a frowsy wife, to peer in maternal alarm. I have the record before me now and I see that Parmelee made a good speech but I cannot recall the emphases, the gestures, the tones. I can reconstruct: he must have spoken levelly and earnestly as he repeated—spiraling infinitely about the fact —that the case against Bryan Talbot was built solely upon inference. He must have been intense, head forward, eyes grim, as he said, "We simply don't know how complicated Louise Talbot's social life was. We do know that she had one lover, and flaunted him; that cohabiting with more than one man was not impossible, and probably not distasteful, to her; how many more there may have been, no man will ever know." That attempt failed, as I recall it; the jury, sunk in heat, fanned itself in a measured flurry of cardboard and straw, twelve men glazed and still, like a church choir during the sermon. Parmelee reviewed the evidence selectively, quarrying out of it every least statement or implication or possibility that favored Talbot: "He would have had an alibi. He would have taken her out of town, staged an accident; any murderer would have. And Bryan Talbot is a notoriously calculating man. He is considered a cold fish, a planner. He is methodical, and appears to be as passionate about money as about anything else. For three and a half years he persevered in his successful attempt at reconciliation. For two years he acquiesced to his wife's adventure in Dallas. Can you believe that after those years this calm, cool, impassive man went home one night—even tipsy—and destroyed the woman he loved? Why? A whim? A sudden decision to annihilate his woman, his future, possibly his own life, all at once? Nonsense. If you believe that then you must believe that he is insane."

And so on. While I suppressed yawns he hammered on, pacing, gesturing: we could not have known whom Louise Talbot might have been teasing; Talbot was eminently not the man, as a type or as an individual, to commit that horrible crime; and—this was his peroration, as expected—no jury had the right to condemn a man to death in the absence of direct evidence. The jury had no choice; the sentence was mandatory upon conviction of first-degree murder; but the jury was not there to judge the law. The jury was there to judge the facts, and there simply weren't any facts. Could they, in conscience, take the life of a human being? Vengeance is mine, saith the Lord. Et cetera. Talbot's blood would be on their hands, and it would not do to share the guilt, like a firing squad with one blank cartridge; every one of them would have to spend the rest of his life wondering if he had done wrong, if he had committed murder himself.

He was sopping when he finished. His shirt was soaked and at the back of his trousers, just under the waist, a stain of sweat was spreading. He was also exhausted. He said, "You cannot convict Bryan Talbot. By all the laws of God and man, you must declare him innocent." He straightened momentarily and gazed at them and said quietly, "I believe him to be innocent. Upon my very soul I believe that." Then he said, "Thank you," and slumped like a wounded bear. He labored to his chair and flopped. He was breathing slowly and deeply and sweat ran down his face. No one moved. He extracted a kerchief from a trouser pocket and sponged himself, and then turned to Talbot and nodded with the weary, somnolent grace of the very old, and smiled a small, tired smile. At that moment the jury might have acquitted; for Parmelee, and not for truth.

Unfortunately for Talbot, the trial was not over. We recessed for lunch. I went home and ate two bowls of chili and packed a bag. I also put on a clean linen suit and felt slightly ghoulish, as though I were spiffing up for Dietrich's summation, like a man in a morning coat at a funeral. My mother sat across the kitchen table and radiated a faint heat of worry and disapproval. "I suppose you think I shouldn't go," I said between peppery mouthfuls. "Let her stew in her own juice, or some equally original gem of folk wisdom. But a girl like that has problems."

"And you don't."

"Now, now. Of course I do. One of them being Rosemary. Another being—would it make any sense to you if I said I was pushing myself to go up there, forcing myself a little?"

"No."

"I don't think I really want to go. I don't like to argue with women about basic matters. I want to go up to the lake and swim, anyway. I want her to come down here. I hate . . . I hate chasing after the world."

"Then why go?"

"Because—well, no man can live that way. You can't just ignore everything. I wish I could. And I— I—" The wrench of desire almost wrestled me out of my chair. I set down the spoon and folded my hands. "All right. I like her. I don't want to bust up whatever it is we have."

"That isn't what I was worried about," my mother said.

"I know that too." I resumed eating. "But I'm going. I can't change anything here."

She sighed. "You'll never be President."

"That's right. But they don't need me. They have Gamaliel. Gamaliel will go on forever. Like Charlie Chaplin. Anything funny enough is immortal. Gamaliel in Alaska. Can you see him, with the cigar, mushing through the snowy wastes?"

"He'll be in Juneau," she said, "and they don't have snow there in summer. And anyway they say he has a girl friend. He can't be all bad."

"I heard about that," I said. "Maybe I ought to write him for advice. Coffee, please."

"You don't need advice," she said. "You need a brisk walk around the block and a cold shower." And then she was serious and pleading: "You shouldn't go. Not today."

"I know," I said. "I'm going. A driven man. It's the prick of fate."

"Language," she said.

I moseyed back to the courthouse feeling rather plantational in my linen, needing only a planter's hat and an eight-inch cheroot, or some belles to bow to. I also felt cheap. Not because of the clothes but because there was nothing wrong with me. My liver did not ache like Parmelee's or my conscience like Talbot's. No plagues afflicted me, coronary, pancreatic, or theological. Questions, perhaps, because I had no idea why I was here or where I was going, much less when or with whom; but there would be time later for metaphysics. Later, when the more urgent demands—clamorous glands, insistent blood, insatiate senses—died. Quiescence then, and acquiescence. Right now I was perky, and the orange flash of a Bullock's oriole in the courthouse square went to my heart as Talbot never could.

So did the bronze apparition of John Digby, rising to meet me as I approached the steps. "What cheer?" I said.

"Where are you going?"

"Albuquerque. On the four forty-five. You're flabbergasted. Don't lecture me."

He stared. After a moment he said, "Two things. First, does Judge Hochstadter know?"

"What does he have to know? Is it against the law? I have things to do in Albuquerque."

"All right," he said quickly. "That's your business. Second, some people want to get married. They were hoping to come to your office at four o'clock. License in order."

"Lovely!" I beamed. "Who are the lucky pair?"

"A man named Golub and a girl named Wendt. Her parents will witness."

"Never heard of them." I smiled. "I'll be happy to oblige." But I used them, and evaded one confrontation: "Would you take my bag to the office? I'll pick it up there."

He saw. "All right." He hesitated.

"Now what?"

"Nothing," he said. "Here comes the U.S. cavalry. See you later."

He was replaced immediately by Colonel Oates, who

hove harrumphing into conversational port. "Well well well. It ends today." The Colonel too was resplendent, in a pleated shirt and what, in tweed rather than linen, would have been a Norfolk jacket. His buff Stetson was freshly blocked.

"It does indeed," I said. "Four days of courtroom Chautauqua. Grand finale this afternoon."

He peered anxiously. "Are you drunk?"

"No. Just confused. Flaming youth. Bitter."

"Confused? He's guilty, isn't he?"

"I suppose he is. I beg leave to point out that you once thought he wasn't. But that isn't what I meant."

"What is it then?"

"Nothing." I grinned a glassy grin and clapped him on the shoulder. "It's just me."

"An eye for an eye," he said firmly. "I hope you won't be sentimental about this."

"Sentimental!" I fixed him in a steely gaze. "Colonel, the law is the law. The safety of the people is the highest law. Hammurabi. Good law means good order. Aristotle. Don't forget that. Don't let Joseph Conrad sap your moral fiber."

"You're spoofing me," he said. "There's something wrong."

"Not at all. At four o'clock I am joining Golub and Wendt. This is a day among days."

"Who are Golub and Wendt?"

"Let's go in," I said. "I hate people who make noise after the curtain goes up."

"Golub and Wendt?" he murmured. "Golub and Wendt?"

I weakened again, and sent a note to the bench: must leave at four. Marriage ceremony. Hochstadter adjusted his pince-nez and read it and nodded and waggled his fingers at me. The courtroom was full and I had not been wrong in my mockery: this was a formal occasion, with markedly more neckties and jewelry in evidence, as well as a more subdued and respectful manner. When court had been declared in session and Dietrich rose, the silence was remarkable. And at that moment I yielded to an almost suffocating nervousness. My muscles twitched; my fingers danced on the back of the pew in front of me; I licked my lips and scratched my head, rubbed my face aimlessly, clenched my teeth. In the great hollow room a rite was about to be consummated and the participants were grave, silent, orderly. But I broke away from them, and wanted to shout, sing, make a speech. I know why, now; I did not, then. I was wrong and bad. Somewhere beneath the skin a lily was festering. My fellow citizens, mes semblables, mes frères, killing ceremoniously. Talbot. Rosemary. Bruce Donnelley of the Chamber of Commerce, unmoved and unmoving, the conscience of the people, the rock of our brief age. Hochstadter in solemn majesty, ha! And the disquiet seemed to be mine alone. As if my own shame (at what? at what?) had lacerated my sensibilities beyond theirs so that only my eyes were restless, only my heart was pounding. But there was no real excitement in the room, not even mild perturbation; a lugubrious assembly but not truly sad; earnest, rather, frozen in sober righteousness. And only one man, me, sniffing the wind in self-judgment, and catching not even the stench of iniquity and corruption, but only a hint of wrong in the warm air, as if a horse had broken wind half a mile away.

Dietrich commenced.

Singlehanded, Dietrich killed Bryan Talbot that afternoon. He began quietly, leading the jury gently away from Parmelee's dramatic admonitions. He reconstructed the crime, and then reconstructed Talbot. And here he displayed a perverse genius: the coldness Parmelee had vaunted became, in Dietrich's description, a very perfect cunning: Talbot was the archetype of the amoral man, whose impassivity masked a contemptuous and diabolical ego. To hear Dietrich every step, even the absence of an alibi, even the drunkenness, had been planned; and the jury heard him. The very senselessness of the crime was a subtle defense; and only the coldest of men would count on that.

Louise Talbot, being the hottest of women, required reconstruction too; and her heat—Dietrich was careful to use the word, informing it with resonances of both whorehouse sultriness and animal oestrus—was the direct and immediate cause of Bryan Talbot's decision, timing, and accomplishment. She drew men, and Dietrich's analysis of that attraction was accurate if moralistic. She drew them by symmetrical features and extraordinary physical proportions; equally important, she radiated availability, and Dietrich spoke a truth when he said that availability was the most insidious and powerful of female attractions. (A truth for that time, at any rate; now that I am a debilitated old crock availability has become, among younger people, the rule and not the exception. Eheu fugaces. Born thirty years too soon. I prefer a golden age to a brassy, though; was kept busy; will not complain.) Her power was a constant threat to Talbot, and his life was a continuing plot to diminish it. Which, out of his own fear, guilt, pride, baseness, he had succeeded in doing. Dietrich did not glorify the victim: she was not a woman he would have liked, he lied, but she was a human being, and the law exists for the protection of the innocent as well as for the punishment of the criminal. (He quoted an English decision, "The law is for the protection of the weak more than the strong.")

Talbot seemed to me to grow pale and rigid as Dietrich progressed, but it may have been my nervous imagination. Parmelee was glum; Hochstadter took a note now and then, for his charge, I assumed. The audience remained silent, attentive, respectful, and frightened me; it was like a beast, a great panther apparently in repose but really screwed to rigid tension by the approach of its prey. Now and then it seemed to twitch its tail as a fan flapped lazily. Bruce Donnelley sat motionless; he had not missed a session since his testimony, and had brooded like Jehovah through the slow, hot hours.

At five minutes of four I left, slipping up the side aisle as quietly as possible. Dietrich was in his peroration, and was quoting Cicero. Barring the unforeseeable —the flash of irrational and sometimes noble independence that every lawyer feared from every juror—he had won. Hochstadter would deliver a solemn charge, and it would be a good one; Hochstadter was a careful man and fair. Then he would dispose of various points submitted by Parmelee, to be added to the charge if the Judge saw fit; then he would have two bailiffs swear to keep the jury incommunicado and comfortable. Parmelee would move again for a dismissal, and probably take exception to the charge, and to any refusal of his points for charge; all that was ammunition for his appeal.

And then the jury would find Bryan Talbot guilty, and Edgar Musgrave would print up a hundred pages in a great hurry, and the superior court would deny the appeal, and then we would have a hanging for the edification of the weak and the entertainment of the strong. A highly moral diversion, with a distinguished cast and a rousing climax and a lesson for all.

Crossing the square I was lucky: on a Gambel oak I saw a walkingstick move. Many people pass a lifetime among walkingsticks and never see one move. I observed him. He was some three inches long, six twiggy legs and a twiggy body, two hairlike antennae whipping back from his head. He sensed my presence, and was still, melting into the rough bark. I looked away—at the courthouse, brown, shining, homely in the afternoon sun; at the municipal building with the high wall embracing the exercise yard where Bryan Talbot would be hanged; at Juano's Stanley Steamer, exhausted and somehow limp at the dusty curb; down Main Street toward the distant corner of Pueblo Street, on which stood the shrine that had once been Connie's place. Then I looked back, and the walkingstick was gone. I found him about ten seconds later, in the same spot; he might have been a roughening of the bark, or a single, wasted, leftover tendril from some prehistoric ivy. I left him there. He would have a short season and be soon gone.

Geronimo stood in his doorway and favored me with a flippancy. "How," he said. "Paleface hanged yet?"

"Almost," I said. "Don't let John hear you talk like that."

"A good boy, John. What are you doing here?"

"My duty," I said. "I have a marriage ceremony to perform. I am a servant of the people."

"What were they doing in court?"

"Dietrich was finishing. It should go to the jury in an hour."

"And come back again in five minutes."

"You think it's that clear?"

Geronimo shrugged. "It's pretty clear. I've been thinking about it." He was in khaki, with a bandanna around his neck to catch the sweat. He was old and lined, blinking in the sunlight. "It's like the World's War," which is what he always called it, "when the atrocity stories came out. Nobody believed them. Not really. Did you ever find anybody who believed them really? No. But we pretended to believe tham because we needed an excuse to hate Germans. People like to kill. You take early man. Prehistoric. He killed from necessity, and he felt good when it was done. So that's a tradition, a deep tradition, no getting away from it. Right? Everybody likes to kill and now nobody will admit it. So they'll punish Talbot to show how they hate murder, and they'll get him hanged because they love it. Right?"

"You sound as though you don't think he did it."

"Oh, he did it, all right. No question. A cold man. But they'd hang him anyway. Because they know why he did it. He had his fun and now they'll have theirs. See?" He waggled a hand at me in impermeable triumph and swept on. "Always. Always it happens that way. When a jury has to acquit, they're disappointed. I'm glad you're not mixed up in this. Talbot did it, all right. No question."

"A deep thinker," I said. "Is that why you're such a good card player?"

He laughed joyfully. "No, no. The cards is from my Jewish half. Pinochle when I was a boy."

"I see. And the thinking is from the Apache half."

"No. From my Apache half is knowing how men love to kill." He smiled dreamily, like a sage, and nodded. It was the repeated, impervious, charitable nod of the man who is sure, whose nod is merely the final confirmation of a truth he has vouchsafed the world. "Now go make your wedding," he said.

Which I did. Clambering up the musty stairs I whiffed again at that faint odor of wrong, but I shook it off at the door and entered my office resplendent and bubbling. A wedding. A wedding! How unique and glorious! Smiles and nods; Miss Wendt giggled, Mr. Golub crushed my hand in his manly grip. Mother Wendt was crying. Father Wendt was slightly embarrassed, slightly uncomfortable: my daughter, he seemed to be saying, will spend the night in this lout's arms. John was a self-effacing usher; but I noticed, with admiration, that he had arranged assorted blossoms in our one vase; the office was all but festive.

I did not hurry the ceremony. These upright young things would, with luck, be married only once; I owed them a pleasant memory, and was therefore properly benign, sprinkling this symbolic pollination with a fine spray of official approval, as though under instructions from the good Harding himself. I performed few marriages, and was curious: why had these fine young Americans not hied themselves to a church? Atheists? Of different and irreconcilable religions? None of my business; I beamed upon them. When I said, "I now pronounce you man and wife," Mother Wendt exploded like a paper bag full of water, showering my threadbare carpet, a cloudburst in the desert. I added, "You may kiss the bride," which was not part of the ceremony but sounded like an order from the State House and some-times inspired a shy groom who might otherwise have felt that the dignity of judicial precincts estopped any such barbaric sexual assault. He kissed her; they clung, eyes closed, sweet and twenty. Father Wendt kissed her. Mother Wendt kissed everybody, blindly, including me and John; her tears wetted my cheeks. I too kissed the bride, and as my face approached hers a mischief al-most burst within me, and I had to check a gorgeous impulse: what would happen, I wondered as the cold, rubbery, moist lips met mine briefly, if I were to seize this unspeakable child and embrace her in Chaucerian enthusiasm, hands on her buttocks, eyes aflame, fever-ishly roaring "Good luck! Good luck! Be happy!"? I withdrew chastely, nodded like a sachem, refused the two dollars proferred by a tremulous groom, and es-

corted them, in a muggy cloud of asphyxiating plat-
itudes, to the door. When John closed it behind them it
was as though a convention had left town.

John would not leave me alone. "You can't do this,"
he said.

"Oh, come on," I said. "I'm doing it. It's not so terrible. I'll be staying at the Bench Club."

"What's he going to say?"

"He won't like it," I admitted. "But what good would
I do around here? I'm sick of the whole business. Just
leave me alone. You're not even a citizen. Why don't
you go back where you came from?"

"All right, all right," he said. "I'll wire you. Back
Monday?"

"Sunday night." Prudently I added, "If not sooner."

It was much sooner.

7

I SCUTTLED OUT OF town. Not lurking in doorways; but I avoided the courthouse and made a roundabout way to the depot. Doubtless prompted by obscure sentiments I cut through Pueblo Street, touching my hand to my heart as I passed Connie's. A shingle outside announced STATE POLICE; a placard in the window advertised NATIONAL GUARD. That window had once been framed in Burgundy swag curtains with a gaudy ball fringe, and afternoons Connie—Consuelo Gracián—sat there crocheting and drinking beer and nodding like a chatelaine, which indeed she was, to friends in the street. Of which I had the honor to call myself one beginning in 1911, September, when upon a sudden high resolve I picked up my suitcase and a stuffed wallet, left the house to go to college, and got on a train three days later, incurring penalties for late registration but bringing to academe a far more rounded scholar than the ignoramus who had begun the journey. Within a week I had a note from my father, one of the three or four he ever wrote me; to wit, Dear Ben, Were you in that hussy shed last week? Your father, Graeme. He was angry because he had heard through my mother, who had heard from Connie through a network of cousins, and it did not seem just to him that he should depend on women for manly news.

He was right. I owed him something. I had made a good impression socially by remembering half a dozen of his paternal asides, enunciated at odd removes and

apropos of random events. My father effused a rough
gallantry all his life because he believed that a woman
was a lady until she lied and he was too much of a gentleman to doubt a woman's word. So when I arrived at
Connie's, gangling, the suitcase banging at my knees,
and entered the parlor with all the blood in my body
momentarily concentrated above the neck, I was prepared to comport myself with at least a gauche good
grace. Though I believe that if the piano had fallen silent, if my three or four colleagues had broken off their
conversation to stare, I would have fled like a jackrab-
bit. The piano tinkled on; the clients, gentlemen to the
marrow, veiled their curiosity; Connie herself welcomed
me. I thanked her, offered beer to the house, and sat
opposite her at a wooden table. The young ladies chatted quietly with their visitors and the music was subdued; barring certain irregularities of dress we might
have been in the parlor of the First Methodist Church. I
won the honors of the house when Connie asked me if I
had made a choice and I observed ruefully that I imagined she herself no longer took an active part. She
grinned then, at the art and not the sentiment, and I
blushed, and she complimented me on my upbringing,
which was her way of telling me that she knew who I
was and considered herself a friend of the family. I said
that maybe she could choose for me better than I could
for myself, which won me another smile, another flash
of silver molar, and also won me Isabel Rosarias, with
whom I spent forty-eight hours of ruinous bliss and
whom I loved deeply, genuinely, blindly, and exclusive-
ly for the next three months with a purity, a tenderness,
and a self-effacement I was never to know again. Isabel
went off somewhere during the war, and Connie, who
was in her fifties when I met her, died shortly after the
Armistice. I missed her funeral but would have attended if I had been home in time. My father told me that

several men of position and respectability were at the cemetery and no one was embarrassed or made a joke. Sometimes it was possible to admire Soledad City.

The train was on time. I swung into the coach and settled down, removing jacket and tie and twisting a kerchief under my collar. Trains were an abomination. I had the classic choice between two asphyxiations: plain Southwest, or flaming air, and fancy Pompei, or hot cinders. I chose the local variety because I was wearing white, and lolled moribund, tongue on chest, for three and a half hours. Clack, clackety, clack, clackety, and the desolate right-of-way, and the sweat dripping off my fingers onto *The Education of Henry Adams*. Every half hour I went to the men's lavatory and unbuttoned and sat over the bottomless pit in Bacchanalian glee while warm winds whistled upward, refreshing. A vulgar and obsolete piece of expertise to be passing along, you will say, but it had survival value, like escaping a fire with a wet cloth over the mouth, and was, to the connoisseur, a small, grifting but soul-satisfying victory over the industrial revolution.

The railroad had one virtue: trains ran fast over a hundred miles of flat, almost waterless plain. We joined the Rio Grande at San Marcial and from there on the view was more various; by then the evening sun lay low, and just the aspect of the river diminished the heat. By Belen, where assorted revelers clambered aboard, destination the big city, I was no longer sweating, and when I swung off the train into the twinkling lights of Albuquerque at dusk I was almost cool. I hired a taxi and checked into the Bench Club, thinking that Bryan Talbot's jury was out, and telephoned Rosemary. She had not dined. Politely, she invited me to chicken salad and iced tea. Her roommate was away for the weekend. I accepted with reserved delight and solemn protestations of continuing respect. It was an ignominious conversation; I was reduced to a Reverend Mr. Collins, gravely informing his Elizabeth, "And now nothing remains for me but to assure you in the most animated language of the violence of my affection." But I slicked back my hair and adjusted my cravat and stepped nervously into the moonless purple night. I walked—it was a mile or so—searching for a florist's, but none was open. I was suddenly very tired. This would be a weary, stale, flat and unprofitable evening, and as I walked a couplet—from what? I never knew—circled endlessly through my mind:

> If a man be so spent
> That his wife keepeth Lent . . .
> If a man be so spent
> That his wife keepeth Lent . . .
> If a man be so spent
> That his wife keepeth Lent . . .

Rosemary was born on a farm, not even a small ranch, not far from Athens, Texas. The Bergquists were hard-working, God-fearing sons of the soil, et cetera, pious Lutherans whose existence was simply bleak. The family had originated, as far as they knew, near a place called Umeå in northern Sweden, not quite Lapland though I had my little joke about that too, which annoyed Rosemary. They did not dance or play cards and refrained from laughter on Sunday. God knows what they did: they worked, they set their lips to keep from pestering Jehovah, they procreated, they read the Bible. The farm barely kept them alive, though they were never in deep debt. Hearing Rosemary talk about it, I congealed, turned away sick and rebellious from the aridity, the grubbing toil, the dry sweat that defined the silent, aching, gloomy Bergquists, whose salvation had never come in this world. Rosemary was born in 1900 and survived, the family's one triumph over a grudging, almost savage, Nature. But the old man wore himself out and ground to a halt in 1905; Mrs. Bergquist found work with the church in Athens and survived ten years more. It was the church that took care of Rosemary from then on, seeing her through high school and into a denominational college, where she took care of small children, waited on table, and made beds in return for her education. A bachelor of arts in 1921, she noted opportunities in Albuquerque—found a squib in a teachers' magazine—and came west to make her fortune. She was highly moral and untouched by human hands.

I met her in 1922, eight or nine months before the beginning of this story. Her eyes were large, brown and direct under brows slightly darker than her hair. Her nose was not neat and Grecian but a trifle too big. Her lips were full and her teeth regular and white. When she moved I saw that liquefaction of her clothes. What a foolish catalogue! I noticed none of that at the time, and knew only that some unformed lust for utter perfection lurking within me as within every man needed no longer be blind and shapeless; here was its object and its fulfillment.

All right: drivel. A purplish way of saying that I saw a woman I wanted immediately, and that in ten seconds I had stripped her and bedded her and taken ten thousand meals with her and grown old happily. What the hell: better that than marrying for money or to win a competition or to make an advantageous alliance. Men marry for hundreds of reasons and I did not know then and do not know now any better reason than to make of life a fruitful orgy. The day I met her I asked her to dinner and she blushed and did nervous things with her hands and said, "Well, I don't know," and at first I thought she was making fun of me with her voice, imitating one of her eight-year-old charges. When I realized that she was not, that she was a natural chirper, I just grinned. I would not have cared if she had bellowed like a bull. In the end I took her to dinner and then to see *The Four Horsemen of the Apocalypse* with Rudolph Valentino. I kissed her goodnight; that was easy because it was unthinkable, and she had no notion of what I was about to do until my lips were touching hers. She pulled away horrified and squeaked "Judge!" and ran inside. For all I knew she would lie awake all night waiting for labor pains. I was very happy and sang a bit on my way to the hotel, no words, just that mandolin serenade from *Don Giovanni*. I had seen it in Paris, only once, and loved it. My French friends told me it was a wretched performance, and I felt sorry for them. That night in Albuquerque I pitied them even more: I had found my Elvira and no one else had, ever. If I had asked her to marry me in those first weeks— but I did not, and then I discovered that she was not perfect, and neither was I. I was so desperately in love with that unformed image of utter perfection that I became petulant, and a pompous masculine surliness cankered my heart. I see all that now. Now I am over seventy. You will not understand why I bundled my mother into an automobile a month later for a two-week visit to Ignacio's. Nor did I at the time. The answer was there, but it wanted finding.

Rosemary lived on the ground floor of a three-story building. Two more teachers occupied the second floor and the landlady, a widow, the third. Rosemary and her roommate had two bedrooms, a living room, and a kitchen with a gas range and an icebox. The furniture was all horsehair-and-maple but the draperies were bright, yellow and red, and the living-room floor was covered by a scattering of pretty Navajo rugs. The girls did not keep liquor or cigarettes, but a large and misshapen fired-clay ashtray announced their emancipation. There were some Audubon prints on the walls, some Navajo knickknacks, a clipper ship under full sail.

I stood outside the building for a moment, warring with an odd reluctance to see her. I was safe on the sidewalk, and perhaps if I did not enter I would never learn the worst. But native optimism, and even a point of dry curiosity, carried me forward. I rang the bell, and she came immediately to let me in. She was smiling. "Hello," she said.

"Hello." I closed the door. "Why the grin? I expected cold silence. Rosemary all in black, buttoned up to the chin." She wore an Indian skirt, imitation buckskin, and a light green blouse. On her feet were moccasins, deerhide, soft soles.

"Now don't be intense," she said. "Please?"

"All right." I smiled. "I tried to find flowers for you but the stores were closed."

"That's better. You're forgiven."

"Will you kiss me?"

"Of course," but it was only a meeting of lips; it asserted nothing. I sat neutrally on the sofa and looked down at magazines: *Scribner's, McClure's, Vanity Fair, The Delineator*.

Rosemary sat in an armchair, smiling, politely, faintly; head high, eyes cool.

Soon I said, "Let's eat. I'm hungry. It's a long, dull trip."

"It's a long, dull trip the other way too," she said, and I grew even more neutral. Would she have preferred that I come here each weekend? To pace the streets of Albuquerque? To watch Tom Mix and take ceremonious leave at her doorstep? She was unreasonable.

I followed her to the kitchen. The table was set. She served chicken salad, went back to chip ice, poured tea. The kitchen walls were white and the light bulb overhead was naked. In the flat brightness flaws sprang out: a tiny mole on her neck, a dry upper lip, a faint wrinkle beneath each eye. But delights too: shadows on the pale green blouse. She wore scent; weak, trailing, it called in whispers. "Now you eat," she said, and smiled again. "You just have to let me be a woman."

"I ask nothing more." Louise Talbot crossed my mind.

"But we don't mean the same thing. Your idea of somebody being a woman is that she flutters her eyes when you walk in, and breathes hard."

"I don't care about 'somebody' being a woman. I only care about you. And you know that isn't what I want."

"I don't know what else you want, if anything. Oh, it's fun." She grimaced daintily at her own weakness. "But it's all you seem to think about."

Silence seemed best. First, because she was right, but in a way she did not yet understand—did I?; second, because she was flagrantly wrong. Sitting before her, munching, calm and tired, not so nervous now, I thought how wrong she might be: forgetting the hours of talk, the books and music and cowboy movies, the long rambles beside the river, the meals and chaffing with my mother, Rosemary now remembered only the moments of what she obviously thought of as assault, which could as easily have been called invitation or fulfillment or just plain love. Right now it was all *she* seemed to think about. She need not worry tonight. We both sensed that, and after a quiet minute or two we smiled again, almost shyly. And then we made small talk for a time, but over dessert I set down the fork and hunched forward. I wanted to touch her hand but did not. "Are you really unhappy? I don't want you to be."

"I keep thinking of a little house," she said.

"Oh. And a little car."

She nodded. "And little kids, and large jars of mayonnaise. And you scare me. You're wild and dark and you have black hair on your back and it scares me. Why is that?"

"I don't know," I said. "I only want you to be happy."

"Then you shouldn't have come here tonight." She sounded sorrowful but her eyes were warm.

"Can you tell me why?"

"After," she said. "Finish your dinner."

Which I did.

We washed the dishes together. Compendia of aphrodisiacs never include domestic chores; but have you noticed that women warm to a man who will put the silver away and take the garbage out? The intimacy of the kitchen sink. That was taught me during the war by an educated private named Sheers from a place in New York State called Tonawanda. His family manufactured bottle caps, and Sheers spent most of the war cleaning out grease traps in the army's more elaborate kitchens. (The alternative, I gathered, was one court-martial after another.) The time, he assured me, was not wasted, and the sacrifice—of dignity and the olfactory sensibilities—not in vain. "Seduction begins in the kitchen," he said. "It is true. The professors say that food and sex are similar satisfactions, but that is not it. A man who does things around the house, when it is not his house, is like a man who smokes a pipe. He is reliable and comfortable. He may be a perfect scoundrel, but to a woman he is reliable and comfortable and when she learns the truth it is too late. Her instinctive approval goes back to January of the Cro-Magnon era. She smiles in her heart because the man who keeps the cave clean is a tender fellow. As the book says, the experience I have acquired during this here war will lead to a fruitful career in time of peace. Hand me that steel wool."

Rosemary smiled. My sleeves were rolled and my tie was flapped in between two shirt buttons. I stacked the dry plates. The silent music of domesticity billowed through the apartment. When the kitchen was clear Rosemary took my hand and led me to the living room; she turned the lights low, propelled me gently toward the easy chair, and settled herself on the sofa. "That was more like it," she said. "I'm not even nervous now."

"I am," I said. "I feel like a defendant. You wouldn't have any of the real prewar stuff in the house, would you?"

"No," she said firmly. "I want you to be a gentleman tonight."

It was an inauspicious remark, and evoked neither anger nor chill, but impatience. Or wry weariness. If I was a gentleman, then how could I not be one tonight? If I was not, then how could she hope for the transformation?

"Very well," I said. "No profanity. No grabbing." And for God's sake be quick about it, I wanted to add.

"Now," she said. "I've been thinking, and I don't think you love me. Not really."

"Oh." I shook my head. "That can't be answered. If I say I do, you'll just say No, you don't, and we'll be like two kids arguing. If I say I don't, I'm lying."

"I think you *think* you do," she said.

"Oh, for the love of God," I said. "Not that, please. Anything a man feels, you can say he just thinks he feels it. That's unanswerable too."

"You said you wouldn't swear," she said. "But I

mean it, about what you think. You have love and sex all mixed up."

"As they should be. Inextricably mixed up."

"Well, not mixed up. I really don't think you know what love is."

I blew out a great, tired, puffing sigh. "Stop. Stop right there. You may not know it, but you've begun a classic, hackneyed speech. Any red-blooded American boy has heard it a dozen times. I don't want to hear it again. I don't have to hear it again. You mean that I want your body, and that I use you for my own pleasure, but I have no true affection for the real you, for the real Rosemary, for your soul, for your mind. That way down deep I consider you a piece of ass and nothing else."

"You said you'd be a gentleman." Her lips were tight; she was blushing.

"Ah, come on," I groaned. "Do you want truth or poetry?"

"All right, truth."

"Then the truth is that I love making love to you. Also talking to you, eating with you, listening to your troubles, and showing you off. But not arguing with you. Not on this level. And all you remember is that we sleep together. You forget all the rest."

"That's not true! And you know it isn't. But you never stop to think how I feel. How every time I turn around you have your hand on me. How I have to sit with your mother and wonder how much she knows. How you make me do things I know are immoral, and even against the law! How——"

"Make you?" She had the good grace to avoid my eyes. "You don't like it?"

"Oh, sometimes. Yes, in a way, I guess. But it's all the time. It's always there. I mean, not every minute, but when I'm with you I always think you're thinking about it. About making love. On the stairs. In the kitchen. On the street, even."

"What would you prefer?"

"I don't know, I don't know. You never gave me a chance to find out. Look." She hunched forward, pleading. Her hair was white in the lamplight. "You know what kind of girl I am. How I was brought up. The way I was when I was little. The church, and all. And when you do things like that to me, I have to—have to—"

"What? Force yourself?"

"No, no." She was impatient. "Well, a little. But it's as if somebody was watching. God, I suppose."

"The fallen sparrow," I said.

"Oh, don't make jokes." She raised her voice. "You *know* it's wrong." Then she blew up. "You know it, know it, know it! Whatever you say, you know that! Don't you have to answer for it?"

"Rosemary—"

"Don't you even believe in God? Don't you think the rules are there for a reason?"

"You can't throw God at me," I said. "You were brought up that way; I wasn't. I don't know what you feel and I don't think you do either. You don't hold back in bed; where's God then?"

"Oh, I know that," she breathed. "But afterward. Afterward. Don't you realize I never knew anything before? I never even kissed a man until I was twenty? And I'm only twenty-three now. I'm only a *girl,* Ben, not a fancy woman, and now I don't even have what I'm supposed to bring my husband. I never had any love so I took it from you, and you enjoyed it. You let me be—be—"

"Dirty," I said. "Dirty is the word you want. It's your word, not mine. I thought you really liked it. I thought you felt good, I thought you felt happy."

"Sometimes I did. And sometimes I hated us both. I

was scared. The first time you got up with no clothes on and went to the window to watch the sun come up, I thought I'd die!"

She sat back and closed her eyes.

My voice was slow and quiet: "And if I say that it would have been obscene to wrap myself in a towel, you wouldn't see what I meant."

"No. Of course not. You've got everything backward. I don't know what's so wrong with modesty. Even the cave men wore clothes."

That was true. The cave men wore clothes.

"Then what do you want?" I asked gently. "Will you marry me?"

"No!" she squeaked. "No, no, no! How could I marry you now? And you only asked me because you feel guilty! Because you want to do the right thing!"

"You asked me to be a gentleman," I explained.

"Don't make jokes," she said. She got up and walked here and there. "Don't make jokes. You've made me feel—oh, God!" She shivered. "I could *never* marry you. And I suppose you'd want your mother to live with us!"

That stopped me short. "Well, I suppose so," I said, confused; and then, "what do you want me to do? Send her to a home? Stake her out in the desert?"

"Oh, I don't care. I just couldn't marry you. Not after all this."

That interested me. And interest was the wrong emotion. I should have been angry and hurt and desolate, and was not. I remembered that later. "Then you'd rather marry someone else and remember what it was like with me? You mean that would be more moral?"

"I don't care about marrying someone else," she said quietly. "And yes, it would be more moral. Or no—I don't know. But I do know that you don't want to marry me. I was kidding myself but you were kidding us both, and you didn't know it and you still don't know it. I think you kid yourself all the time. That's why I let you come here tonight. Somebody had to tell you that. I'm young, and confused. But you're a lot younger, and I think a lot more confused. You're a big man when you have your robe on, but you're a little boy underneath. I didn't see that for a long time."

I drew away. I coiled up like a diamondback and sat stiff and sullen, hating her. Women! They wanted someone who was so busy paying bills and getting ahead that he had no time to annoy them with love. Automobiles and position and tasteless mayonnaise in two-pound jars.

"I'm sorry," she said. "But it's no use. You scare me. I don't know why. But you have no shame. You don't even know right from wrong. You hurt me, and you took something from me."

That was all I could stand. Of her, of the genteel apartment, and of course—but God! we never know these things at the time—of myself. "I see," I said. "You wholesome blondes all think alike," and I picked up my jacket and went away, not pausing at the door for any limpid look back. In the street I took a deep breath and swallowed a minuscule lump in the throat, but do you know what I was thinking? I was thinking, Well, I tried. I tried. I walked a bit faster and then, because it was good to be in the open air, broke into a trot. When I reached the Club at eleven o'clock I asked Paul to bring me a glass of bourbon, and I called the station. No one answered. Paul said there were no trains this time of night, but he recommended a garage, and I got the owner out of bed, finished my drink, checked out, and left Albuquerque at about midnight in a handsome Packard touring car. I fell asleep at about four and ran off the road, jolting through soft sand until I snapped awake. No harm done. In Deming I parked

in front of a café and fell asleep again, and when the
man came to open he woke me thinking I was drunk or
dead, and I let him serve me four fried eggs with bacon
and muffins, and I drank many cups of coffee, and entered Soledad City in stately disarray at about eight-
thirty. There seemed to be no excitement at the courthouse so I went directly to my office. I was plenty tired
and I wondered how Bryan Talbot had slept.

Geronimo was on the sidewalk eating sardines from
a can; he whistled and goggled over the Packard and
managed to spill fish oil on one fender. "They're still
out on Talbot," he said. "How much does this cost?"

"God knows. I got it for the weekend. John been
around?"

"Not yet. Hot today. You look tired."

Tired. He little knew. "I better get over to the
courthouse."

"Yah," he said. "I'm surprised they took so long."

"You never know about juries," I said.

He shrugged. "Everybody knows he did it."

Everybody knew a lot of things in those days. Thunder would curdle milk. Jews had tails. Tomatoes were
poisonous. Wobblies were paid by Russia. Eagles carried off sheep. Hanged men died with erections.

I went to Hochstadter's chambers and knocked, and
he said to come in so I came in; when I saw the relief
and surprise on his face I knew that John had made
lame excuses for me. "Good morning, Ben," the Judge
said heartily. "John said you had big business in
Albuquerque."

"Just something personal. I came right on back."
Now I felt shame—not at having run off, but at falling
in with my own lie. Why not say, Yes, and if she'd been
my old Rosemary I'd still be there, sleeping, a hand on

her rump and the hell with Bryan Talbot? Why not? "What about the jury?"

"Nothing yet. I got them off to bed about ten last night; no point in these all-night sessions. They're back together now. No questions. I suspect they know he's guilty but they want to talk for a while. Nobody likes to hang a man, and they generally like to go over the ground two or three times, and chop up the responsibility in twelve equal pieces."

I nodded. There was not much to say. I yawned.

"You need coffee."

"God, no. I've had a gallon this morning. When's the hanging, if he's guilty?"

Hochstadter cocked his head with a sharp glance at me.

"No," I said. "I wasn't being flippant. I want to know."

"I thought the sixth of July," he said. "Give him plenty of time for the appeal. You know," and great distaste crossed his ruddy, jowly face, "I sort of hope the appeal wins. There's nothing evidentiary and nothing statutory to work on, but maybe a technicality somewhere. God damn it. The way that man says he didn't do it, that bothers me. I half believe him. And I know Oliver believes him, and Oliver's no fool. I wish to God I had some choice in the sentence."

"Maybe the jury'll call it second-degree."

"They can't." He scowled. "Not on what they've got. If it was murder at all it was first-degree."

"It's a bad law," I said. "Nobody's death should be mandatory. But I think Parmelee made a mistake. He could have made a deal. Something. Anything. But he bet the whole roll on one throw."

"That's why he did it," Hochstadter sighed. "He thought his man was innocent, and in any case he thought they'd be too squeamish to hang a man without direct evidence. But Dietrich was good. Dietrich nailed him to the cross."

Someone knocked and the Judge called, "Come," and John stepped in.

"How," I said. He stared. "You're supposed to be an inscrutable redskin," I said. "You look like you'd lost your breechclout."

"Good morning," he said. "Good morning, Judge Lewis, sir." To Hochstadter he said, "Chief Harmsworth has brought Talbot in. Nothing yet from the jury."

"Thank you," Hochstadter said. "We'll be here when they need us." John looked at me again, wonderingly, baffled, and went on out.

"How did the charge go? I'll read it; but how did they react?"

"Very well." Hochstadter nodded. "They followed carefully, and I'm sure they understood about premedit-ation. I think they also know that they can't hold his tomcatting against him or even his sloppy approach to public health." He smiled. For Hochstadter it was a well-turned phrase. "Oliver made the usual motions, and I turned him down, but he expected that. His points for charge were sort of—well, upsetting. They weren't good points, and I refused most of them, but they bothered me. He knew they were bad, almost un-professional, but he had to do all he could. Like one that went something like 'If the jury find that there is no evidence placing defendant on the scene of the crime at the time of the crime, jury cannot convict.' Well, he knew damn well that was silly, and I covered circum-stantial evidence in the charge; but I didn't feel right just the same. And I covered second-degree, if they be-lieved the accused had gone instantaneously into an un-controllable rage, but Parmelee wanted me to tell them that lacking evidence of premeditation they must acquit because the state's case required premeditation. It was

as if he was trying to get at me, and not at the jury. And
there isn't a damn thing I can do, unless I want to dis-
miss altogether. Of course he asked for that, too, in a
motion, and also for a directed acquittal. I tell you, I
squirmed a little. It's that damned law. If I had my way
I'd never hang him. I think he did it, all right, and I
think doubts would be unreasonable. But just the same
I wouldn't hang him. I just hope they make it second-
degree but I don't see how they can. If it was murder at
all he had damn well thought it over more than once."

I grunted agreement, and John stuck his head
through the doorway and said, "They're coming in."

I put on a robe and sat below Hochstadter at the end
of the bar, unobtrusive. That morning, May 26, 1923,
we had discipline. The courtroom was full; it was also
orderly. When we walked out they rose immediately,
with a direct attention, a solemn respect, that they had
not previously shown; it was as though we were priests,
or matadors. And yet this was not the critical moment;
it was only the dramatic moment. What moment in the
trial most demanded solemnity no one could say; just
when the last juror had decided, no man, including the
jurors, would ever know for sure. Just what fact, what
supposition, what prejudice, what inference had resolved
which juror—and those moments, twelve of them, were
the climaxes. This, now, was simply an announcement.
One way or the other. My stomach pitched a bit anyway
and my muscles were tight, and naturally the coffee
chose that moment to clamor.

Talbot was white, and what clamorings assailed him
we could not know. We could not imagine. Half hours
of my own life had perhaps not been too different; pull-
ing a platoon through a mile of thunder—that war was
all noise—not knowing at what moment a piece of that

thunder might crystallize, solidify, be transmuted by
pure chance to a lightning sliver of metal. But that was
chaos and chance; this was order and purpose. Talbot's
thunder would be words, and the transmutation not
random but ordained. Parmelee too was livid. The spectators were blurred, their faces identical blobs.

The jury returned in awkward procession. Hochstadter recited formulas. Bryan Talbot rose. So did William
Sawyer, the foreman.

Hochstadter spoke to Harvey Bump in clear, unhesi-
tant, yet neutral tones: "You may record the presence of
defendant and counsel. Then you may take the
verdict."

Harvey stood up. An extra, a spear carrier, a walk-
on; but this was his moment, and a hundred of his fellow citizens who had ignored him for four days now
paid him homage: they stared, unmoving.

Harvey cleared his throat. He was short and stocky,
balding; his ears stuck out and his rumpled suit was of a
sleazy purple cotton. But his voice was steady and he
did his job: he was an agent, a messenger, a Hermes
and no Apollo and if his wings were frayed and stained,
what matter?

"Members of the jury," he said, "look upon the accused. Accused: look upon your jurors."

And that was honorable. Every hour we judge one
another; and how often do we look?

"Members of the jury, have you come to a unanimous verdict in the proceedings of this state against
Bryan Talbot on the charge and count of murder?"

"We have," Sawyer said.

"And how say you: do you find him guilty or not
guilty?"

Sawyer looked straight at Judge Hochstadter and
said, "Guilty of murder in the first degree."

PART TWO

8

IN ALL MY LIFE I CANnot recall another month as oppressive as June of 1923. The last spring rains had dried on the first of May and by June first Bryan Talbot's cell was the coolest chamber in Soledad City. My mother's house was large and usually airy, with tall, wide windows and overhanging eaves for shade; but that June it was an oven. The heat seemed to roll down like a bland, transparent, indifferent solar lava; it flowed into corners, filled basements, rose through parlors and kitchens and bedrooms and attics. Most of the year the town smelled good, even if it looked terrible. Exhaust fumes encroached slowly, but the desert supplied a regional perfume, cactus and cholla and prickly pear, Spanish bayonet and sage, nothing overpowering but a good clean dry sandy smell. That June we smelled of whatever was in the street. The air just hung, and the horse apples and dead cats decomposed fitfully; so, it seemed, did grass and shrubs and even people. Hochstadter was played out, as though he had been drained by the trial and now *this,* no breeze, no cloud, only a stinking town with pigs on the dirt roads and cars on the paved roads and oily streetcars on their tracks and the tracks embedded in ribbons of black tar that bubbled like bean soup. Drinking was no help. Geronimo drank hot tea. He said that was what the Chinese did. He and I went to Alonzo's for dinner one night—a Chinese restaurant, and Alonzo's real name was Charlie Quong—and asked him about it, and he said yes yes, red tea. The British drank black tea and the Chinese drank green tea, but in very hot weather, red tea. Yes, he had some. I bought a couple of ounces and brewed it at noon the next day. After two cups I was hotter than before but I had learned a valuable thing: bad as a hot day is, it will be worse if you drink red tea. Geronimo said it cooled him off right away.

Even my mother groaned and complained. She was alert and curious for a few days, waiting for my account of the visit to Albuquerque, which was not forthcoming. She admired the Packard, which hung around until the following Wednesday, when I got Phil Moens to take it back; he was an electrician and his wife's folks were in Albuquerque and I imagine he was delighted to pile the kids into the car and come tootling up to the in-laws' like John D. himself. And the Packard sharpened her appetite for news. "Must have been a fine fight," she said. "What time did you leave Albuquerque?"

"Poincaré has resigned," I said, "and Stanley Baldwin has replaced Bonar Law."

"All right, don't tell me. I'll just imagine it."

"We talked about William Jennings Bryan," I said. "He wants to ban Darwinism in Presbyterian schools and their general assembly won't let him. Rosemary was furious."

"I read that." She smiled. "And the Sunday paper had a funny thing. Two headlines. Page . . . four, here it is." She adjusted her reading glasses and sat there like Benjamin Franklin. "Two headlines side by side: Presbyterians ban views of Fosdick; and Baptists in uproar silence Doctor Straton. How's that?" She looked up. "Can't take it, those Protestants."

"Unlike you folks," I said, "who have free and open debate on all matters."

"Touché," she said. "But the Protestants are *supposed* to. That's what they turned Protestant for."

"You are an ignorant old Dago lady," I said. "In their best days the Catholics never dotted the i's the way Calvin did. In writing, too. He gave Servetus a safe-conduct and then burned him alive. For whistling in the street, or something. I guess for taking the Reformation seriously."

"Who was Servetus? What happened with Rosemary?"

"She just didn't feel like screwing. Hand me that newspaper, will you?"

"Ben!" Real anger; I looked up. "Don't be rude to me. Obscenity has to be redeemed by a high elegance, and you don't always have it. I don't like that kind of language. In certain essential respects I'm a lady. Here." She passed me the newspaper.

"Sorry." I smiled half a smile. "Very sorry, really. I'm tired, and we had a dust-up, and it's hot, and Bryan Talbot has to hang, and I just don't feel like talking about that particular virgin goddess. All right?"

And I still have two reports from that newspaper; I ripped them out and slipped them into a ledger where they yellowed until I grew old and began reminiscing. They were not dramatic. One simply stated that Larry Semon, a comedy star of the films, had signed a three-year contract for three million dollars. Remember what three million dollars stood for in 1923. Obviously Larry Semon would never be forgotten. A true immortal. Who? What was that name? The other report also concerned the films. The British censor had unburdened himself of a few rules to be applied to American movies. Sixty-seven of them, "Any one of which will cause a film to be banned. The board will not permit materialization of the figure of Christ, cruelty to children and to animals, disparagement of public characters or officials, prolonged death bed scenes, too much revolver shooting, or a picture which holds up as laudable the sacrifice of a woman's virtue.

"The censor will not allow little boys to tie cans to dogs' tails, and he will not let trained 'movie' dogs pretend that they have been hurt. He allows the bad man in the film to say 'Go to Hades!' but not 'Go to Hell!' Girls taking part in crime, women drunk, and women being branded are not allowed to be shown on films, and no one may say 'What the Devil!' on the screen."

What the Devil! The man had left us nothing! I wished him in Hades! I think I kept those reports because they summarized human foolishness; and that week, that month, the human race seemed to have little to recommend it. Thwarted in her busybodying, my mother fanned herself and took to drinking with the Colonel; and the Colonel annoyed me beyond measure because he was devoid of honest lechery. Altogether. He could monger rumors with the fellows, and he was avid of transgressions; but other people's, and not his own. He was a nosy, rigid, disciplined, bloodless officer in the army of permanent righteousness. He was, God save him, pleased that Talbot would hang. "The sins of the flesh always, always, always demand retribution. I have never known it to fail." Well, I had known it to fail, but you could never be sure; you never knew what remorses, what frustrations, what bladder troubles might be the wages of sin. Death was everybody's wages and so did not count. Though payday was coming a trifle early for Bryan Talbot. The Colonel liked that, and he sat on our porch swilling my bourbon and chattering, instructing, preaching; his horsy nostrils flared and contracted, his glossy skin dulled in the heat, his slightly yellowed eyes rolled and flashed. That my mother tolerated it was a measure of her own disarray.

He drove me out of the house, and there was little

judging to do, and I would have felt only moderate surprise if the world had come to an end. The town was torpid. We squinted against the sunlight, gaped sleepily, nodded like robots. Business fell off everywhere. Henry Dugan worked overtime and ran out of ice. The river was low. Judge Hochstadter was troubled by indigestion and John Digby at last renounced his jacket and tie. We tried one card game and quit because the cards were slippery with sweat and limp in twenty minutes. Oliver Parmelee composed his appeal and Edgar Musgrave printed it and off it went to the superior court. Geronimo had a fight with Bosko because they were both selling Za-Rex fruit juice concentrate, which Bosko thought unfair. But Bosko was selling sanitary napkins. At Peter Justin's Billiard Parlor a customer played "Bambalina" twenty-two times and was knocked unconscious with a pool cue while winding the machine for the twenty-third; when he woke up he ripped the baize off a table and Peter had him arrested. I dismissed the charge when he paid up, including seventy-five cents for a new record.

Ebb tide. Soon, the summer session, Judge Lewis presiding. Hochstadter was planning a trip to Montana for most of July, to a place where Mrs. Hochstadter could sit with refined ladies while the Judge disappeared with a guide and lived on trout, bourbon, and cigars. "There is a glacier," he lusted. "A small glacier but a glacier. And the water of the lakes and streams is cold, and rushes. And sometimes it actually rains."

"Take me with you. John can handle the court calendar."

"I'd like to." He cocked his head, amused. We had been spending more time together; meeting as if by habit at the Territorial, sitting in quiet communion while the afternoon burned out. Juano joined us now and then; he had drawn up a chronological list of the states ratifying the Eighteenth Amendment, and had declared a thirty-six-day period of mourning, each state to be honored in turn. Ordinarily Hochstadter would have spurned such juvenile recreations, and it was in surrender to the heat that he fell in with the ceremonies. We were a bit hazy one afternoon when he said, "You know, I wasn't expecting you back, the morning the jury came in."

"It was the least I could do."

"But I didn't think you'd do it. I didn't know you were out of town until about eight-thirty and I was pretty sore. How do you feel about it now?"

"About the verdict?"

"No. About being a judge."

I thought it over, and then shook my head. "I just don't know. It was an honor, and all that, and I couldn't have said no to the Governor. And then my mother was proud, the little old lady with the boy who makes good. I even had a girl I wanted to impress, just met her the day the Governor asked me. And the Colonel—you know the Colonel? a damn fool—honored me with the formal approval of the War Department, law and order et cetera. Even old Goldman got owlish about it. You know what he said? Pour me another, will you? He said, 'In those days there was no king in Israel; every man did that which was right in his own eyes.' And he slapped me on the back. So I said, what the hell was that? And he said, It's from the Book of Judges. Don't forget it. Then he said if I could find out why Ehud had to be left-handed he'd appreciate it. Who was Ehud? He spelled it for me and I had to go home and look it up. I still don't know why he was left-handed. But I found the verse, and I noticed that it was the children of Benjamin who lived that way. So even that seemed to fit. If I was superstitious I'd have said it was a sign. You know? But even so, have you noticed that

nobody calls me Judge? Only John." I raised my glass
to him and drank.

"And then?"

"And then . . . well, I had to decide important
things. Whether a man spent ten days in jail or thirty.
Whether he had a right to beat his wife. To kill his
neighbor's chickens. To break a contract. Do you know
what I liked best in the war?" He waited. "I mean in
the fighting. What I really liked best was a few days in
Paris. But at the front what I liked best was patrols. Because on a patrol there were four or five of us, and every man did pretty well what was right in his own eyes;
but when the whole company moved up I had to give
orders. To my thirty men. I had to say, Let's go. And
thirty men would go and ten come back, and I was the
one who had said, Let's go."

"Responsibility," he said. "You can't duck it forever.
You can't always be a lone hand."

"Maybe." I rubbed my eyes. "I don't mind responsibility up to a point. But I don't like power. I don't
trust it. And a judge has a hell of a lot of it. My God,
what a good man a judge ought to be. And I'm not a
good man. I'm an upright, downright, foursquare, kind-
hearted, easygoing, red-blooded American boy."

"You've got real trouble," he said, serious and sym-
pathetic. "If it helps any, a judge has got to be human,
too. I mean he's got to be pretty much like everybody
else or he won't see through the shams and evasions
and such. I think you underestimate yourself. A judge
can't be a saint, you know. He has to be above it all,
but if he's never felt temptation he can't judge the fallen. And god damn it, boy, better a man who knows his
own stupidities than a man who's too sure of everything."

" 'I wish I were as sure of anything as my opponent
is of everything.' "

"What?"

"Something like that. Melbourne. Or Macaulay. I can never keep them straight. Well"—I grinned at him —"you've made me feel a little better. Let me buy you a drink."

"A pleasure," he said. I poured. He raised his glass. "Here's to an easy summer term."

"Thanks," I said. "I'd like that fine."

You agree that I was querulous and petulant, a boy-man. I have been trying to set down the story of a trial and it twists and writhes like an unruly sunflower glaring always at me. Autobiography, after all. Facts are hard and understanding is harder and wisdom is hardest. So we read a book or a magazine and look in the mirror and then, complacently, describe the world. We say that Dostoievski was epileptic or Carlyle impotent and listeners say oh ah really, but we never tell them about our own seizures or limpnesses. I have not been honest. Not said that Bryan Talbot's fate was of no real concern to me; that I observed him, did my duty as a young judge, and did not care. Not said that as I strutted and sulked before Rosemary other haunches, other bosoms, other fair faces caught my eye, my mind, my loins. Or that the heat of day was as nothing beside the heat of night; lying alone, frenzies upon me, the corrupting odors of desert and river roiling my blood like coriander in a lusty soup. Or that I was lonely, not unloved but unloving. Despising, deep within me, the cast of cardboard characters I called friends, understanding them no more than I did Congreve's: MADAM DOTING, a mother; COLONEL SEBASTIAN ENTRENCHING-TOOL, a prurient and gossipaceous officer; MR. SEIDLITZ PERUNA, a sentimental pharmacist; SIR SUSPENSUS P. COLLUM, a gouty judge; LOINCLOTH GAITERS, a reformed savage; Miss Messalina Rondeur, a laetificant and temulating temptress; and Senorita Nina de la Tierra, a wall-eyed princess.

And the embarrassment, the shame, that racks me now, forty years later, is secret, exquisite, and agonizing. The walls of my study (once my father's) reproach me: they are lined with plaques and scrolls and photographs, some merely pompous (clubs proclaiming that I am a good fellow), some serious (a letter from Harlan Fiske Stone), some downright subversive (an award from the CIO and a photograph of Franklin Roosevelt shaking my hand). Now I am venerable, and no one knows or cares that I passed the crisis of adolescence at the ludicrous age of twenty-nine; a crisis for which there is no medical name but which the knowing might call generalized tumescence. I was swollen with garbage and bitterness, the litter of the soul, and saw no possibility of relief in a world of grubbing egos. My own ego was monstrous, mainly because I had never done anything for anyone and could justify my uselessness only by assuming that the world was not worth my energies. But I did not see that then. Certain rebukes I will not accept: that I failed to join, or to attack, or even to take seriously, this or that political or social group. Middle-class I was, and lazy, and living in a small corner of the world, and not for me were starving millions and oppressed masses and kings and bankers and jack-booted heroes. Mostly I wanted to be left alone. With Rosemary, or someone like her, conveniently to hand.

Well, they grow up a lot faster nowadays, don't they? Which means that they early commence killing and owning. Most of them never make it all the way; they live to be a hundred and are still twelve or thirteen when they die, hoarding goods and triumphs and vital juices, fearfully squaring up the edges of home, community, nation, God. Existence assaulted me late, but I think perhaps the assault was successful. Otherwise I would not be writing this. Otherwise I would have nothing to tell you.

And what do I have to tell you? Well, I had intended to save it for later, when I had established to your grudging satisfaction my small right (in your terms) to speak at all. But I will tell you some of it now, and be brief, and not explain. I do not like you. You have submitted yourselves to things, and soon they will kill you (all of you in fifteen minutes, they tell me), and you are half dead anyway because even your passion is a sort of trader's ecstasy, and those you say you love are acquisitions to be measured against the acquisitions of others and cherished accordingly. You worry lest your children love the flesh, and will not teach them how; but you rejoice when they are taught to kill and become sergeants. You join culture clubs and lament taxes; but you will not strike, picket, stand up and shout for the simplest of human decencies like not killing little children in Sunday school with homemade bombs. You see a pair of splendid breasts in a film, and you stare and form committees; slouching doom sneers on every doorstep, and you avert your eyes and go your way. Your poets have told you that you are locked and frozen in your desire, unroused; and you are too busy to listen. Or afraid that love will cost you money; you have created a God who approves of moderate interest rates. There is not one among you with the heart to walk naked on a sunny day.

On the fifteenth of June, being burdened by no murders, rapes, arsons, boys tying tin cans to dogs' tails, branded women, or excessive revolver shooting, I turned the office over to John, hustled my mother into a hired car, and pointed my finely chiseled nose into the afternoon sun. The car boomed along, creating its own exhilarant wind, and we never even stopped for a drink in Nogales; just checked in at the border and fled south. As we climbed we left behind the cottonwoods and desert willows and mesquite and yucca, the dun and yellow, and wound between fields of buffalo grass and groves of piñon and juniper and then through a forest of quaking aspen and scrub oak, green and silver, and a breeze came up. We stopped at one high, jutting curve and left the car in its ruts to sprawl on the grass and drink from the canteen, and we could see fifty miles: valleys and washes and distant mountains, and the late sun on it all like a bank of flame. Ruddy golden grasses, and stretches of blue-green, and in the hollows and canyons a heavy blue-purple. Four mule deer came browsing through a stand of oaks; a red-tailed hawk wheeled over the car, intent, raptor's beak cutting the wind; when he was gone the thrashers revived and swooped and called, and a buckeye butterfly stopped to rest on my foot. The sun was a friend again, and the earth itself —land, sky, mountains, groves—was luminescent. My mother broke the silence, and the enchantment: "Let's go," she said. "I need a bathroom." Poor, sad human beings. When I started the car the mule deer fled and the thrashers vanished.

Ignacio bounced out to greet us, yelling and burbling over his shoulder to rouse the servants, and threw his arms around my mother, kissed both cheeks and then her hand, kissed me, purled and plashed and susurrated, and then actually spoke, with the effect of Bach in an iron foundry: "What a long time it has been! What a long time it has been!" He pushed us to the house and sent small boys scurrying after the bags, herded us to our rooms, saw that we had water, and commanded us to grace the drawing room in half an hour. We were all laughing and gesticulating, spraying Spanish, nodding and slapping. Welcome home.

I was downstairs in twenty minutes and there she was, formal and cold as I kissed her—and God! how lovely she smelled—while Ignacio beamed. "Have you missed me?" I asked her.

"One always misses one's family," she said politely.

"True," I said. "Many nights I have longed for the warmth of this house," and Ignacio slapped my back again and roared, "Ah! Ah! Ah!" meaning, what a well-spoken man this is. He was not putting it on. Dinner was an event, fish and goat and his best wine, and after dinner he unveiled a prize, a new gramophone, and insisted that we dance, he and my mother like something out of the Spanish court, circa Charles Five, Rafaela and I more grave and Victorian. She kept her distance, and was cool, and I knew she was right. It had, as Ignacio kept insisting, been a long time, and I had not been a gentleman: one letter, as far as I could remember, in all those months. And she was older, stronger, disconcerting. But Ignacio bore all before him; we danced and drank and gossiped—Ramón had a new son—and tumbled to bed exhausted. He poked me awake at about six and I enjoyed his pleasure so much that I decided to add to it: when we had eaten eggs and beans and drunk coffee with milk I suggested that we go shooting, and we did, the two of us on leggy paints, high in the hills, sitting on the grass and banging away at some sort of mountain cony, dozens of them popping up, insatiably curious, at the lips of their holes. Ignacio was in a state of percolating ecstasy, and when we cantered into the yard and saw Rafaela, still cold and distant, he bellowed, "What a man this is! What a man this is!" and dismounted, and bobbled into the house to see about lunch.

It was our first moment alone. She turned away; I followed. We sat on a stone bench; before us the sun danced up off a muddy fishpond. We were surrounded by junipers.

"I heard you were married," she said.

"Married! Where did you hear that?"

"From Jorge. My cousin. He saw Luis Nava, who said that your wife had come to live with you."

"Not true. I am not even engaged. I had a visitor at the house a few times. My mother was always with us."

"As she and my father have always been with us here. All right." She smiled sadly. "It is really not my business. Welcome."

"Thank you." I kissed her. "It is good to be here."

"Don't kiss me again," she said. I waited. "We have had a visitor too. A friend of Ramón, young and quite pleasant."

"Oh." What could I say? Slack and lifeless, I sat. She rose and walked to the edge of the pond. She was wearing a long summer dress, and she was small, a cameo, her black hair trailing long and gathered only by a ring. A bird swooped low over the pond, shot away.

"I am twenty-one," she said. "A woman."

Yes. And I was twenty-nine and a boy, and all my turnings led to rebukes and malignity.

After a while she went into the house. I sat at the pond for another few minutes, old, stiff, and gray. And then wonder assailed me, that I could be so badly hurt, my heart shrunken and cold, my lungs tight and my belly griping. I never knew, I thought; is this love? God, how it hurts!

And Rosemary? I barely remembered Rosemary; but then I saw her face, and the golden hair, and the hills and valleys. I must be insane; I love by geography; that was in another country but tomorrow I will be in that

country again. And then will I remember Rafaela?
What do I love? One for summer and winter, one for
spring and fall? Do the names matter or the faces or is
it only lips and hips and maidenhair and am I nothing
more than a blind and nervous organ? Is that all? Is
that all I am? How do you learn to love?

So that too died on me, though Ignacio never noticed
and when we left, Sunday morning, the trunk was full
of wine and two hundred cigars. I said goodbye to
Rafaela quietly, memorizing the shape of her nose and
the curve of her lips and the depths of her dark, dark
occhi di venere; I knew there was pain in my own eyes,
and I thought I saw it reflected in hers. I was glum all
the way home. My mother's first words were sharp:
"Have you been fooling with that lovely girl?"

"Of course not," I said.

"She's a princess," my mother said vehemently. "If
you rebounded from that Swedish girl—"

"Her name is Rosemary."

"—and did any canoodling with Rafaela I'll tell Ignacio to shoot you."

After some ten miles of difficult downhill curves I
said, "I like Rafaela. I like Ignacio. I'm not sure I like
you. You giggle and titter about your lover-boy son as
long as he works his wiles on people you don't care for.
You're a snob. Rosemary's okay, and I suppose you
know all about that—"

"It shook the house," she said.

"—but let me get near a nice high-class Mexican girl
and oh, no. Hands off. That's different."

"It is. Besides, you're related."

"Yeah. What? Tenth cousins? With Luis Nava in
between? Anyway I plan to enter a monastery. I'm sick

of the whole god damned business. Maybe I'll marry the Colonel. Down deep he'd like that."

"You're a cold man in many ways," she said. "You don't know that; but you are. You have no charity."

"I spend all my time trying to be nice to people. Carrying on polite conversations with my mother when I'm tired and sad. But maybe you're right. Most of the time I just want to be left alone, but that's impossible, I guess. A fellow has to make a living. I have to live up to the Governor's idea of me. And laugh at Geronimo's jokes. And bow to the Colonel. And sit at Hochstadter's feet. And let John sit at mine. Do you remember Bill Carter?"

"Yes."

"Why can't I be nice to him for a change? God knows he could use it. He never even set foot in my house. But everyone else—oh, hell. I don't know. I was happy yesterday morning, with Ignacio fizzing and rumbling and shooting the heads off little animals."

"And what happened?"

"I guess a delayed reaction to Rosemary. I never did get around to screaming and kicking."

"Is it all over with her?"

"Maybe." We were racing across a flat toward Nogales. "The trouble is I don't react enough. Maybe you're right. Maybe I'm a cold fish. Rosemary gives me the gate and I say, All right, so long. That's no way for a tragic young lover to behave. And do you know *why* she did it?"

"Because you wouldn't propose." That smug tone.

"No. Because that hermaphrodite of yours had to make a speech about the clap. The little girl got the horrors, with the wages of sin spread out in front of her like a rash. And all she could think of was a long line of lantern-jawed, constipated Swedish preachers thundering about mortal sin from the depths of their frozen balls."

"You have a foul mouth," she said.

"I was badly brought up."

She surprised me then by saying seriously, "Yes. In a way you were. You know, you have to be a very natural man to be like your father was. Either that, or a great actor. You have to *be* it so you can't be anything else, or learn how to carry it off so nobody can tell the difference. And you're kind of caught in the middle."

"The blood runs thin in the second generation," I said bitterly.

"No. The blood's there. But you want something, and you don't know what. When your father swore it was like a volcano. Variation. Poetry. The wild Welshman. Couplets and quatrains on the stormy night air. But sometimes it comes out of you like a screechy nastiness. Because you haven't got the whole heart behind it."

"All right." I turned my head to smile at her, and I could see that she was grateful. "That's true. Whatever it is I'm going to turn out to be, I am not it yet. So mostly I want to be a lazy tomcat because that's easy. But it's impossible too because I'm like a little boy with a lot of relatives who pat him on the head when he gets medals at graduation. Everybody *expects* something. I don't even have time to find out what I really want. Hochstadter expects industry and uprightness. John expects praise. The Colonel expects gossip and phony manly wisdom. You want some kind of Paul Bunyan bringing home blonde maidenheads. And what do I want? A few women and a library. Because that's all they've left me to want for myself, without having to feel that I probably want it because somebody will approve of my wanting it. A hell of a thing."

After a while she said brightly, "Well, there's no music without frets," and I could have strangled her, but we were in Nogales.

And there was a new man on at the border station so we had to go to the hotel and unload the wine and cigars on the Mexican side and have the boys cross the border in the basement. Then we went through customs and drove around to the side door of the hotel and picked up the contraband, and it cost me two dollars in tips. Cheap enough; and, oddly, the smooth success of that criminal act restored my spirits. I was no longer above a joke or two and the rest of the trip was pleasant. My mother had picked up a Sunday paper in the hotel and announced that Stambulisky had been assassinated in Bulgaria. A bandit in Canada had escaped from a crowded courtroom and killed two constables and was still at large. More earthquakes: in northern Persia six thousand people, and possibly twenty thousand, were dead. The Cabinet had met to wish our President Godspeed. "Ah!" she said. "The Prince of Wales has been voted first among the dancers of the world by the National Institute of Social Dancing."

"Thank God," I said. "The suspense is over."

"And the President has been initiated into the Tall Cedars of Lebanon. And the Barling bomber is to be tested. It will carry seven guns and five thousand pounds of bombs. Oh, and here's one for you." She read it silently. "Chief Justice Harry Olson of the Chicago Municipal Court says that mental deficiency is— this a quote—'the root from which criminality springs.' He says the law should use modern science and weed out defective stock. Eugenics, he says."

"Does he say how?"

"No."

"Gelding shears, I imagine. Does he say what crimes?"

"No."

"Hell of a price to pay for a shot of whiskey. I think he just doesn't like Catholics."

"What?" She vailed the newspaper and looked up.

"All those rumrunners and bootleggers. In Chicago they're mostly Irish and Italian. You got to look behind the news."

"Olson," she said. "One of those damn Swedes."

"All right," I said. "Drop it."

After that she recited some advertisements ("Lady Sealpax Dainty Athletic Underwear") and soon enough we were home. That night I read some Gibbon and was much comforted. "The art of man is able to construct monuments far more permanent," he wrote, "than the narrow span of his own existence; yet these monuments, like himself, are perishable and frail; and, in the boundless annals of time, his life and his labours must equally be measured as a fleeting moment." Stambulisky and Bryan Talbot, Harding and Harry Olson, the Prince of Wales and I, we were small potatoes.

But not that small, I thought, drowsing, not that small; that can't be right; and I fell asleep with one arm around Rosemary and the other around Rafaela.

9

BRYAN TALBOT'S AP-
peal was denied by a unanimous superior court on June
28th, and Oliver Parmelee immediately sent the record
to the Governor. The event was noted, and honored by
a day's speculation, but the town had, after all, other
cares and considerations. President Harding, for example, was moving west, and was cutting grain in Kan-
sas just three days after the American State National
Bank of Wichita reported a shortage of one million five
hundred thousand dollars and one cashier. And then a
Presidential automobile soared off a cliff near Denver,
two killed. To my mother such cosmic happenings were
of little importance, but she very quickly found the
counterpoint to Bryan Talbot's imminent demise: a
turtle branded in Tonga by Captain Cook in 1773 had
been found alive. "One hundred fifty years," she said.
"How old is Talbot?"

It was a strange season. The newspapers were full of
death and I was preparing to take the bench. A sharp
drop in the suicide rate was credited to general prosper-
ity and I was studying the documents in a hotly contest-
ed condemnation that Hochstadter had held over for
me. While I pored over injunctions and restraining orders four Labour members of Parliament were sus-
pended for calling various other members of Parliament
murderers because children were dying of starvation. I
took the bench, robed and dignified, on July second,
Monday, at ten in the morning, having read at breakfast
that a Mr. J. C. Gomez of Venezuela, vice-president,

brother of El Dictador, had unfortunately been assassinated. I labored for arbitration, for a settlement. Mr. Hewlett, an irascible rancher of sixty or so, was about to be deprived of eighteen of his three thousand acres, object a new highway, and was, quite obviously, trying to hold up the state for more cash. In the end I got him to settle for twenty-two dollars more an acre than the state had offered. Then I had to get the state's agreement. Then a man in Florida, decent and honest and wanting no skeletons in his daughter's closet, confessed to her fiancé that he had long before escaped from a Georgia chain gang, on which he had been serving a monstrous sentence for a petty crime. The fiancé promptly turned him in, earning, to my taste, a permanent niche in Dante's lowest, iciest circle of Hell. My mother went to her room and did not emerge for a whole afternoon. The man himself was philosophical, telling the newspapers that he would rather spend twenty years on the chain gang than have his daughter married to a traitor. Meanwhile a successful duelist in Russia was tried for murder. He had fought the duel over a woman, who had witnessed it; she was tried as an accomplice. President Harding, near Spokane, had driven a locomotive twelve miles, realizing a boyhood dream. You see what sort of summer we were having.

On the Fourth of July we had a parade. Bruce Donnelley contributed the hot dogs and was seen to smile. He liked giving. He had come out of the east—Ohio, they said—twenty years before and prospered among us, and what he could not give in laughter and tears he made up in money; his heart was locked, his purse open; gaiety was damnation but charity was the mark of a good man. He was everybody's stern rich uncle, and everybody's civic ideal, and nobody knew him. He patted children on the head and sat on the dais during the more inspirational proceedings. To a captive au-

dience Mayor Cathcart made a speech about the land of
the free and the home of the brave and of course no one
dared walk out. A small Mexican boy lost an eye when
he lingered near a four-inch firecracker. I was at home
that night wondering if independence was a good thing,
and reading, when the telephone rang. My mother answered. I thought of Rosemary and listened, but heard
only one end of an enthusiastic exchange of greetings
and protestations of affection. I went back to Anna
Christie. Shortly my mother called, and sailed smiling
into the room. "Ben. It's the Governor."

I went quickly to the telephone. "Governor. Hello."
My mother hovered.

"Ben," he said. "Nice to hear your voice. Everything all right?"

"Just fine, sir. Couldn't be better. How are things in
the capital?"

"Under control. Everybody getting rich but me. Ben,
I've been going over the record on Bryan Talbot."

My hands and feet prickled. "I wasn't sitting, you
know."

"Yes, I know. But Parmelee's letter was impressive.
Trouble is, there's nothing in the record for me to act
on. Talbot sounds like a bad apple, and even if the evidence is all circumstantial, it's pretty damning. I've got
nothing against hanging a murderer, but I don't want to
be casual about it."

"I see."

"I know Parmelee by reputation," he said. "He's an
honest man, and if I turn him down I want to be sure.
You were there all the time?"

"Yes. I missed an hour or two. I didn't hear Hochstadter's charge, but I read it. It was good. Fair. Even-
handed."

"Then you think the superior court was right."

I paused for a long moment.

"What is it, Ben? If you think they were wrong, tell me."

"No, it isn't that. I—why are you asking me? Why not Hochstadter?"

"Oh, I've asked Alvin. I've asked several people."

Better. Relief washed over me. "All right," I said. "I'm not one hundred per cent sure, but I have no reasonable doubts. I know what you mean about Parmelee; and there was something about the way Talbot handled himself that made me not so sure. But it was a fair trial; I think he did it. I wouldn't mind if you could find some reason to commute, but I can't give you one."

"No. There's nothing to act on. It's a hell of a thing. But it always is. It was a lot more fun when I just had to arrest them. Well, thanks, Ben. Anything I can do, let me know. It's been nice talking to you. Eulie sounds the same as ever."

"She is. It's a shame."

He enjoyed a boisterous laugh and said, "So long, Ben."

"Goodbye, Governor."

I hung up. I was covered with sweat.

My mother was not entirely beyond redemption. "Let me get you some coffee," she said quietly, and I was grateful.

And so we approached Friday morning, July sixth, and the death of Bryan Talbot. Judge Hochstadter had set his vacation for the seventh, in an ancient and honorable tradition: he had passed sentence, and would not spare himself the personal consequences. Though God knows the true consequences were Bryan Talbot's alone. Hochstadter prepared the orders and talked awhile with Alfred Harmsworth and Willie Waite. The execution was set for six, and Edgar Musgrave's request to be admitted was promptly denied. Hochstadter and I,

Dietrich and Parmelee, Alfred and Willie. That was all. And Bryan Talbot, and a preacher if he wanted one.

I thought of Talbot. I thought of visiting him but did not. He was now not a man but a sacred object, or a damned, which was the same. I mean that I was timid and, unreasonably, ashamed. There must come to every man who is part of an apparatus a moment when the apparatus functions without him, in spite of him, unheeding; the moment when he must say, You take the king's shilling, you fight the king's war. Either that or he deserts. But the moment is a hard one. You join up because they need a man and you think you are a good one, and suddenly you are not a man at all but one small dumb erg in a monstrous blind force. I wondered if congressmen felt that way when they declared war. I knew lieutenants did when they said "Let's go." And knowing about death, its inevitability, a favorite discovery of so many young poets, was not enough; we all knew about death. We were engaged to marry her, and as we grew old and the ceremony approached, we made friends with her. But Bryan Talbot's was a shotgun wedding.

Yet I slept well, and woke with the alarm at five, and ate a hearty breakfast, wondering what last breakfast Bryan Talbot had ordered. The heat still lay upon us but not so heavily in the early light; the sky was pink and blue and yellow when I left the house and the air was almost cool to my cheek. Not to be born is the best for man. Something else from Sophocles plucked at my mind, something about death not being the worst; it was worse to want to die and not be able to. But who wanted to, really? Only those who believed in a blissful hereafter; and they did not want death so much as birth. Timor mortis conturbat me. A bookish lout. I walked with my head down. I had never seen a hanging. I might throw up. Thou owest God a death; a demand note. But hedged about with options and renewals. Not for Bryan Talbot, though. Foreclosure today. Timor mortis conturbat me, my own or anyone else's. Had he made a will? No living relatives. The end of the Talbots. Dust.

Judge Hochstadter joined me in front of the courthouse and we walked to the jail in silence. Inside, we nodded to Alfred and Willie and the two attorneys. Judge Hochstadter drew the orders from his pocket and I signed them and handed them to Alfred. The attorneys inspected them. Parmelee was dead white. "This is wrong," he said. "I know it's too late but this is wrong." Dietrich was silent.

"I'm sorry," Hochstadter said. It was ten minutes of six. Inside the jail it was cool. The overhead lights were still on. Alfred was glum and avoided our eyes. Willie Waite stared at nothing and twisted the hood. I wondered if it was the hood he wore to Klan meetings.

Five of us stepped outside into a beautiful morning while Alfred went to fetch the prisoner. Hochstadter gazed up at the sky and shook himself. He drew in a deep breath and let it out with a hoarse clearing of the throat. His eyes were not quite focused, as if he were looking back over the years and remembering dead men. The courtyard was bare and stony, with the platform at one end and the rope in place. The wood of the platform was raw, fresh white pine from Donnelley's lumberyard, stark and unfinished and temporary. Willie climbed the steps and tugged at the rope.

Talbot came out of the jail screaming, hanging limp while Alfred and the preacher, a Mr. Morrison, dragged him. At first it was just noise but then we heard the words. "No! No! I didn't do it! Don't kill me! No! No! I didn't do it!" Without his glasses he seemed much younger; shirt open at the throat, hair mussed, eyes wild, pleading, desperate, furious. His knees hit the ground and Alfred hauled him up. Talbot's hands were behind him in steel handcuffs. Willie stood patiently on the platform. The sun was high enough to rim the far wall, a streak of yellow light on the stone. Parmelee shuddered. Dietrich was staring sightlessly at the ground. Talbot was still yelling but he shut up when they reached the steps, and went limp again; Alfred and Morrison tugged him up on his knees, a step at a time, and then they were there. Talbot had wet his pants.

We uncovered. I looked. I owed it to myself, and to every man who would ever stand before me, to look. Morrison bowed his head and so did the others but I went on looking. I was looking into Talbot's eyes but he was staring at Willie Waite. Morrison was saying, "The mercy of the Lord is from everlasting to everlasting," and Alfred had the hood in one hand, the other on Talbot's shoulder, when the sunlight struck the arm of the gibbet above Talbot's head, and the others were standing with their heads bowed and their eyes closed so that only I saw Talbot move; with a swift sidewise glance at Alfred and then a quick, jerking motion he was free, hands locked behind him, and he shot forward screaming with his head down and rammed Willie Waite in the belly. They tumbled off the platform with Talbot on top. Morrison stood there with his mouth open. Alfred cursed and leapt to the edge of the platform and then down, but he was too late. Willie's head had smashed against the cobblestones with a rude, hollow crack and Talbot was up, stomping at Willie's neck, blubbering and keening and stomping until Alfred jumped on him and dragged him down. Parmelee ran forward yelling "Bryan! Bryan! Bryan!" and we, the other three, stood frozen; but deep inside me a monstrous atavism stirred; I could feel my eyes glitter; and I knew with horror and exultation that I was blessing him because he had done what all men should do. Odium mortis conturbat me.

10 "HE'S DEAD," DOCTOR

Schilling said. "Skull smashed like a sugar bowl."

"Oh, Jesus," Alfred said. "Oh, dear God."

Oliver Parmelee went on shaking his head. "Gentlemen, gentlemen," he said, and shook his head. "Gentlemen." Then Dietrich too shook his head and they stood in the now sunny courtyard like mechanical dolls.

"Oh, Jesus," Alfred said. "Oh, dear God."

Schilling entered the office and said, "Talbot is all right. He's out cold but he'll be all right. That Morrison is with him."

"Did Willie Waite have children?" That was Hochstadter.

"A couple," Alfred said. He was seated at his desk. "My God. Who'd have believed he'd do that?"

"Emil," Hochstadter said, "it would be the decent thing for you to tell Mrs. Waite. You were his boss, in a way. As soon as she's ready to look around again, you ought to tell her she can petition the state, and sue if she's turned down."

Dietrich nodded.

"Next time we put the hood on first, and then do the praying," Alfred said. "But who could've known? We never had a hanging here before. And there's no *rules* for it; just hang him by the neck until he is dead. And what do we do now? Tell me that, Judge."

"We call the capital and ask for a new hangman. And we hang Talbot tomorrow morning. Ben will give you an order."

"Oh, Jesus," Alfred said. "Oh, dear God."

The street door creaked open and slammed shut and we heard footsteps in the corridor. Then Edgar Musgrave marched in, bright-eyed, wattled: "Well," he said cheerfully. "Is it all over? Can I view the remains? You sure don't look as if you enjoyed it. How did it go?"

"There is no proportion in life," the Judge said a few minutes later. We were talking in the sunny, deserted square and it was six forty-five of a summer morning. "Do you know what I was thinking in there? I was thinking that I planned to leave tomorrow at about noon and I can still get away all right. Provided the new man gets here today, and I'm sure he will. Now isn't that a hell of a thing to be thinking? What do you suppose Bryan Talbot would say about that? And what do *you* say, my young friend? All this is happening in your term."

"I haven't been able to think. I've been numb."

"Poor Willie Waite. Poor Alfred. Alfred will always feel responsible."

We walked on in silence.

At the courthouse we separated. "If you need me just call," he said.

"Thanks."

We shook hands. We were alone in the street. I felt like a young Roman parting from a senator before a temple. At least I was not worrying about women today. I entered my chambers and stood for a moment reading the sampler: DISCITE JUSTITIAM. My mother had fabricated it in a burst of domestic solemnity, and it hung like a warning, the capitals in red and the rest in black. Learn to do justice.

I sat down. I was still numb, and my mind was empty of all that I had so assiduously stuffed it with. I did not want to die, ever.

When John came in I was still sitting there.

"How did it go?" he asked.

I told him, and we sat looking at each other for a long time.

I went home for lunch. Doubtless they were waiting for me at the hotel and I did not want to talk. My mother's thoughts were for the widow. "Willie was no good," she said, "but the woman has two little ones and shouldn't be left to starve."

"Willie was a live human being," I said. "She won't be left to starve." It was seven hours since breakfast but I was not hungry. "Hochstadter thought of that right away. Willie wasn't even cold, and the Judge was telling Dietrich to be sure the widow got after the state."

"What will they do for her?"

"They'll vote her a pension, I imagine. Because she could sue for a good sum. Simple negligence. Or maybe they'll just give her a lump of money. I don't know. Maybe Talbot will make her his beneficiary."

"What happens to Talbot?"

"He hangs tomorrow morning."

"This is a bad summer," she said. "It's one of those years we'll date things from. Remember the Chinese curse? 'May you live in interesting times.'"

"Mmm." But I was not listening. I was remembering Talbot's eyes.

So it went all that day, with questions and answers and unsolicited advice. The Colonel said that discipline had become lax everywhere: there was one way, and one way only, to accomplish a hanging, and if it had been done properly . . . Geronimo said there was a curse on us all. "Burning for burning, wound for wound, stripe for stripe," he intoned. "The land is full of bloody crimes, and the city is full of violence."

"And the rabbis are loose among us. You're a great help. Get out of here now." I was in my chambers, killing time; the courthouse was full of loiterers, and John was detouring them but a few were heedless and rude. I had signed the order for the next morning's work, and Hochstadter had called to say that we would meet at the same time and place, he and I, and the afternoon wore along and then Goldman deigned to visit. "I have it figured out," he went on, settling lumpily into his chair and beaming behind his spatulate pink nose. "The new hangman will arrive this evening and will be Jewish, which means that he cannot work on Saturday. *You* cannot work on Sunday and there would be hell to pay if you hanged a man on Sunday anyway. We are already at Monday, by which time something else will come up. The new man will get the gripes or the glanders. Mark my words. Satan is abroad."

"Get out of here."

"I just came in." He was grossly offended.

"It's been one of those days. I need a drink."

"Why don't you go home? What are you accomplishing here?"

"I'm waiting for the new man."

"Ah. The angel of death. Then I'll leave you. I don't want to be here when he walks in. Drop by the store on your way home. I'll give you a drink."

"Goodbye."

"You should be more gracious to an old man."

"Goodbye."

He waddled out, injured, pouting. Soon John came in and we played cribbage halfheartedly. At the knock we both looked up in sudden excitement, as though it might be Santa Claus or the Second Coming or President Harding. He came in. He stood about five feet four, and weighed about one hundred and twenty pounds, and wore glasses, and was at least sixty-five. He was wearing a brown linen suit with an unnecessary vest and a red bow tie, and with his straw suitcase he looked like a traveling salesman for Congress gaiters.

"Here I am," he announced cheerfully.

I tried to read that night, but unsuccessfully. Gibbon offered his "register of the crimes, follies and misfortunes of mankind" and when I opened Calderón the first verse I saw was "Pues el delito mayor/del hombre es haber nacido"—man's greatest crime is having been born. I could not sleep; I could not read; there was no one to love; the heat was oppressive. I sat naked at the window, in the dark, and looked out over a silent city. I tried to remember the passage about alms for oblivion, and could not; my liege, I did deny no prisoners, and could not; oh happy dagger, and could not; the barge she sat in, and could not. I had rather be a kitten and cry mew than one of these same metre ballad-mongers; I remembered that; and to pluck bright honor from the palefaced moon.

It was no use. What I thought about was Rosemary and Rafaela, and I ached until the tears came. I felt quieter then, and slept until an evil dream shook me, and death was grinning at my shoulder as bells pealed. My eyes opened to darkness and the bells were still pealing; I flung on a robe and dashed downstairs, flipping light switches as I ran, blinking, waking, death's face still at my shoulder. My heart pounded, and I took the receiver from the wall with a shaky hand; was I awake or asleep? The clock in the hall: three-thirty.

"Ben? This is Alfred."

"Yes. What is it?"

"Oh, Ben. Oh, my God, Ben."

"Alfred! For the love of Christ, what is it?"

"It's Bruce Donnelley, Ben. He just killed himself. He left a note. It says he killed Louise Talbot."

PART THREE

11 A MAN NEEDS EIGHT
hours' sleep. Without it he can function but people and
rooms and objects and conversations are off center,
elusive. I remember dugouts where great decisions were
made, whole companies sent to doom; but it is not the
decisions that I remember. It is the hostile yellow light
of a gas lantern at four in the morning, the lantern oscil-
lating gently on its hook so that soon the dugout, the
men, the chairs and tables also swayed; or the flat and
watery taste of bad coffee; or the major blustering with
his fly open; or the map I knew so well transformed
before my eyes to a menacing and meaningless jumble
of signs and symbols, a zodiac, a chart by Merlin with
fate in every whorl and loop but indecipherable in the
sickly light. Alfred's office was like that at four in the
morning. The light was white and not yellow but Alfred
was no longer real, or Doctor Schilling, or the lawyers
when they arrived, or Hochstadter; or I. Wax dummies.
Tableau.

Alfred reported in a hopeless monotone. "Mrs.
Donnelley called at about three. I got dressed and
hurried over. She had heard the shot and knew he
was dead. It was an old forty-four and he had it at an
angle so there was a sizable hole in the top of his
head and some brains around."

"He died immediately," Doctor Schilling said.

"He dropped in a heap and the gun was under him. He wasn't holding it but his hand was jammed up against it. No question but it was suicide."

"That's something," Dietrich said.

"This is quite a community," Doctor Schilling said. "I wish somebody would kill somebody during office hours."

"The note," Hochstadter said.

"Right here." Alfred opened a drawer and extracted a sheet of paper with great care. Hochstadter read it, looked sick, and passed it to me.

> July 7, 1923
> 3 oclock A.M.
>
> To whom it may concern.
> My name is Bruce Donnelley of Soledad City and I am writing this letter. I have done terrible things and I do not want more killing.
>
> I killed Louise Talbot and now Wm. Waite is dead too. I killed her because she laughed at me loving her. I knew it was a sin but I could not help it. But I had already sinned in my heart looking through the window. Matthew says that. Whosoever looketh on a woman to lust after her hath committed adultery with her already in his heart. Then I went into the house and said I loved her and I tried to hold her. I told her I would do anything for her. She said for me Bruce? For little me Bruce? She looked down and she could see how I was and she laughed at me and said I should not go around looking in windows. Then she opened up the bathrobe. How does it look close up, she said. What am I supposed to be? The town harlot? But she did not say harlot. Then she stopped laughing and told me to get out. I said no, I

cant, and I took hold of her. She fought and said she would tell everybody. I had her neck in my hands and I only wanted to pull her close to me. I was not trying to kill her but I had to have her close to me. So help me God I was not trying to kill her. When I let go to touch her she fell down. I was afraid then and did not want to touch her again so I went out and went home. I did not know she was dead. I do not know why I did that but I am an animal and could not kill the devil in me. I have not slept right since then and I can not pray.

I do not want anyone else to die. And I am damned. I know that. So I must do this. It is the wages of sin. I hope my wife and sons will forgive me. Because I love them. I hope my sons will stay close to God and will not sin. Not ever. I hope God will have mercy on this sinful animal.

Tell Bryan Talbot I am sorry. Let him go.

I never did anything like that before but I know now the devil was in me all my life. My will is in the desk.

That is what happened.

Sincerely,
BRUCE DONNELLEY

We all read it and no one spoke. Soon Doctor Schilling picked up his black bag and went out. We just sat there, on Alfred's straight-backed chairs.

"It's cooler," Hochstadter said after a time. "Maybe the heat's broken."

We all looked up like dogs sniffing the wind.

"I think you're right," Dietrich said. Parmelee was looking thoughtfully at me.

"How is Mrs. Donnelley?" Hochstadter asked.

"She seemed all right," Alfred said. "Somebody's

with her. Doctor Schilling gave her a pill and said he'd be back at seven. The boys never even woke up."

"My God," Parmelee breathed, and then he said it angrily, "my God."

"What now?" Alfred asked. "What about tomorrow morning?"

"This morning, you mean," Hochstadter said. "It's off. Ben will give you an order."

"And what about Talbot?" Parmelee snapped. "What about him now, after all the fine justice you gave him? I need time to think, but I want him free tomorrow. Today, I mean."

"He killed Willie Waite," Hochstadter said.

"And suppose he hadn't?" Parmelee was working up to a fury.

"Well, now, just a minute," Dietrich said.

I interrupted. They swung toward me as though I were a stranger; all but Parmelee, who subsided and watched me narrowly. "Alfred," I said, "you have Talbot in court at ten o'clock. You gentlemen can be there then?" They nodded in some surprise. My voice was sharp but they did not know how angry I was. "I don't think we ought to try cases here, and I'm not sure you—any of us—realize what's involved. You'll forgive me for the impertinence. The issues aside, I doubt the propriety of a heated discussion right now." Nor did they know *why* I was angry; nor did I. "There's nothing we can, or should, do here. I suggest we adjourn."

"He's right," Hochstadter said.

"Who sees Talbot first in the morning?" Parmelee asked.

"Old Whitey," Alfred said. "With breakfast. He's out there now, probably asleep."

"Well, I want you to talk to him before you leave,

and tell him that he's to tell Talbot about Donnelley's letter; and the execution's off; and I'll be here about nine; and he's not to talk to anyone until I get here. I want him told all that the second he opens his eyes."

Parmelee looked at me again with that same ruminative expression.

"So do I," I said, and then I put my head up and said, "but he wasn't a judge," and while they wondered what I had meant I got up and walked out.

"What a race we are!" I snarled over breakfast, eggs, beans, whatever it was, tasteless, rubbery. "How can they feel the beat of their own hearts and still kill? How can they fight? or quarrel, even? How can they not know what they have, and always want more? Don't they know what a god damned miracle it is that their organs work? That the sun warms them and they can eat and make love? I can see it when people are starving. When they're hurt bad. When they have nothing, only trouble, and just being alive is a curse and not a blessing. But these people. Here. Donnelley."

"People," my mother said. "People do all kinds of things. That's why we have laws."

"I know, but Donnelley. Three people dead because he looked in a window and saw four circles and a triangle. What he could have seen on the wall in any barbershop."

"Not the same," she said, "and you know it."

"Yes, I know it." I pushed the plates away, pushed back my chair, slumped. "There but for the grace of God. But to let an innocent man be hanged——"

"Because he was damned anyway. Donnelley." She blew smoke and there was pity in her voice. "He was damned even before he looked in that window. He was damned when he was five years old and they told him not to touch himself. They never gave him a chance. A little more damnation was meaningless because it was too late."

"No degrees," I murmured. "Who's they?"

"They," she said, waving her cigar in disgust. "Them. Out there. They're all over. I guess I like your dirty mind better after all. So what did it matter if another man died? Besides, he may have hated Talbot. Talbot had those circles and triangles. Donnelley didn't."

"He had Mrs. Donnelley. Mrs. Donnelley is a handsome woman and she seems warm. All right, all right. I know. That doesn't matter."

"It's the women who suffer," she said. "Always. Men made up that story about Adam and Eve. They had to blame Eve for something so they could feel better about what they do to their women."

The bitterness in her voice startled me. "That, from you? The one complaint you never had—"

"Who says?"

I was speechless. Shock, outrage: I wanted to rush to his defense and there was nothing I could say. I shriveled.

"I'm sorry," she said. "I didn't mean that the way it sounded. And it wasn't anything serious. But men are men, Ben. They hurt women. You too. You have and you will. You chase a fat bubby here and when you get it you chase a fat tail somewhere else. The worst men do because they don't care and the best men do because they care too much. Any man good enough to be loved is going to be loved by more than one woman, and somewhere along the line he's going to love back, and he can't love two at a time. I don't care what the poets say: he can't love two at a time. If he's lucky he gets finished with the wrong one and gets back to the right one. Either way some woman gets hurt."

By then I could talk: "And men never get hurt?"

"No." Scornfully. "They feel bad for a little. Sorry for themselves. Then they figure she was no good anyway, or they meet another one. And I'll tell you why." She leaned forward, grim and glum. "When a woman makes love she feels it for hours, for days. But a man can kiss his sweetie goodbye and step out into the street and see a skirt and he's ready. And ten thousand years of rules and regulations hasn't changed that one bit."

"I'm sorry," I said. "This is all—I'm sorry. I never dreamed. Anyway you can't mean all men."

"No," she said. "No. That was just stupid talk. And I didn't mean your father either. You Lewises. A long line of connoisseurs. You know my trouble?"

"What?"

"I was just so damn happy with your father. Oh, I was, I was. And when he died, he hurt me. Past all repair. You don't have to be a Talbot or a Donnelley to hurt a woman." I looked away from her sudden tears. "And you still don't understand," she said. "You think I'm an old lady with a bruised heart and a lot of happy memories. Love is for the young, you think. You're too stupid and naïve to think that I've got a bruised body too. And I lie there at night and hurt just the way you do. Damn that man! And damn you too, sonny. Women love more and they get hurt more. Remember that," and she blundered out of the kitchen.

She went to visit Mrs. Donnelley that afternoon. Dressed up, in what might have been called festive

black, quite formal, and walked to the Donnelleys'
slowly, greeting friends and being slightly ostentatious. She opened the gate, entered the front yard,
and swept regally to the door. Helen Donnelley
opened it, and for a moment they stood unmoving
and silent; then Mrs. Donnelley looked past my
mother to the three or four rubbernecks across the
road, and stepped aside to admit her guest, and
closed the door. The house was almost unbearably
suburban, the guest reported later, like something
transplanted from the east, with odd touches of New
England like a captain's chair. Much chintz, many
flounces; an upright piano; embroidered mottoes;
mission magazines; half a dozen books. The living
room was dim and cool, and Mrs. Donnelley too was
cool, defensive and wary.

"I came to see if there was anything I could do,"
my mother began. "I'm awfully sorry."

Mrs. Donnelley said, "Oh."

"I lost my husband two years ago, and whatever a
man was, losing him is the worst thing that can happen to a woman."

"Yes," Mrs. Donnelley said in some wonder. "Yes.
I didn't know that before."

"I won't stay long. I wanted to tell you that you
must not worry about your friends and what they
may think. Some are afraid that you may be embarrassed by visits, but we're all very sorry."

"I can't face anyone," she said. "I didn't want to
let you in." She was whispering.

"I'm glad you did. How can I help?"

"I don't know. Would—would you like some tea?"

"No, thank you. Do you have food? Can I cook for
you? Take care of the boys?"

"Oh, no. We have everything. The boys are
upstairs."

"It must have been terrible for them."

"They're bewildered. I didn't tell them everything. I suppose everybody knows."

"Yes."

"We'll move away." She seemed almost asleep. "He left insurance. I have to see a lawyer. No one's been here since the doctor."

My mother asked sharply, "Your pastor? The people from your church?"

Mrs. Donnelley shook her head. "No one. Just that nurse."

"Do you want me to stay?"

Mrs. Donnelley hesitated.

"That was a silly question," my mother said. "Of course you don't. You have to do two things: take care of the boys, and take care of yourself."

"Yes." And Mrs. Donnelley looked up abruptly, pleading: "Do you really think he did that?"

"It doesn't matter. It's all over now."

"Looked in her *window?*"

Afterward my mother was sorry to have made the visit. "It was awful," she said. "I can't do that, commiserate. The funny thing was that I never remembered until I got home that the house next door was the Talbots'."

But that was later. That was the afternoon. The morning was much more difficult. To begin with I was exhausted. And there were too many elements. Two murders and a suicide; trial and verdict; misfired execution; miscarriage of justice; two lawyers who did not think much of me. Two ladies who did not think much of me, and of whom I should not have been thinking at all. And I had to contend with John, who was full of questions I could not answer.

And I was not feeling well. The stomach. A slight indisposition, coupled with an explosive nervousness that verged on hysteria now and then and had to be beaten down. I was assailed by the willies and borborygmus, and my mind refused to compose itself, leaping about from the hanged man in a tarot deck to a haunting line from George Moore ("I wonder why murder is considered less immoral than fornication in literature") to Geronimo Goldman and his minor prophecy and then to my father, who had had the bad taste to die and hurt my mother. The world was full of a number of things and I was very unhappy.

Hochstadter met me at the courthouse and said the wrong thing immediately: "Don't hesitate to call on me if you need help." John seemed rather offended but I said "Thank you" and we marched in. It was a hearing and I thought we could use privacy, so I had Harvey lock the door. Harvey was out of sorts. Working on Saturday. The steel companies had just refused to shorten the twelve-hour day but Harvey was grumpy because it was Saturday and he could not fish, or read a magazine. Also, I was tired of the same old faces. Here we were again: Hochstadter, Parmelee, Dietrich, Harvey, John, Alfred, Talbot, I.

Girded in a robe I took my place at the bench, opened my portfolio, and cleared my throat resoundingly. I looked at Talbot and nodded. He returned the nod. He glowed. He radiated life this glorious summer morn. A prisoner, a widower, a killer, he was in fine fettle. Parmelee seemed at once determined and excited, and Dietrich was suspicious of us all. I could not see Hochstadter's face but I imagined he was solemn.

"This will be informal," I announced. "I expect we'll have a more official meeting this afternoon. We have to get certain things straightened out this morning and I want to stick to the agenda. Please try not to fly off on tangents. Time for that later."

"My only concern is to see Bryan released," Parmelee said.

"You're jumping the gun," I said. "As of now he is still a prisoner, still guilty of murder, at least on paper, and still under sentence of death." Talbot's face darkened and I went on quickly, "No. No, Mr. Talbot, there is no danger of that particular sentence being carried out. All I mean is that certain forms have to be observed before you can be cleared of the one charge. And as you must know, you are to be charged with another murder."

"Now see here—" Parmelee began.

"No! Please, Mr. Parmelee. That's what I meant by a tangent. You agree that Bryan Talbot killed Willie Waite intentionally and by violence."

"Yes, but—"

"The 'yes' is all that matters this morning." Dietrich nodded in satisfaction. "Now. Mr. Dietrich. Has the state any reason to oppose a dismissal of all charges against Bryan Talbot in the murder of Louise Talbot?"

"Well, no," he said. "But now I think *you're* jumping the gun. I assume that Donnelley's death was by his own hand, and that the note was genuine, and that it told the truth. But none of those matters has been established by law."

I nodded. "Fair enough. I expect the coroner's jury—you called them?—will deal with Donnelley's death this morning, and I don't think we have any reason to doubt that they'll call it suicide. For the note, I assume that you'd be content with proof that it was in Donnelley's hand. Do you need proof of his soundness of mind? You could complicate matters badly if you wanted to."

"He certainly could," Parmelee chimed in, "and it would be cruel and unusual punishment. Ordinary decency—"

"I have no desire to complicate matters," Dietrich grumbled. "But I am not doing my job if I assent to sloppy procedure. I'll accept verification of the handwriting as proof of authorship, and I won't ask for an alienist to examine a dead man."

"The question of truth remains," I said. "I don't believe there's a jury in the world that wouldn't acquit Talbot on a retrial, but you have the right to point out that we never know what a suicide will do or say in his last moments. But you know the maxim, too—no one is presumed to trifle at the point of death. Can you give me any possible reason short of insanity why Donnelley would have confessed to a crime he hadn't committed? And if you can, you must also hazard a reason for his suicide."

"I can't," Dietrich said promptly. "You've misunderstood me. You're a young man and you haven't been on the bench too long. I've had murders before, you know." I might have spoken, but did not. Parmelee glanced quickly from me to Dietrich, who was still speaking. "If these loose ends aren't tied up, and I just agree to a dismissal with no questions asked, it almost amounts to misfeasance. I have obligations to my office."

"And I imagine it's embarrassing," Parmelee said innocently. "You did such a fine job at the trial. Shame to let it go down the drain without a fight."

"Mr. Parmelee," I said as dryly as I could, "I think that remark was out of order. I ask you to withdraw it."

"I withdraw it," he said, "and apologize."

"All right. Then I may take it that if the coroner's jury brings in a finding of suicide, and if Mrs. Donnelley—or even some of Donnelley's business associates—will verify the handwriting, state will not object to an immediate ruling by the Court."

"That's right," Dietrich said.

"Good enough. Now: the other matter." The other matter! Willie Waite with his skull in small pieces: the other matter. In re Willie Waite.

Dietrich rose immediately. "I have here an information charging Bryan Talbot with the murder of Willie Waite. I now submit it."

"What are you talking about?" Parmelee cried. "You can't submit an information at this hearing."

"I don't know why not," Dietrich said. "I can submit an information any time I want to."

"That's correct," I said.

"But this is outrageous," Parmelee complained. "I've been so busy with Donnelley's death that I haven't had a minute to think about Willie Waite. I don't even know if there's a legitimate objection I can make to this."

" 'This' is simply the submission of an information," I said, "which under the circumstances will serve in lieu of an indictment. Technically you haven't even been told about it; the District Attorney could have submitted it privately any time after Willie Waite's death. Without eyewitnesses you could demand a grand jury, but with two or more eyewitnesses an information has been held to suffice. Even in murder. The murder of Willie Waite was not a Federal crime, and the first clause of the Fifth Amendment has been held repeatedly to apply only to Federal prosecutions. The states operate by their own codes or statutes provided they grant roughly equivalent protections, and in this state the information is enough provided the eyewitnesses exist. Their existence here is not, I imagine, in question. Now whether this procedure is altogether just, I can't say, but it's legal. I wish we had a Federal code to guide us, but we haven't. So if you like we can set a time now for the arraignment, and I'm sure Mr. Dietrich will join me in obliging you with whatever reasonable delay you require."

Parmelee blinked up at me, vexed. I could not restrain a glance at Hochstadter; he nodded gravely.

"Well, what's in the information?" Parmelee asked.

"The specifics of the murder, and the charge that Bryan Talbot committed it," Dietrich said. "And the names of the witnesses."

Parmelee said thoughtfully, "Including the Judge, here, and the arresting officer, and Judge Hochstadter, and the District Attorney."

"That's right," Dietrich said, "and if you want to move to disqualify everybody and get a change of venue, go right ahead."

"Never mind that now," Parmelee said. "All right then. We're charged with murder. I'd like a little time to think."

"How about Monday at ten?" I asked him. "You can have more time if you want it."

"That'll do," he said slowly. "But if I need more time I'll ask for a postponement."

"Fair enough. All right with you, Mr. Dietrich?"

"Sure," he said.

"Good. We'll adjourn until four o'clock this afternoon, at which time I imagine we can dispose of the old business. Mr. Talbot, I'm sorry you have to go back to your cell. I've explained why you must; and I should also point out that if you were cleared of the first charges now it would be Alfred's duty to arrest you on the spot for the murder of Willie Waite."

"I understand," he said calmly. "Can I have a decent lunch brought in?"

"A decent lunch!" Alfred was outraged, and on that note of low comedy we adjourned the hearing.

I went to my chambers and hung up the robe, and settled to my scrivening while John unburdened himself of character analysis: Dietrich would bear watching and did not respect me, Parmelee was tricky and the surprises were not over. Hochstadter dropped in to announce his imminent departure. "This ought to be very hard or very easy," he said. "A man can't run around cutting down agents of the law. I'll make you a bet. I bet Parmelee takes an offer of second-degree, and Dietrich asks for a light sentence."

"That might save trouble," I said. "I don't know if you've thought it through—"

"I am on vacation." He smiled, blinking lazily.

"And second-degree gives me leeway; ten to life."

"That is right. What would you give him?"

"We'll worry about that when we get to it. No offense." I smiled politely.

He waved a hand. "Of course not. I hope that's how it goes."

"Me too. It seems likely."

"Hot again," he said. "I was wrong." He looked out at the sycamores behind the courthouse. "No breeze now."

"You should worry," I said. "This time tomorrow you'll be—where? Colorado? Wyoming?"

"Colorado," he said. "No hurry. Mountain air. Ah. Montana Monday."

"Should have gone earlier," I said absently, my

mind on the orders: non obstante veredicto. Peremptory command. Ringing phrases. Subject, verb, object. The adjective is the death of the noun. The adverb is the death of the verb. Well, no. It was a rich world and a rich tongue and why impoverish either? Why kill? Why demean? Why prune and slash and dominate? In what fear? Why geld?

"Earlier? What for?"

"Dempsey and Gibbons."

"Ah," he said, "fighting. Who cares? Fishing, that's the sport. What are you going to do this afternoon?"

"N.O.V.," I said.

"Good. Saves expense. You going to let Talbot have bail?"

"Yes."

"Poor fellow. Poor you. Saddled with something like this the first week. Maybe you'll have an easy session afterward."

"I hope so. By the law of averages this town ought to be a safe place for a long time to come." I wished he would leave.

"You've got my address up there," he said. "If anything goes wrong, you send me a wire. It may take a while to get to me. I'll be out there with the Blackfeet."

"Blackfoot, sir," John said.

"What? What's that?"

"They're the Blackfoot," John said. "Singular or plural."

"Is that right?" Hochstadter was delighted. "Never knew that. Never knew that." And he bubbled on for half an hour, and the farewells were ceremonious, not to say sentimental. He stood in the doorway and said, "I know you think I'm an old gasbag—"

"That isn't true," I said flatly. "My doubts are of myself."

His eyebrows soared. "Hoo," he said. "Sorry. I wanted to give you some advice, and I wasn't sure how you'd take it."

Well, I experienced affection for the old puffer. You never know what irrationalities will assail you without warning. "I'd take it very kindly," I said.

"You surprise me." He smiled, and a bashful look came over him. "I was going to say, if you have any tough decisions to make, make them strong. Whatever you rule on, rule firmly. Don't be afraid of reversals and such. Because if they're going to reverse, they'll reverse a lot quicker if you've been wishy-washy. And a judge who hedges is no judge at all."

"Thank you," I said. "I'll remember."

"One other thing." He squinted away from me, and wetted his lips. "Don't take this badly, now. You're one of the smartest people I know. You have a quick mind and you don't miss much and you're a damn good kid. But sometimes I think your, ah, intelligence is a little separated from your life. You know what I mean? You've got to have confidence. You've got to figure that if you feel strongly a certain way, and you're a good man, the feeling has a good chance of being right. Sometimes I think you don't get into things feet first—you kind of hang around the edges. That doesn't work."

"You're a smart one yourself," I said, between anger and rue.

"That's all." He smiled. "Good luck."

When he was gone John said, "Gros Ventre. That man is a Gros Ventre."

"That man is a good judge," I said sharply. "I

don't think he needs criticism from people like us.
Let's get some lunch. He only wanted to help."

"You don't need help," John said.

"The hell I don't," I said.

Shortly before four o'clock I donned the robe and
stepped from my chambers into the vast and virtual-
ly empty courtroom. Seated at the defense table
were Parmelee and Talbot; Alfred was behind them
in a folding chair. Harvey Bump sat below me,
expressionless. Dietrich leaned on an elbow at the
prosecution's table. None of them had bothered to
rise. I remained standing and stared coldly.

After a moment Harvey stood, and the others followed him lazily, and he said "Oyez oyez" and recited
his incantation. The flag hung limp and a muggy, silent calm hovered in the room, as though we were
the only survivors of a freak summer hurricane and
were gathered together in its eye; as though its leading
edge had passed and no man knew what might come
after.

"Bryan Talbot," I said. "Please rise."

Willie Waite had been dead for ten hours; it seemed
weeks.

Talbot came to stand below me. He had stood on
that spot when Hochstadter sentenced him. I read off
my first judgment of the session, and this was most
of it:

"Court has this day entered an order acquitting
you of all charges in the matter of the murder of
Louise Talbot.

"Court has done so in accordance with Section
94, paragraph C, of the Criminal Practices and Procedures of this state, permitting a judgment non ob-

stante veredicto in defendant's favor at any time before sentence is executed.

"An acquittal non obstante veredicto is more than a convenience available to the Court: upon introduction of irrefutable and uncontested evidence of the defendant's innocence, such a judgment is a peremptory command of the law, rooted in ancient doctrine and ancient faith. . . . Judgment carries the full force of an acquittal upon retrial, and may not be appealed; nor may defendant ever again be placed in jeopardy of life, limb, or liberty on the instant charge. . . .

"You now stand acquitted of the murder of Louise Talbot, in common justice and by order of this Court. You are free."

Talbot smiled and said, "Thank you, Your Honor."

Alfred set a hand on his shoulder and said, "You are under arrest for the murder of Willie Waite."

freedom shocked the local experts. I continued the bail
Parmelee had put up and let the prisoner go home.
Home was not, however, his destination. He stopped
off to pick up clothes and then, displaying more gall
than wit, checked into the Territorial. At dinner he
enjoyed lonely splendor while a large and subdued audience—Ettore made money that Saturday night—pretended to be drinking and chatting. Colonel Oates was
naturally among them, and confessed to a paralyzing
conflict. "My impulse was to say hello. But the man was
a murderer! And impulses are not trustworthy. Against
my better judgment I caught his eye finally, and nodded.
I should have known better. He waved ostentatiously
and raised his glass to me. It was bad taste, bad taste.
A simple nod would have sufficed. Talbot was just not
a gentleman."

The prisoner passed a pleasant weekend at the
city's best hostelry, like a retired businessman. My
own weekend was also quiet. I reread *Jonathan Wild*
and spent two hours over the Sunday newspaper. I
also fended off an impulse—untrustworthy—to call
Rosemary. Bruised pride, of course, but much more:
a split vision of her, one eye seeing her clear and
cold and twenty years ahead; the other clouded by
the usual glandular viscosity and distinguishing only
—well, circles and triangles. No young lover was
quite so calculating, and the suspicion burgeoned
that I was either no longer young or no longer a lov-

er. But I was enough of both to sleep badly. How do you know when, or how much, you have hurt a woman? How can you tell when the last rending moan is a lie? If you have given as good as you got? Hard questions and even if the answers are in your favor you may have inflicted hurt. I could remember Tommies, relieved in both senses, heading for the rear and roaring "She was poor but she was honest, And her parents was the same, Till she met a city fellow, And she lost her honest name." Who are you? I once asked Rafaela, when she was ten or so and masked, sombreroed, holding us up at gunpoint, and she said, I am Montemayor; give me your watch and your money. You should never tell your name, I warned her, my hands in the air, and she said, It is a good name and mine. Ignacio approved, but reminded her that Montemayors did not rob their guests. We were grave and did not mock her. I could remember her at ten because of that, the mask coming off to reveal those wide, disquieting black eyes and the face of an angel.

Go to your bosom; knock there, and ask your heart what it doth know. No answer; so I slept badly.

On Monday I saw Dietrich first. He knocked at a quarter of ten and entered my chambers briskly, like a professor about to lecture. "Parmelee has something up his sleeve," he said. "There was a look in his eye, and he wouldn't bargain with me."

"Should you be talking to me this way?" I leaned back in my chair.

"I don't see why not."

"I do. I don't believe I should see either of you alone until the case is decided."

"Oh." He stared down at me.

"You're the stickler for procedure."

"All right. I won't argue." He lingered, hesitated.

"Look: are you sure you can handle this?"

I stood up, four inches taller than he and a good deal angrier; but my voice was calm and obliging. "Why don't you ask me in open court?"

His eyes were steady, but he made no answer.

A sprinkling of spectators this time, Edgar among them with his notebook, the Colonel of course, and Geronimo; I wondered if he had left the store unattended. All rose as I entered, and once more I suppressed the impulse to grin and wave, to jig, the actor's impulse or the high priest's, the politician's, any man's who stood alone, the solitary oak in a garden of eyes.

Oyez. And Dietrich concentrating on Parmelee, watchful; and Parmelee on me, thoughtful, with that same narrow, measuring regard. And Talbot's glance skipping about: the murderer in spite of himself, guilty, guilty. I would postpone sentencing for at least a week.

"Mr. Talbot, will you please rise. Counselor? Please."

They came forward. Dietrich was frowning now. Harvey read the information in his gravelly, matter-of-fact monotone, and sat down.

Parmelee was not pensive now but excited, head thrust forward, eyes glittering. I became aware of my heartbeat, the tap of blood at my temples, a fluttering of foreknowledge, almost alarm.

"You have heard the information. Do you understand the charge?" Talbot nodded. Oliver Parmelee said, "We do."

"And how do you plead?"

"I plead not guilty," Bryan Talbot said.

I stared. No one moved.

Oliver Parmelee smiled gently and said, "By reason of self-defense."

PART FOUR

13

"FURTHERMORE," OLIver Parmelee said, "the defense at this time waives all right to trial by jury and moves for trial by the Court. The facts and evidence are not at issue; we stipulate those. We also move for dismissal or immediate acquittal."

No blurred vision, or roaring in the ears: a moment of pure clarity. Too pure, as on mistless mornings when through the cold desert air buttes loom and arroyos wander, too sharply outlined to be real, too minutely speckled and stippled and striated to be so distant. A crystalline moment, unnatural: trompe-l'oeil, trompe-l'oreille, trompe-coeur.

Bryan Talbot was calm, but his eyes were cold and hard. He seemed, at that moment, alone and stark, in the lonely quiddity of a man whose life had been reduced to one struggle, one meaning.

I leaned back, and the motion restored one or two of my mental processes. Not credulity, not yet, not even resentment, certainly not coherent thought, but at least professional reflex.

I turned to Dietrich, inquiring silently. He made no move. I held his gaze for ten seconds or so; he looked away. I returned to Parmelee.

Parmelee stared into my eyes like a hypnotist in a vaudeville.

"Today is Monday," I said. Under the circumstances it was a memorable epigram, a brilliant jeu de mots. "Court will rule on these motions Wednesday morning at ten o'clock. Bail will be continued. Court is adjourned," and I rapped feebly. There was a stir in the audience, and as I rose I saw Dietrich's fretful face.

Oliver Parmelee smiled sympathetically.

14

angel for two full days.

On the one hand I did not believe that the life of any man should hang upon the word of another, or that facts ever spoke for themselves—never accurately, never fully. I wanted twelve good men and true to make this decision, and my dominant reaction to Parmelee was resentment. These questions should simply not have been posed to a nervous and inadequate young man with problems of his own.

But on the other hand lay my rudimentary sense of fitness, duty, rightness, and even a whisper of pride, the truculent pride of a shavetail in a world of gouty generals. "Judges are best in the beginning," Tacitus wrote; "they deteriorate as time passes," and that was some comfort. But Edward Coke answered the more important question; he told me that "judges do not answer questions of fact, juries do not answer questions of law," and evasion became impossible. Either I was a judge or I was not.

Before I entered court Wednesday morning I had decided that I was.

And then Dietrich made me prove it, and I am still grateful to his shade. He got up and he shook his head and he said, "Your Honor, the state would like to express serious doubts of the propriety of submitting so cruel and complex a decision to a Court so tender in experience. It does so with respect, and I hope Your Honor will understand that this is not a reservation as to your quality as a person."

I suppose he had more to say, but that was enough. "Mr. Dietrich. You presume." I spoke with the voice of a lion, and I glowered frankly, and all at once I was not two people, one painfully aware of what the other said and did; I was angry and did not care who knew it. "You've reversed the natural order of relevance, Counselor. What you think of me personally has no bearing. When I preside over this court I represent the people of this state as much as the Governor does, as much as the flag does, as much as the Constitution does. From the first day of my appointment I am entitled to the respect and credit you would grant me if I had been on the bench for half a century; not for what I am but for what I represent. If you have legal or moral arguments for my disqualification, you would be remiss not to state them, and I ask that you do so."

"It isn't that," he began.

"Then I must tell you that your personal doubts of my age, experience, or competence are, when here expressed, contempt of court." He reddened, and I was not above a surge of satisfaction. "I warn you not to repeat them, and I will not warn you again. Do you have anything more to say on this?"

"No." He sat down. Parmelee sat with his head bowed, but he was not neutral; he was demure. I suppressed a smile.

"Now," I said briskly. "We'll forget about that. I have considered your motions, Mr. Parmelee, and I think they are well-founded. The issue does seem to be more one of law than one of fact, and therefore more properly the business of a judge than of a jury.

Your motion for trial by this Court is granted. I remind you that while you may, by statute, reverse yourself later and move for trial by jury, it is most unlikely that this or any court would respond favorably to
such a motion, barring flagrant error on my part."

"I understand that," he said.

"Your motion for dismissal is denied, and so is
your motion for immediate acquittal. I won't require
printed briefs, but I would like them typed up. How
much time will you need?"

"A week from Friday all right?"

"Mr. Dietrich?"

He nodded.

"The record will show," I said dryly, "that the District Attorney assented to Friday, July twentieth, as
date of submission of briefs."

"I apologize," Dietrich said with a wry smile.
"Yes, Friday will do.'"

"Court is adjourned," I announced, and rapped
three times, and returned to my chambers, where I
buried my head in my hands and briefly contemplated suicide, or at least exile.

John came in to worship. "Wow," he said.

"Exactly. Do you understand the issue?"

"Duly authorized agent of society proposes to
commit legal but immoral murder. Victim resists,
commits illegal but moral murder."

"There is no moral murder," I said. "And I am a
judge and not a preacher. The question is legal,
John, much as we might like it to be moral or emotional. Remember that."

"Custer," he said.

"What?"

"George Armstrong Custer."

"Oh, come on. And the Sioux weren't a part of the society that commissioned him. It was a just war, if you like, but not—"

"They were so," he said. "They'd signed treaties and acknowledged the government's authority and kept their word. That Custer was after gold and he got what he deserved."

"All right, all right." I surrendered. Digby on Indian affairs was Calvin in a Montmartre boîte. "But I don't think we'll get very far with it. Will you see if you can find something more relevant?"

"I will," he said, and marched out immediately. My faithful scout.

It was the loneliest week I can remember. I was hedged about with taboos, and walked in a golden glow of divinity, like a primitive chief with a bagful of enemy eyes or big toes hanging from his belt. The experts deferred; more, they avoided me. I had a quick chat with Geronimo and when I asked, "What do you think?" his glance darted here and there and he mumbled, "How would I know?" Colonel Oates's reticence was almost pathetic, and his humility almost human, but at the last moment he was a prancing stallion again: "Ah, yes. Yes. The most difficult of human decisions. I remember sending men to their death. A dreadful decision," and you could see that there was nothing he had ever enjoyed more than that power. "Mind you, I had fought well myself, and been wounded. I knew what I was sending them into. Good boys, they were," and so on and so forth. We parted amicably. My isolation had softened the critical sense; these people were not so bad after all, just people, and I would have enjoyed a drink with Hochstadter. In the street my fellow citizens nodded respectfully, and made way for me. I wandered alone, or conferred with John, or sat on the veranda thinking. I had no faintest notion of an answer. John was not much help because there was little in the books that applied. Which meant that the briefs would be more interested than interesting, more partial than informative. My burst of confidence died quickly, and I was left with a void, infiltrated now by worry, now by frustration, now by dread, now by helplessness or the fear that whatever I did would be wrong. An outsider might have said that I was well prepared, but an outsider would have seen no more of me than my mirror saw: a tall dark stranger with a strong nose that might someday be bulbous and a middling chin that might someday recede and good teeth that might someday be replaced. Inside me were a heart and a brain and various efficient systems, at least one of which had been neglected for too long; and on such frail elements, subject to unexpected malfunction and inevitable decomposition, rested my burden.

I thought of my father often, because I had been linked to all this forty years earlier by what I can only call an accident of love. My father had saved the life of the man who was now governor of our state. Not in a great blaze of heroism, villains dying by the score, but with the patience and persistence of a nurse. "You'd be surprised how seldom a man has to shoot," he had once told me. "In the first place these pistols"—the old .44s, like Donnelley's—"couldn't hit a wagon full of hay at more than about fifty yards, much less a moving target, and much, *much* less when you're moving yourself. You're hot stuff with tin cans on a fence, but try it sometime at a gallop. You do better than one in ten and I'll make you a deputy on the spot. In the second place a marshal or a sheriff or a ranger generally goes into trouble with his gun in his hand, where it'll do him some good, and if you come up on your man that way it looks like a cannon and he comes along quietly. If he's holed up somewhere, then you shoot and shoot and shoot and he shoots and shoots and pretty soon he gets thirsty and comes out, or he knows he will sooner or later so he does it now. And in the third place there was nothing worse in my time than killing a marshal or a ranger. If you did that you knew they'd come after you for the rest of your life and your only chance was to go down to Mexico and settle there for good. That old story about the one ranger—'Ain't but one riot, is there?'—was true, but not because he was so powerful or a dead shot or anything like that. It was because he stood for hundreds more, for *years* more, of rangers, and people didn't want to fight that. Of course, some of them did. But most of the shooting was right on the spot, if you happened to come along when a crime was being committed. Then they'd shoot and try to get away, and you'd shoot back and try to stop them." It was when they were sent out after a man that he had saved the Governor. Fifty miles from men, at the edge of a desert, the one had poisoned himself with bad water and the other had wiped off the vomit, improvised a shelter, medicines, and bedpans, sponged away sweat and urine, poured precious water—taking none himself—cupful by cupful into the gibbering mouth to flush out the agonizing body, and, when the fever broke, tied the half-conscious patient on his horse and led him thirty miles to a river. It is easy enough to say that in those days that was how men behaved, but that was not how men behaved in those days or any days unless they were very good men. That was the cardinal act of my father's life and it was not Davy Crockett or Sam Houston; it was Walt Whitman. And because of it—half in thanks, half in the confidence that virtue was heritable—I was a judge.

Thank you, old man.

Thursday, the nineteenth, I did what my father might have done, thinking of him as I changed to jeans and an old denim shirt and dragged out my boots that I hadn't worn for half a year, blew the dust off them and put them on and stuffed some canned goods and bread and cheese and a pillow into an old potato sack and jammed a blanket in after them. The pillow was from my father, too: he did not believe in unnecessary discomfort. I filled a canteen and snapped it on my belt, and finally turned up an old jackknife. I left a note for my mother and walked down to Santiago's, a mile and a half and none too comfortable in the boots, and picked out a horse. "His name is Rickets," Santiago said.

"What kind of name is that for a horse?"

"What's the matter with it?"

"Do you know what it means?"

"Don't mean nothing. Just a name. He's strong and gentle."

He was, a chestnut gelding about eight years old. We followed the river south for seven or eight miles and then hooked west for ten more. It was longer that way but we were near water, and as the crow flew we would have had to cross a bone-dry, sandy, twelve-mile flat. This time of year there would be none of the red and yellow cactus blossoms, and who wanted twelve miles of nothing? Along the river we had grasses and alders, and flushed some scaled quail; killdeer hopped and swooped and woodpeckers fell silent. After we swung west the trees were mostly desert willows, and there were patches of mesquite and cholla, and once we saw a badger. In a couple of hours we reached the first slopes and climbed into a modest range of hills humped around Toussaint's Lake like buffalo around a waterhole. We came down on the lake shore and I made for a small grove of Gambel oaks. I emptied out the saddlebags and scavenged enough wood for a fire while Rickets browsed. Then I watered him and tethered him. Hobbles are all right if you know the horse but not otherwise. A good horse can go miles overnight in hobbles, and I was no tracker. I could have followed a mule deer through a mud flat but not if I was more than ten minutes behind him.

The sun was low but not setting. I stripped and walked out into the lake. Cold. When it was thigh-high I flopped forward and wallowed like a stranded whale. It was shockingly cold but the shock passed quickly, and a pleasurable tingling set in.

I was alone. I was probably ten miles from a human being. The world was water and hills and trees and a dark blue sky, and it was world enough. It was peace. Rickets had grass and I had beans, and it was peace. I amost fell asleep floating, like a man in a snowdrift. I lay on my back and thought that I would have liked to take Rosemary there. Rosemary. But she would have brought a bathing suit. Rafaela, then. Peace. Gli occhi di venere. Et la tête. Et la bouche. Et le cou. Et toutes ces choses-là. Y pues? El galanteo. Y pues? La paz.

It was a lovely thought but I was cold again, and waded ashore peering about like the first amphibian. I rubbed myself warm with the blanket and stretched out on the sunny bank. Peace. Within a mile of me skunks were eating turtle eggs, and foxes were eating silky pocket mice, and coyotes were eating desert squirrels. Not to mention birds eating insects and fishes eating fishes. Peace.

I too had to eat. I dressed and built a fire and opened two cans of pork and beans. When the beans were ready I ate them and the sun was setting. I heaped more wood on the fire and lay back in the cool dusk and thought.

Which means not that I wrote myself an essay, but that for a couple of hours, while the fire snapped and Rickets shuffled lightly in the darkness, ideas and images thronged my mind. Words and pictures and a little music. But I will not subject you to impressionism and palimpsest. I thought about love, and the law, and the world I lived in and the world it was likely to become, and shortly I sat up to give that world my full attention. I thought about privacy and tolerance, and about their deadly cousin, indifference. The early moon rippled silver off the lake and washed the spurs and boulders in ghostly white; before me as I sat Indian fashion burning oak glowed orange and crackled gently; wood smoke perfumed the night; outside my little circle of light it was dark, dark. I thought of my own future, and of the little use this world had for the weak; and I was weak, and realized that night that I preferred weakness to strength. And that not only Bryan Talbot's life but my own depended on the next few days, and I could not flee, because certain questions require answer and my moment had come.

Thus my vigil, and I do not mean to romanticize it. I have liver spots on the backs of my hands now and white hair on my head, and I am sitting in a warm and well-appointed study. My belly is full. I know, as I knew on that night, that the law is made by full bellies; but now I know too, as I did not know on that night, that empty bellies crowd my world, each with its pair of beseeching hands and pleading eyes. In the world of my youth, the world of privacy and indifference, one man could water his lawn with old brandy and die fat and go to heaven while another hewed wood and died sick and went to hell: but Bryan Talbot's life was of value. Now no man dies alone, and we may all die together, and there is no heaven or hell, and we do not give a damn about the death of strangers. We have learned to speak to one another but without affection because indifference has won out; politics is one long meddling, but with the mind and not the heart, and if now and then we dispel the ultimate indifference—to annihilation—it is not because we love but because we fear; or not because we will miss the miracle that man is, but because we have just paid off the bank and it would be a shame to go now. But we will go, unless we learn to care. We banded together to stave off murder and to seek the beloved republic, and we have found the perfect defense against murder but it is not the beloved republic: it is suicide. I tell you: I would blame no man today for murder, and neither can you. To kill everyone is bad, we are told now; to kill only half the world is better, and to kill only a quarter of it is evidence of care and compassion. On that scale to kill only one man is an act of virtue and restraint, the act of an ascetic.

I exaggerate. A crusty old gaffer, grumbling. Like Jeremiah's, my soul is wearied because of murderers. But that night at Toussaint's Lake all things were still possible, and the race was worth saving. Talbot was a threat to it but he was also a part of it, as each of us has within him something that threatens the whole man; and what we do about that makes us or destroys us. So I searched for my flaws, because Talbot's life was bound up with them, and I found many; and I tried to decide what to do about them, because that might be what I would do about Talbot. The stars were bright, the air chilly; I wrapped myself in the blanket and lay warm, looking up at the stars in a soundless night. Many, many stars. Rosemary and I had looked at the stars. What revulsion had overtaken her? What bitterness? What despair? Was I indifferent, and did she know it? Was she no more to me than a trophy? My loving cup? Recesses gaped, thoughts tumbled. Perhaps the Morales in me had to straddle a blonde goddess; vanity, vanity, the rebellion of the slaves: on my back was thick black hair but I had conquered. And Rafaela, what was she? My dark concubine, not trophy but chattel? What had I given to either, and what did I deserve?

I groaned aloud. I knew nothing. I was a poor half-man with Bryan Talbot's life in my palm, and even this lonely communion was a childish cry for help that would not come. From where? Those stars? The army of unalterable law; no help to mere man.

My last thought was of Willie Waite, and then I slept.

But in a dazzling dawn, and damn cold, I was stronger, and cheerful, and had a fair idea of what I was. I washed in the lake, gave the horse a short drink, ate bread and cheese, and rode back to Soledad City.

15

WE CLIP-CLOPPED
home and I tied Rickets to the outdoor faucet. My
mother was inhospitable. "Don't let him trample my
poppies."

"What's for lunch?" I asked her.

"Catch any fish?" she said.

"Fish? That's Alvin's line. What do I look like, a mil-
lionaire sportsman?"

"You look like a bum," she said. "Get those boots
off before you fall down. Buffalo Bill."

Over lunch—cold chicken and beer—she asked me
why.

"I needed to think. I thought if I got off alone . . ."

"Did it help?" Her voice was low and diffident.

"Come on, now," I said. "Don't go all over respectful. No. It didn't help. Or maybe. I suppose so."

"You look a little different," she said.

"Like a bum."

"No. Happier."

"Because I met a girl up there. She said her name
was Sacajawea. Fellow named Clark had run off with
her clothes."

"Oh, you're a lot happier, you are."

And I was.

I never even changed, except to slip on a pair of

moccasins. I rode Rickets back to his home and rubbed his muzzle in fond farewell, and walked to my office. John was studying the briefs and when he saw me rigged out like an unemployed farmhand his face fell into lines of deep sorrow and disappointment. "Yes?" he asked politely. "Can I help you? The Judge is out."

"Be quiet," I said. "I'll have you deported. To Siberia. Is it true that you came from Siberia?"

"Careful," he said. "My ancestors were eating raw meat and wearing skins when yours were still writing books. You look like a kid today, you know? Where've you been?"

"I just got a good night's sleep. Are those the briefs?"

"Yes. They came in this morning. I'm afraid you're going to be disappointed."

"Why?"

"There's nothing much in them. Nothing conclusive, I mean."

"Did you dig anything out of the books?"

"Yes, but that's not much help either. Nothing *really* relevant. A lot of cases that almost apply but don't. I felt pretty bad about it, but you don't seem to mind."

"No, I don't mind. I didn't expect much."

"Well." He rubbed his hands and spoke briskly. "I have some notes here. Parmelee talks about doctrines, necessity and coercion, but I don't think he's on solid ground. He's just throwing everything into the pot. Sit down." I sat down. I was amused but impressed, and I liked John fine. I liked preactically everybody that morning. "Let me see. Here. 'When irresistible natural forces create the choice of losing all or saving some, lesser evil may be committed without incurring liability.' That's very weak, and it should really apply to numbers of people and not one man. He doesn't say so, but what he's talking about is that lifeboat case, United

States versus Holmes, twenty-six Federal three-sixty—"

"Eighteen forty-two," I said.

"Show-off. That's the one. He didn't mention it because the conviction—manslaughter—was upheld. It was only upheld because the poor people who got thrown overboard weren't chosen by lot. Court agreed that the boat would have sunk if they hadn't done it, but they should have drawn straws and not just dunked the nearest weakling. But anyway I don't think he has anything there. Unless you assume that Willie Waite's life was worth less than Bryan Talbot's; then it would be the lesser evil. But you'd also have to assume that Willie stood for an irresistible natural force."

"Maybe he did. Did you ever try to resist the state?"

"My ancestors did."

"And they died for it. And it wasn't their state."

"We're back to Custer," he said.

"So we are. What about coercion?"

"That's a lot closer to what Parmelee needs. A threat to kill someone unless he commits a designated felony. But Willie never came up and said, 'You better kill me or I'll kill you.'"

"Didn't he?"

"No. Willie stood for—well, I don't know. Did he?"

"No," I said. "You're right. Coercion requires that the felony be committed at the express command of the coercer and not simply because defendant felt that its commission would free him of pressures. If you were being kidnapped and you shot a cop because you thought your kidnapper would like you better and let you go, that's not coercion. If he has a gun at your head and says, 'Kill that cop or else,' that's coercion."

"Isn't that what happened to Talbot? Nobody gave him the order, but there's a kind of human necessity—"

"Which we call self-defense," I said. "And that's what I have to decide. Because society has necessities too; and if human need were all that mattered you could rob a bank and say you needed the money."

"I've thought of it," he said. "Nobody can live on a clerk's salary. If I didn't do beadwork at night——"

"A Siberian Bolshevik," I said. "Let me see the briefs."

He passed them to me. "There's one other thing," he said. "Parmelee doubts the constitutionality of prosecuting on an information in a capital case. He goes back to the Fifth Amendment. I think if he has to appeal he's going to do it on that basis."

"We talked about it in court," I said. "The law is damn sloppy there and I wish we had a Federal code. The states have to make their own laws; I saw girlie shows in Chicago that would have got everybody in sight arrested down here, and that's what they call local variation; but procedures ought to be uniform. It would save higher courts a lot of work. They do too much remanding on procedural grounds."

"Anyway he makes that point," John said.

"Not much of a point. Not substantive, and only for appeal. Well, I'll look at these."

"When do you plan to hand down decision?"

"Monday. Will you call Dietrich and Parmelee and see if ten o'clock Monday is all right?"

"Monday! Then you've already decided!"

"Oh no," I said. "No, I haven't. I've got a lot of books to look at and a lot of thoughts to think before I decide. Now get out of here and call them from your own desk."

"You're lying to me," he said.

"No, John." I was serious and spoke quietly. "I've come to a couple of conclusions, but not the big one; and I'm not even sure that the small ones are material. But at least I know that I *can* decide. That's something."

"I believe you," he said. "You're the boss."

"No. The people of this state are the boss, and it doesn't matter that sometimes I have little use for them. Do you know why the Governor made me a judge?"

"Your father?"

"Well, yes, but I meant, why does he create judges at all. Because he needs protection. The people elect him but they've got to be able to walk the streets at night or there won't be any state for him to be governor of. The state is a great pain in the ass but it's better than blood in the streets. Poor old Willie Waite! He died to save us all. You call the lawyers, now."

Man comes first, with his lusts, and then the law, usually in the form of an intricately reticulated mechanism that serves variously as strait jacket, leg iron, or chastity belt. Or that should so serve; but in its preventive function it usually fails and thus becomes merely punitive, the rationale for thumbscrew or dungeon or guillotine. Which is to some extent why legal language is incomprehensible to laymen. To state plainly that the theft of 12.001275 cents by Mr. Charles Brown of Detroit demanded his incarceration for five to fifteen years would not relieve his hunger and would court contempt for all law; so Brown was apprehended, charged, and convicted of a felony against the state of Michigan, to wit, petty larceny, and after much polysyllabic due process he was jugged. Those who write laws, and often those who write decisions, must obfuscate; and "in every page our taste and reason are wounded by the choice of gigantic and obsolete words, a stiff and intricate phraseology, the discord of images, the childish play of false or unreasonable ornament, and the painful attempt . . . to astonish the reader, and to involve a trivial meaning in the smoke of obscurity and exaggeration." Old Gibbon knew. In all the history of law there are not two dozen decisions set down in truly noble prose. The one I like best is Lord Justice Crewe's on de Vere—should the name lapse, or go to a cousin when the direct line died—delivered in a great time, when man was outsize and every capillary full. He read it aloud in the House of Lords in 1626. "I have labored to make a covenant with myself, that affection may not press upon judgement, for I suppose there is no man that hath any apprehension of gentry or nobleness, but his affection stands to the continuance of a house so illustrious, and would take hold of a twig or twine thread to uphold it. And yet time hath his revolutions; there must be a period and an end to all temporal things—finis rerum—an end of names and dignities, and whatsoever is terrene; and why not of de Vere?—for where is Bohun? Where is Mowbray? Where is Mortimer? Nay, which is more, and most of all, where is Plantagenet? They are entombed in the urns and sepulchres of mortality! Yet, let the name of de Vere stand so long as it pleaseth God." Ah. That rings. But de Vere was not Bryan Talbot, and you have noticed that I was no Crewe.

So the books I took home that night could not answer my questions. They were heavy, and I was asweat when I arrived; they were leather-bound and close-printed and in them was some wisdom; they told me what I must not do, and for that I was grateful; but it was not enough. Nor were the briefs. My mother continued deferent, and did not try to make conversation; now and then, as I read through dinner, I allowed myself a "hmm" and she adopted a respectful expression of patience and expectation. When I left the table and went to the telephone she assumed that I was engaged upon business of the highest importance, but her curiosity was too much for her and after a minute she followed me, just in time to hear me say, "Rosemary. This is Ben."

"Oh," Rosemary said. "Hi," meaning, Oh yes, I remember you.

I laughed. I guffawed. She was a beautiful woman and I should not have made fun of her but I laughed. I wished her well but I laughed. "I'm sorry," I lied. "Forgive me. I don't know why I laughed. Will you meet me at Tobias's for lunch tomorrow? I promise not to make trouble."

"Tomorrow?"

"Yes. Saturday. I want to talk to you, and I won't be a bother."

"All right." She sounded cheerful. "How are you?"

"I'm fine. How are you?"

"All right," she said. "That Talbot thing must have been terrible. I read about it. What's going to happen to him?"

"That's what I want to talk to you about," I said.

"Me? You're fooling."

"Yes," I said. "I'm fooling. Twelve-thirty be all right?"

"Yes. Yes, that'll be fine. It'll be nice to see you."

"It'll be fun," I said. "See you then."

"Bye bye," she said.

"Bye bye," I said, and hung up.

My mother's mouth was set in hard lines. She vanished into the kitchen.

She condescended to join me after half an hour. I was sunk down in a stuffed chair, immersed in Barron v. Baltimore, a decision not only irrelevant to my problem but downright silly on its own merits, or demerits: old John Marshall, the Pooh-Bah, holding that the first ten amendments had to be honored by the Federal government but not by the states!

"You just can't do it," she said. "You can't go chasing off after a skirt at a time like this."

"Please."

"What's the matter with you, anyway? You've got a good mind and no sense at all. Sometimes you act like an old man and sometimes you're still a child."

I set down the book, and studied her. "You really think I'm chasing a skirt."

"I know you are. I know you and I don't understand you."

"That last is true enough," I said.

We sat in silence for some moments.

"You've got a man's life on your hands," she said.

A sigh was all I could manage; then I said, "Be quiet now and pay attention."

"That's what I want you to do," she said. "Pay attention."

"Shut up," I said. "Listen, for a change." She was distrustful. "This is a remarkable house, full of good things, good people, good echoes and shadows, and a man can be comfortable here. But maybe I should have gone somewhere else a long time ago. Because you're hard to take sometimes. You're a professional mother the way John is a professional Indian. You have to be wiser and stronger than anybody, so I have to humor you. Pop did too, and he didn't mind, but it made him uneasy—I know that—that I never told you off. I think he half expected some wild coming-of-age declaration from me." Her face was troubled; she set down her cigar and folded her hands in her lap. The light was behind her and she resembled a stone idol, grave, unmoving, but her eyes were bright and alert. "I thought it was fun, though, and I still do. Like a vaudeville act.

But right now isn't a time for vaudeville. Not a time to make me feel like less than I am. I don't need advice, and I don't need wholesome maternal solicitude. I don't even need love, and the last thing I need is Rosemary. What I need is a cloud to sit on so I can see everything that's ever happened. I have Bryan Talbot to worry about, and the sovereign authority of this state, which I have sworn to uphold, and the future of the human race, and my own life, my own rock-bottom self. All dumped in my lap at once because in a certain month of a certain year I happen to be exercising a profession I wasn't even sure until this week I cared for. All I need from you is 'Ben, I never realized until now how deep and wise you are, and I know you can handle this.' So what do I get? Lectures on morality. I don't mean to hurt you; you're a hell of a good kid and I'd do anything to keep you from pain and I don't want to inflict it myself. But you've got to stop being a high priestess. You can start again next week. Right now you've got to leave me alone."

"You're a nasty boy," she said. "Insulting an old lady like that." She got out of her chair and came to kiss me on the cheek. "Sorry," she said lightly, and tightened her mouth to keep back tears, and quavered, "Damn it, I wish Graeme were here."

"I'd have to send him away too," I said wearily.

"No. He'd keep out of your way. And he'd keep me out of your way. That's why I wish he was here." She was crying. "I miss him and I'm going to read in bed." At the door she turned and blinked, and tried to smile. "Ben," she said, "I never realized until now how deep and wise you are. You can handle this," and we grinned and she went on upstairs, blubbering.

I drove to Albuquerque the next morning, my mind full of Talbot, and when I parked near Tobias's I had almost forgotten what I wanted to say to Rosemary. I was early and ordered a glass of pineapple juice and sat reading a newspaper. The waitress was a pretty Indian girl of about eighteen with a magnificent dimpled smile. I could not help comparing her with Rosemary and remembering Stendhal: It is passion that we really want; beauty only furnishes possibilities. But the waitress did not linger. Overhead fans drew lazy circles; the customers were cool and quiet and the checkered tablecloths were fresh and summery. From my corner table I could see the street, and Rosemary was handsome striding in the sunlight. She wore a dark blue dress, some sort of small print, and I remember my wry surprise at her white gloves. Also at my own calm. She smiled when she saw me and I stood up and we shook hands, at arm's length; whether she was afraid that I would sweep her into my savage embrace and bend her back over the oysterettes I never knew. We sat facing each other.

"Well!" she said. "You look very good. I thought you'd be all nervous."

"About?"

"About Talbot and everything."

"Oh, yes. That's quite a case. How have you been?"

"Just fine."

"Shall I get you some fruit juice?"

"Oh, yes."

I beckoned the waitress and ordered.

It was a pleasant luncheon. A tall, dark, presentable gentleman with a flawless blonde companion. Old ladies would cluck and simper. The head waitress interrupted twice to be sure we were happy, and blessed us with her eyes. Rosemary chattered. She was hoping to spend two weeks in California. She had never seen the ocean. We discussed a recent tragedy in New York: eight hundred and thirty-six thousand gallons of beer, plus four thousand of ale, had been flushed through the city's sewers when a disused brewery was sold. Mr. Rockefeller had celebrated his eighty-fourth birthday, attending services on his estate; there were fifteen children present and after church he had presented each with a shiny new nickel.

We were on the ice cream when she asked, "Are you mad at me?"

"No."

"Why did you want to see me?"

"Well," I said, "I think I wanted to apologize."

She pouted. "That's not very gallant."

"Not for that." I smiled. "I wouldn't apologize to God himself for that. No. It's just that I think you were about half right, what you said last time. But you were also half wrong. I feel, well, responsible for you."

"You shouldn't," she said. "I think we were very nice together in some ways. I didn't mean that you took advantage of me or anything like that."

"No. That isn't what I meant either."

The waitress brought our coffee and I smiled at her; she was obliged to smile back and I saw the pretty dimples again.

I leaned forward to touch Rosemary's hand. "Look. I don't even know you and I never tried to. That's what I wanted to apologize for. I don't know if you're a Democrat or a Republican, or if you roll toothpaste from the bottom or flatten it out, or if you have moods, or if you loved your father and mother, or even if you want children, or how many. I thought I was taking you on faith but I was really not even man enough to be interested. That's what I'm sorry about. That's what you were right about. I made love to you and even there I never asked you what you liked or didn't like." She blushed and sipped at her coffee. "I was a lousy lover, wasn't I." That may have been what hurt most.

"I don't know," she said. "I have no basis for comparison." I really don't believe she knew what I meant.

"But you were wrong too," I said.

"I know. I didn't know much about you either. You kind of swept me off my feet." She met my glance. "You know, most of it was my fault. Because I let you do things that were going to hurt me, and then I blamed you for it."

"It was more than that," I said. "You didn't like me from the start, except as something exotic. And maybe a chance to find out what it was all about, and I suppose it seemed somehow safe, because I was a judge. You're a scared little girl, though, and that's bad. Do you know, you would never look at me? At—well, you know. At the *real* me." I grinned.

She turned fire-engine red and looked around like a thief. No one peered through a lorgnette or brandished a parasol; thunder did not roll.

"I want you to have a good life," I said. "You've got to learn to prance." I hesitated, searching for words that would not frighten her, and scratched my head absently.

"Don't scratch your head at the table," she said.

"Yes. That's what I mean. Let's see." I stared off at nothing for a few seconds, and saw the waitress again. "Here. You were really talking about a kind of respectability, and how it was wrong of me to love, or to *think* I loved, if I couldn't go all the way, with a house and a car and pretty curtains. And then I got sore and walked out. I wondered about that later. And I think I was mad because you were making us less important than things. Listen," and I took her hand, "maybe you were right about making love on the stairs and such; but it's better than being a thing. Don't be a thing. Don't ever think there's anything more important than loving somebody. Mayonnaise or cars or a handsome face or anything else. That's what I came to tell you because I'm afraid I may have spoiled love for you. Please don't let that happen."

"Oh, I'm sure I'll marry," she said, and smiled, sweetly and imperviously. "Did you ever notice that men always look *into* a cup when they're drinking coffee, but women always look *over* it?"

That was the last time I saw Rosemary. I left her in defeat and almost in despair, and I remember her not because I loved her so well but because I loved her so badly.

I was home by five and called John, who told me that Dietrich and Parmelee would wait upon my pleasure Monday morning. I took a quiet highball with my slavishly silent mother, and shared with her a thick steak and mounds of soft-fried onions. Then I returned to the briefs. At about eleven that night I went into the study and placed paper, pencils, pen and ink on my father's desk. I am there now, seated at the same desk, and I remember rubbing its worn, smooth surface as if I hoped that its virtue would pass to my right hand. I went to the kitchen for a glass, to the pantry for a bottle of Ignacio's harsh red wine, and to the living room for a box of his cigars. I returned to the study, and sat down, and poured a glass of wine, and lit a cigar, and wrote for nine hours. Early of a Sabbath morn I went to my office, and for two hours I typed, and it was done. I strolled home wearily in a shower of sun and church-bells.

16

I WAS ALONE IN chambers. I had sent John away. My chest was tight and my limbs were heavy; toes and fingers tingled, and I was conscious of each short, shallow breath; like a man in fever, fearing hysteria, I clenched my hands and concentrated, counted the knots in the paneling, the books on the shelves, the beat of my heart. Discite Justitiam. A glass of water eased me. I removed my jacket and went to the closet, groping for the robe; it slipped off the hanger and fell, and lay wadded on the floor while I stared down at it. I picked it up and brushed it off and carried it to the window, and stood looking out over an empty lot and the sycamores like sentries. Sparrows fluttered and gossiped. No angel descended on a shaft of light with words of cheer.

Monday morning. And our hero heavy with regret: for a misspent youth, for a reckless heart and a feckless mind, for stealing fire. It is stage fright, I told myself. Nothing more. And the omens are good: you have a cool day and a cielo aborregado, the mackerel sky of good augury and fair weather. That you could not eat breakfast is only to be expected. Stage fright and nothing more. Now robe yourself.

I emerged woodenly from the wings and entered a full courtroom. Faceless, they rose. Eyeless, they stared. Enthroned, I nodded; they sat. Harvey chanted. I smoothed the folded sheets of paper. "Is there anything you wish to say before I proceed?" The lawyers said, "No, Your Honor." Talbot was intent. I met his eye.

My voice held steady as I identified the decision; for that I was grateful. It would be gratifying and wholesome now to remember that I thought of my father, or of some great man, and took heart; but I thought of nothing and no one. I was conscious of silence, and as I read my voice grew stronger against the silence before me; I seemed to feel larger, and higher, and the people below me seemed to dwindle, as though I were addressing them from a mountaintop. This is the greater part of what I read to them, and toward the end I could taste again the wine and cigars:

". . . In the instant case the facts are not at issue. Defendant was indicted and duly convicted, in open court and by a jury of his peers, of murder in the first degree. The sentence of death by hanging was mandatory, as was appeal. Appeal was denied. During execution of the sentence, by a duly authorized agent of the state and in the presence of the required witnesses, defendant freed himself momentarily and attacked that agent, deliberately and with malice aforethought. As a direct result of that attack the agent died, and execution of the sentence was postponed, as required by statute. Within hours new and irrefutable evidence proved beyond doubt defendant's innocence on the original charge. Defendant was immediately acquitted by order of the Court, non obstante veredicto, as permitted by statute. He was then charged with the murder of the state's hangman. He pleaded not guilty by reason of self-defense. He moved to waive his right to trial by jury, and he moved for immediate judgment by this Court. Motions were granted. . . .

"The cases cited by counsel are apposite but not perfectly so. In Dennison defendant, driving alone at night, was flagged down by an officer in civilian dress driving an ordinary unmarked automobile; frightened, fearing robbery or other danger, he refused to halt, committed several violations of the law in his flight, and inadvertently caused the death by accident of the pursuing officer. He was held innocent of manslaughter, and indeed of all violations committed subsequent to his first encounter with the officer. But here the charge was not murder, and defendant could not reasonably have been expected to know that the authority of the state was involved. In Somerville defendant seriously wounded a uniformed officer in resisting arrest for a crime he had not committed, and was found guilty on several counts; but he had declined to avail himself of the many reasonable safeguards and opportunities for exculpation and redress provided by law, and his life was not at stake. Perhaps Hastings, in the cold print of the record, best approximates the instant case: defendant, apprehended on his farm by a sheriff and arrested for the crime of murder, resisted arrest, shot the sheriff to death, and wounded a deputy. He was later executed though it had been shown that he was innocent of the original murder and that the sheriff had known of his innocence. What the record does not emphasize is that Hastings was a Negro in the Deep South, that the sheriff was known to have vituperated him publicly again and again, and that he had little if any expectation of escaping execution for the original murder; that society was clearly—to any reasonable outsider—in the process of violating Hastings's natural and legal rights: of, in short, murdering him. We suggest that Hastings is no precedent at all. . . .

"We have no precedents. We have only our own precarious humanity. Humbly but without hesitation—because a human life is at stake—we must do what courts should never do: we must make the law. Aristotle wrote wisely, 'It is best that the laws be so constructed

as to leave as little as possible to the decision of those
who judge.' When they are not so constructed, those
who judge fall under an awful responsibility. The law is
light, says the Bible; and in a darkness we must make
our own light."

And I paused, and drank.

"The covenant by which man creates a community is
an agreement to forgo the perilous gratifications of animal existence for the more permanent advantages of
human fellowship; and the law is a detailed statement
of that covenant. In a state of nature man is ruled by a
lonely violence, a violence not merely characteristic but
essential to survival, not merely an attribute but a right.
And because survival is the ultimate value of the lonely
beast, the right to survive implies all other rights: the
right to steal, the right to rape, the right to kill. But in
accepting the company of his fellows, man yields a
measure of that violence in the name of a general tran-
quility; and society assures him that he has not dis-
armed himself—that his survival, once important to
him alone, has become the care of all. That is the covenant, and it was born with the most primitive social
unit of the earliest men. In time that unit acquired com-
plexity, and so did the covenant, and so did the law; but
at the heart of all three, however deeply buried, lies one
value: survival.

"License ends where civilization begins; the one is
the price of the other. Man yields up his right to steal,
though certain modes of self-enrichment, hallowed by
custom or expediency, are sanctioned. He yields up the
right to rape, often to the extent of assigning his goods,
services, and affections irrevocably and in perpetuity to
the objects and products of his procreative urges. He
yields up his right to kill except upon the express command, usually justified as self-defense, of the society he
has created. In return for these abdications he is offered

certain sureties. His goods are not subject to arbitrary confiscation. His family will not be sundered. He will not be assassinated. Those assurances would be vain without another: when there is error, redress will not be denied. Under the slow but benignant processes of essentially just and disinterested law, the confiscated goods may be restored, the family reunited, the dead man—ah, no. We are brought up short: the covenant has its limitations, and of these the most brutal is death, because the promise of the covenant is survival. . . .

"So when society kills arbitrarily, with or without due process, we call it tyranny; and it is as much tyranny in our time as it was in the time of the Pharaohs. When the individual does so, we call it anarchy, and it is as much anarchy in our time as it was in the time of Cain. But tyranny is far the more common, because in creating society the covenant confers upon that society vast powers, even as it restricts those of the individual. In a stable society anarchy, though often conspicuous, tends to be self-limiting; tyranny, though often inconspicuous, tends to be self-aggravating. The famous dictum that 'power tends to corrupt, and absolute power corrupts absolutely' applies to both states and men: but the state begins with far more power. That differences in degree become differences in kind no one denies, and an important purpose of the law is to determine and explicate those differences: so a merger is not necessarily a monopoly, nor political opposition treason, nor killing murder. The question is almost always one of power and its uses, and the conclusion seems inescapable that a far greater threat to the covenant lies in tyranny than in anarchy. The political and legal struggles of the past have been a shifting battle between the two, and the significant outcome of those struggles has been the growth of popular government under law, of which the main concern is to compose differences—

to resist tyranny without surrendering to anarchy. Nowhere has that concern been more nobly cherished than in this country. We more than others, relatively unoppressed by nature and committed in writing to life, liberty, and the pursuit of happiness, have succeeded in humanizing the state; it is that success, and not some administrative convenience, which accounts for the most significant of all legal fictions: the fiction that the state is a person, and may be petitioned, sued, openly criticized and brought to public account for its actions. We have acknowledged redress of grievances to be a natural right and an essential article of the covenant.

"But the dead have no redress. Certain abrogations of the covenant are final and absolute, and take us beyond the possibility of composing differences. So the one right that may not be waived by the individual or rescinded by society is the right to life. That right is the root and heart of the covenant: when it is denied a man by society, with or without reason, that man's obligations are discharged and the covenant is dissolved. That denial is fatal to the covenant itself. If carried to an extreme that denial would be fatal to the survival of humanity, and we are justified in considering the extreme: the covenant is our answer to the question. 'What if everyone did it?' That the right to life may not be waived or ignored by the individual is implied by laws making felonies of attempted suicide and of murder. That society's rescission of the right, even by due process, is not taken lightly—is, indeed, a source of awe, horror, and mystery—is better illustrated in less sophisticated societies than our own: we permit the condemned a hearty meal and a last speech, but among less inhibited peoples he was often granted twenty-four hours, or even longer, of absolute sensual license, of the free play of his primitive vitality, during which time nothing—save, again, life itself—was sacred or taboo to him. That we are now less awed, horrified, or mystified by legal executions is another difference in degree; we must take care that it does not become a difference in kind.

"We retain our horror of murder, that final and absolute abrogation of the covenant, though we tend to forget that in the deepest eschatological sense murder is monstrous even when committed pursuant to due process. The Sixth Commandment is not hedged about by qualifying clauses. But when survival is the paramount value, the value upon which the covenant lives, self-defense, by the man or by the society, becomes a virtue. And survival is still the paramount value, the root, however camouflaged by centuries of social foliage. When the state executes a felon it offers the justification not of revenge but of deterrence, or self-defense; though in the swell of passions that attends great transgressions, motives are rarely so simple. How necessary and how effective such executions may be are not, or not immediately, the judgments we are here asked to make. Their legality and their necessity are presumed by past and present law, to which we must here submit."

And I paused again, and drank.

"But past and present law presume that self-defense is an inherent right also of the individual. 'No man,' wrote Thomas Hobbes, 'is supposed, at the making of a commonwealth, to have abandoned the defense of his life and limbs, when the law cannot arrive time enough to his assistance.' This commonwealth has not long been a state; its traditions are rooted in the more violent and primitive mores of the frontier, and only a short time ago self-defense was not a legal concept but a daily necessity. Now we are asked to decide whether an innocent and inoffensive man may exercise the right of self-defense against society itself, when that society has been not arbitrary but only misguided, not malicious but only mistaken. The state has maintained that some error is inevitable in human affairs, and that the law has allowed for error as far as it may without abdicating its functions; but in view of the finality of death, that argument loses force and becomes highly legalistic. The state has also attempted to fix responsibility for the original miscarriage of justice, implying strongly that defendant's conviction and sentence were the will of society as a whole. The argument would be rejected by Blackstone, who wrote, 'It is better that ten guilty persons escape than that one innocent suffer'; and in this Court's view of the nature of law, the argument is a justification for tyranny. Gibbon, too, would reject the argument; he saw the race of men as petty and foolish, but his dour judgments were intermittently brightened by flashes of pity and fellowship, and in one of those flashes he wrote, 'Whenever the offense inspires less horror than the punishment, the rigor of penal law is obliged to give way to the common feelings of mankind.' It may be argued here that horrifying as the offense was, the punishment would be far more horrifying; the one was a justified act of despair and instinct, the other would be a cold and remorseless revenge by a society that may with some logic be held to share the guilt for the crime. The state has also argued that the purpose of capital punishment is the protection of the innocent; but who protected the innocent defendant? Simple equity would seem to require us to sanction murder by an individual for the same purpose; if it is an obligation of the state to assure the survival of the innocent, surely it is also an obligation of the individual. The state's arguments turn upon themselves: if self-defense justifies killing, then defendant was justified; if deterrence is the state's purpose, surely it was—and how much more immediately and effectively—defendant's; whatever justification the state proposes, defendant may claim as his own. . . .

"If an innocent man is, for whatever reason, brought to the last extremity by society; if, as we maintain, his historic obligations under the covenant are then discharged; if, as we maintain, survival is the instinct that informs man, society, and the covenant; then it seems impossible not to conclude that he has a perfect and inalienable right to preserve his life at whatever cost—more, that he has an absolute duty to do so under the articles of the covenant itself. . . . At some times and in some places such self-defense has been called heroism, and when unsuccessful, martyrdom. The renunciation of it has often been considered the highest flight of man's spirit, accessible only to saints—which indicates forcefully and clearly the supreme value placed upon self-preservation by ordinary mortals. Defendant is an ordinary mortal, and must be judged by the standards of other ordinary mortals. Threatened with arbitrary extinction, he exercised his human right and fulfilled his human obligation; he reminded us that there was man before there were men; in defending himself he defended us all, and the covenant by which we survive.

"It is the judgment of this Court that defendant is not guilty. He stands acquitted, and is free."

17 WHAT ASTONISHED ME

was the silence; it persisted unbroken for many seconds, almost half a minute. I glanced at Talbot, at the lawyers, at the spectators; I set down the last sheet of paper and eased back on the bench.

Bryan Talbot stood up, faced me squarely, and said, "Thank you, Judge Lewis. Thank you. Thank you," in a wondering, almost dreaming voice, and nodded several times with his mouth half open, and then sat down and cried. He bawled, and put a hand on Parmelee's shoulder, groping blindly. Parmelee put an arm around him but went on looking at me, and he too was nodding gently. After a moment he disengaged himself and got up and called to Dietrich. They came to the bench slowly while the audience found its murmur and then its full voice, a babble, but many were nodding and Colonel Oates was pounding the floor with his cane.

I used the gavel, and they subsided abruptly, as though they wanted an encore. "This court is still in session," I announced, "and I want order. Sit down and be quiet."

And they did. Quick.

Parmelee reached up to shake my hand. "I really don't know what to say," he mused, almost to himself. "You have done justice, and it couldn't have been easy.

I don't know if there's any higher compliment to offer a man."

"I wonder if the District Attorney feels that way." I smiled.

Dietrich blew out a long breath. He looked exhausted. But I saw much in his eyes: relief, good humor, even—well, I couldn't be sure, until he spoke. "That was pretty good," he said, and his mouth quirked. "For a young judge, I mean."

"Your apology is accepted," I said, fighting down a crazy laugh.

"You know—" and he paused.

"Go on."

"I could have raised hell with you. I never gave formal consent to trial by the Court."

"That's true. Do you remember my looking at you after Mr. Parmelee's motion?"

"I do."

"I took your long silence to mean consent. So did Mr. Parmelee, and I think the absence of objection, of even a request for time to think, would have hurt you. Mr. Parmelee and I would have fought you hard on that; and if you'd objected today I would have ruled that you were too late; that by implication your consent was a matter of record."

He nodded. "We could have had a hell of a fight."

"Thanks for not making it necessary. But you didn't want to."

"No," he said. "So you knew that too."

"So did Mr. Parmelee."

Parmelee nodded.

"And I don't blame you," I went on. "You did your job just the same, and it couldn't have been much easier than mine. Except that I had what my friend Gibbon calls the labor of composition."

"That was a nice quote," Dietrich said. "What is he, the source of all wisdom?"

"Hell, no." I grinned. "He also said that corruption was the most infallible symptom of constitutional liberty. You see?" I was serious again. "A man has to question everything. Everything."

"You may make the law journal, you know," Parmelee said.

"My impeachment, you mean."

He smiled. "I doubt that. I don't know who'd want to make trouble."

"We'll worry about that when it comes," I said. We all shook hands again. "How about dinner tonight at the hotel? Think it would scandalize the population?"

"The hell with them," Dietrich said. "You, Oliver?"

"Good idea," Parmelee said. "Seven-thirty?" We nodded. He smiled again. "It's on me," he said, and they went back to their chairs.

I adjourned court, and stepped sedately to my chambers, and went straight to the bathroom, where I sat retching on an empty stomach for half an hour.

18 TO HAVE LEFT TOWN

immediately might have seemed cowardice, or at least timidity, and I confess to curiosity too, so I strolled the city more than usual that week. "You let him off," Geronimo said. We were lazing in front of his store and nipping an execrable soda pop.

"I didn't let him off. I gave him justice. This stuff is awful."

"You want some whiskey?"

"No." I lit a cigar instead.

"Where is he now?"

"Gone. For good." This was Wednesday, and Talbot had moved along, out of our lives. He had called on me the day before, at my office, shaken hands with John and then with me, sat down, lit a cigarette, and launched a tedious speech of thanks. "You don't have to do that, you know," I told him. "What was done was done not for you but for all of us. You were the beneficiary, and I'm happy for you; but even the District Attorney didn't want to hang you."

"He could have tried, though," Talbot said, owlish and reflective behind his glasses.

"Yes. But you still see the law as a weapon. I don't blame you, after that first trial, and I admit that it has a tendency to become a weapon, but I hope you'll remember that it's also a shield."

"A shield." He was in tan gabardine, with a white shirt and a flowery brown necktie; quite managerial, a vice-president in charge of. "Well, I'm not so sure. I can still see Willie Waite looking at me as if I didn't exist."

"Yes. To him, you didn't. Your existence had been canceled by other people. I don't have to apologize for that. A miscarriage of justice is something like a lost battle. It's hard to assign blame. I'll tell you what I am sorry for: that you had to kill. Not because of the law; just because—well, because it's not something that a man ought to be forced to live with. I hope that won't haunt you, and I think part of my decision was directed at you: for you to remember, and sleep well. Bruce Donnelley killed Willie. Remember that."

He nodded. "I'll be all right."

"What do you plan to do now?"

"I'm leaving tomorrow," he said. "California. I've got a new idea for making ice." He perked up and raised a professional finger. "Cheap manufacture of ice. Wholesale, or bags full of cubes, things like that. It—"

"I wish you luck."

"Yes." He saw that commercial discussions were not in order, and he rose and stood before me, the Americano, the little man, the booster and the go-getter; and then we shook hands and he thanked me once more and left, migrated, disappeared into the vast national limbo to find his level and have his picture taken for trade magazines. Exit Bryan Talbot, who had shaken the foundations. The Colonel had also spoken with him, and duly reported. "So you let him off."

"And what would you have done?"

"I'm not a judge," he said complacently.

"No," I said, and checked a savage comment; why bother?

"Amazing, that one woman could make so much trouble." He glowered.

"It was hardly her fault."

"She was a temptress."

After a time I said, "Colonel, I want you to do me a favor, and listen to a miserable lieutenant."

"Your servant," he said.

"Louise Talbot was a temptress to you. And to Bruce Donnelley. Remember: there but for the grace of God went Sebastian Oates of the Carolina Oateses." He flushed slightly and looked fierce. "To Talbot she was a wife and all in all a good one, and the most beautiful woman in the world. To that young fellow she was a mistress and all in all a good one, and they giggled and she told him lies and he believed them. To her parents she was a daughter and all in all a good one, and a wronged woman. To my mother she was a face in the crowd, but possibly a woman who had been hurt, badly misjudged, forced to play a part she wasn't suited to. There was truth in her and falsehood, and there was truth and falsehood in every separate opinion of her. Beauty is in the eye of the beholder, and she was many different women, the more so because she knew it. And she had a sad time and not too many people ever went out of their way to make her happy. So judge not, that ye be not judged."

"I'm not a judge," he said again.

"Yes you are," I said. "You judge every day of your life, and you judge by the rather narrow views of a retired army officer and a stuffy patrician. I said judge not, that ye be not judged, and there's only one way to avoid that trap, and that is, if you have to judge, judge yourself first. I don't believe you've ever done that."

"You are an impertinent puppy," he said. "I shall tell Eulalia."

"Eulalia worships me," I said lightly, "and will not take kindly to criticism," which made him very grumpy.

Saturday morning I packed my white linen suit and my father's string tie, and hired a car and pointed it west. I reached Ignacio's at about four-thirty and as I stepped out of the car Rafaela appeared on the veranda. She flowed down to meet me, and we kissed formally. "Where is your mother?" she asked.

"I am alone this time," I said. "I want to talk to Ignacio. Business." I tucked her hand into the crook of my elbow and we strolled slowly. "Are you well?" I asked.

"Yes, very. You?"

"Very. Now."

We approached the fishpond; stately, we were, and calm, almost courtly, and my heart beat strongly as I wondered if all things were understood. We seemed to have nothing to say; perhaps nothing needed saying. We took a turn about the pond and went to the house. She ordered refreshment and sent a child for my bag. Soon Ignacio caromed in, hawking and spluttering in pleasure, and Rafaela made as if to leave us, but I asked her to stay and said we could discuss serious things later. We chatted, and I told them about Talbot, and Ignacio was impressed; his experience of judges was less happy, and his idea of gringo justice was not flattering.

I changed for dinner and was pleased at my image in the glass: the suit and the old-fashioned tie were becoming, and in my face I thought I saw a new repose and perhaps a new power. Rafaela was gravely suspicious but obviously taken with me; I had the air of an hidalgo of thirty years before, and I escorted her gravely to the table. We ate fine mutton from the best plates and drank Ignacio's wine from splendid goblets, and the candlelight flickered; I half expected a guitarist to emerge from the shadows. It was all warm and elegant, and Ignacio was so caught up in the regal mood that he became intelligible.

When coffee and brandy had been served, and a box of cigars placed at his left, he said, "Now. What is this business?"

"I have come to ask the high honor of your daughter's hand in marriage," I said, and he choked and turned scarlet and emitted lallations.

"What!" Rafaela said passionately. "You have not asked *me!*"

I stared intently across the candles at her and said, "I have been asking you every day since you were ten years old. But I did not understand the question until now. Does a man ask the sun to rise? I have loved you as a man loves the sun, unknowingly because the sun never fails him, and I have loved you for many years," in a deep and slow voice, and in the finest Spanish because only that was as beautiful as she was.

She drew a long, audible breath, as if sudden pain had assailed her; her face softened and her eyes glistened; and then she favored this poor forked worm with two melting words, "How beautiful," and a smile that may have been the one Adam saw just before he chomped down on the apple. Then I could not speak, and only sat gazing ravenously at her dark loveliness and gli occhi di venere, gli occhi di venere.

"But it is you who honor us!" Ignacio shouted. I had forgotten him. "The eminent American jurist! Bringing us such honor!" And then he remembered his manners and yelled, "Paco! Paco!" and when Paco came dashing in from the kitchen Ignacio said, "Take this horsepiss away and bring us the eighteen-twelve!" Then he gave himself over to beaming and chuckling, and got up to kiss me, and kissed Rafaela, and sat down again and bubbled.

"I'll get fat," Rafaela said.

"Please. Oh, please get fat. But slowly." And I was drunker then than I would ever be, and even the eighteen-twelve was like water because Rafaela was all the liquor I would ever need.

Ignacio had one worry, which he confided to me later when we were alone. "I understand," he said fretfully, and halted. "That is. What I mean to say."

"Yes, my father?"

"Well," he said. "Well, then. I have heard that the gringos use two beds. One for the man and one for the woman. I ask you now, as one man to another, is that reasonable?"

"Don Ignacio," I said, "I am no gringo," and he exuberated.

Then Paco ran into the room and blurted that Pancho Villa had been assassinated that day, and waited like a bumpkin for Ignacio to say something. So did I. Ignacio went pale and stared into the candle flame, and finally said, "He was a man, and men die," and then in outrage, "but how could it happen on this great day? Why today? Why?"

"Bad news," my mother said as I stepped into the house. "Pancho Villa was assassinated."

"I know," I said. "I heard. Rafaela and I are being married on the tenth." She stood like an idiot.

Finally she said, "Rafaela who?"

"You heard me," I said, and she let out a whoop. She did Ignacio's work for him, the announcements and such, and was full of advice on handling Mexican women—I ignored it—and neglected no opportunity to express snobbish approval, which I rebuked. But as the day approached her high spirits drooped, and when President Harding died she wept, which was hysterical because she had not cared for him. But I knew what was wrong: she was losing her son, and with him her motherhood and many years of her life; to be at once evicted and reminded forcefully of her own mortality was not easy. I was kinder then, and took her to the movies and played euchre with her.

Rafaela and I were married in my house by Judge Hochstadter, in the presence of my mother, Ignacio, Mrs. Emily Hochstadter, John Digby, George and Fanny Chillingsworth, Sebastian Oates, Bernard Goldman, and Mr. and Mrs. Juano Menéndez. Edgar Musgrave wrote it up for his newspaper. The Governor sent a telegram and promised a party later. The ladies cried and John gave us two ceremonial silver drinking cups that had belonged to his father. Rafaela wore white lace two hundred years old and was straight out of Cervantes, or Velásquez: her face a cameo, pale, the dark eyes hot and the skin of her face glowing and silken to my fingertips, and then the slightly dizzying décolleté of the old-fashioned gown, and the tiny waist, and the petit-point slippers; John could barely speak, and Fanny kept an eye on George when he kissed the bride. So did I. Then we had a drink and everybody kissed everybody else, or almost, and Rafaela and I held hands and slipped away as soon as we could, leaving our guests to their maudlin revels. "My mother is going to Spain for a year," I said. "In November. When she comes back she will live with us."

Rafaela was puzzled. "And?"

"And nothing. I just wanted you to know."

She was still puzzled. "But where else? Where else should she live?"

"We will have to make less noise at night," I said sternly.

She smiled demurely: "Yes, my husband," and then she said, "in the afternoons, too," and bit my lip.

There was more celebrating in the fall, when the Governor gave a reception for us. He said it was the only way he could get Eulalia alone. We drove to the

capital, where Ignacio admired the skyscrapers, all of
six stories high, and that evening we arrived at the Governor's mansion in full panoply; Ignacio too, like a San-
cho Panza elevated to the peerage. Rafaela wore cloth
of gold, and was a princess; the women fluttered and
cooed, and Rafaela, my voracious little baggage, was all
charm and innocence. When the Governor was not
dancing with Eulalia or fetching her punch he was arguing with Ignacio, the two of them snorting and thundering like Mutt and Jeff in a new language, a bastard
Spanish-English and a triumph of the human imagination. The Governor had made the mistake of mention-
ing land reform, and my reactionary father-in-law
boiled over. "You should know," he warned me later,
"that your Governor is an anarcho-syndicalist." It was
good of the Governor to do all this for us, and I
thought I saw a more generous motive still: he was telling the state that he too had acquitted a murderer. But
even there I underestimated him. Late in the evening he
hustled me into his study, an oak-paneled room with a
fireplace and a desk and three and a half walls of
mounted heads, crossed sabers, and racked rifles. In a
moment we were joined by State Senator Deming, a
small, extremely old man with severe blue eyes and a
drooping white mustache from the 1880s. The Governor introduced us. "How do you do," the Senator said.
"May I congratulate you. Your bride is an extremely
beautiful woman and the essence of femininity. I hope
you will have many daughters because women these
days are going downhill. Do not let them bob their
hair."

"Thank you," I said, and we were silent for a time,
three generations. The Governor opened a cabinet and
extracted three small glasses and a decanter, and
poured. We held our glasses to the light while he said,
"To the bride," and I said, "To our fathers that begat

us," and Deming said, "To the three branches gathered here," and then we drank.

Deming spoke to the Governor: "Will you tell him, or shall I?"

"You tell him," the Governor said.

"Very well." To me he said, "We have a wedding present for you. With the Governor's support I am about to introduce a bill making capital punishment optional with judge and jury, and not mandatory. It is a step toward civilization and I think it will pass. I shall refer to it in my speech as the Lewis Bill. I am very proud of you because this country is going to hell but you are not."

Well, there have been many moments. The moment of the acquittal and the moment of my marriage, moments later of birth and death and war and peace; but of them all that one was most mine. It was yours too, but it was very much mine, because the load that man was born to shed had been lifted from me, and not by chance, but because I had refused to bear it, and had been heard. Little enough? I'm not so sure. I never agonized with Aeschylus and Job, and sometimes at night I regret that, the fierce exaltation or wrenching agony of those who measure themselves against the gods. But I was born to duller work, and have too little vanity, or too much humor, to take gods seriously. I suspect that when a man challenges the gods, they are gods of his own creation, born of his own fears, and his victory or defeat is proportional to his fear but is of little help to anyone else, except perhaps as a reminder that fear too is vulnerable. Death is the only god I have ever glimpsed, and the only one I ever wrestled with. I pinned him once and he will get me for that, but until he does I will jeer and jab and let him know what I think of him.

So we were married and lived happily ever after. Hoo. Like hell we did. We committed all the stupidities that you have committed, but we shared a kind of love that had nothing to do with the half inches and quarter inches that make the grand bosom or the noble jaw. (Rafaela got fat, but slowly.) It was an Antaean love, so to speak, that fed on the earth, on touch, on sunlight; that made whole again Keats's weighty pearl. It fed even on death, because they all died, Ignacio and Eulalia too, they are gone now, the Colonel and Geronimo, the Governor, Hochstadter, even John, killed in a war; and their death diminished us but enlarged us too, and exalted us; we turned from death to each other, from nothing to everything, from the inescapable void to the earth and the fullness thereof. We loved and we made love because they are not different, and we were one flesh and the flesh is life; and the sun beat down on us and said, it is good. More, it is the only good, because what is not living is dead, and there is no love among the grains of sand, or among the stars.

Not much of a moral to a long story? But it is all I have to tell you, so listen:

Wiggle your fingers. Wiggle your toes. Go naked to the market. Rejoice in all mornings. Join hands and kiss. Laugh. Love. If you cannot love, pity. If you cannot pity, have mercy. That man is not your brother; he is you.